"Hamrick makes her debut with this erotic novel that pulses with *Black Swan* energy. . . . Hamrick offers up a thrilling meditation on the tension between love, desire, and art by combining the artistry of *The Red Shoes* with the eroticism of *Fifty Shades of Grey*."
—*Entertainment Weekly*

"Addictive. Hamrick weaves a fascinating portrait of the darkness behind the curtain in professional ballet. Perfect for fans of *Black Swan* or those who love forbidden romance."
—Emma Noyes, author of *Guy's Girl*

"Emotional and enthralling."
—*Woman's World*

"*First Position* is a largely authentic portrayal of the world of ballet and the life of a dancer. . . . I loved Sylvie's tale and her journey to redemption. . . . A challenging story that is reflective, dark, and emotional."
—Tessa Talks Books

"Possibly the most frustrating character since Scarlett O'Hara, [Sylvie's] narration is filled with shocking scandal and [an] incredibly loving description of a professional dancer's lifestyle—and I adored every page."
—The Southern Bookseller Review

"Hamrick weaves a dark and scandalous web around the often-glamorized portrayal of professional dance. . . . The writing flowed effortlessly, as did the storyline. . . . Anyone looking to add something a little different to your TBR will not be disappointed in *First Position*."
—Chick Lit Central

BERKLEY TITLES BY MELANIE HAMRICK

First Position
The Unraveling

THE UNRAVELING

MELANIE HAMRICK

BERKLEY
New York

BERKLEY
An imprint of Penguin Random House LLC
penguinrandomhouse.com

Copyright © 2024 by Melanie Hamrick
Readers Guide copyright © 2024 by Penguin Random House LLC
Penguin Random House supports copyright. Copyright fuels creativity, encourages
diverse voices, promotes free speech, and creates a vibrant culture. Thank you for buying
an authorized edition of this book and for complying with copyright laws by not reproducing,
scanning, or distributing any part of it in any form without permission. You are supporting
writers and allowing Penguin Random House to continue to publish books for every reader.

BERKLEY and the BERKLEY & B colophon are registered trademarks of
Penguin Random House LLC.

Library of Congress Cataloging-in-Publication Data

Names: Hamrick, Melanie, author.
Title: The unraveling / Melanie Hamrick.
Description: First Edition. | New York : Berkley, 2024.
Identifiers: LCCN 2023051454 (print) | LCCN 2023051455 (ebook) |
ISBN 9780593638163 (trade paperback) | ISBN 9780593638170 (ebook)
Subjects: LCGFT: Romance fiction. | Novels.
Classification: LCC PS3608.A69657 U57 2024 (print) |
LCC PS3608.A69657 (ebook) | DDC 813/.6—dc23/eng/20231102
LC record available at https://lccn.loc.gov/2023051454
LC ebook record available at https://lccn.loc.gov/2023051455

First Edition: August 2024

Printed in the United States of America
1st Printing

Book design by Kristin del Rosario
Interior art: Ballet shoes © Stephen Orsillo / Shutterstock.com

Again, to my love,
thank you for encouraging and loving my wild dreams

THE UNRAVELING

PROLOGUE

Wʰat . . . what is this?"
A woman's voice.

I blink slowly, over and over again, trying to get my eyes to roll back to where they're supposed to be. I can't see anything. I can only feel the solidity of the man who holds me and the icy, freezing floor beneath my bare skin. Am I naked?

Oh god. Please don't let me be naked.

"Fuck," says the man's voice.

"What the hell is this place?" the woman asks.

My head lolls and I see sparkling high heels on the bathroom floor a few feet away, then the slender legs of the woman wearing them.

"Can we not do this right now? We need to get her to a hospital."

"A hospital? What's wrong with her?"

"She's what's wrong with her."

"It's not my fault," says Arabella. "She was like this when I found her."

"I don't understand, I thought this girl didn't have any money. Explain what the fuck is going on!"

"Not *now*, we don't have time for this. Go call nine-nine-nine, *now*!"

I try to sit up, but my body feels like it's been hit by a train.

"Deal with your whore yourself," says the woman.

I see her shoes turn and go the other way.

"Dammit."

The man lets go of me, and I feel my body fall onto the ground as he leaves the room.

Then I hear laughter.

CHAPTER ONE

FOUR MONTHS EARLIER

I pinch the skin on my inner thigh between freshly manicured fingers. Blood rushes through my legs as I watch the dancers onstage. It's nearly killing me to be in the audience, trapped in the middle of my row. I can't tell if I'm claustrophobic or if I'm afraid I might lose my mind and climb onstage. Am I jealous I'm not up there, or am I just not ready to be a spectator?

As if he can read my tense mind, Jordan puts a hand on my knee and gives it a gentle squeeze. He asked if I was sure I wanted to come to *The Nutcracker* tonight and I acted like he was ridiculous for asking. But, as usual, it looks like he was right. It's the snow scene and I notice a young woman in the back line of the corps de ballet. Her ribbon has come slightly untied. I can't take my eyes off her. I'm worried for her. She dances as if she doesn't notice, but I know she does, and I just know she's freaking out about how much trouble she will get in. She's wondering if it will hold until the end of the scene or if it will completely untie. She'll be in trouble either way. They will take money out of her pay-check.

I feel bad for her but also annoyed. If I was up there, that would never happen to me.

I close my eyes to block out the beautiful shapes onstage.

The act ends and the curtains come down. I burst out of my seat like a rocket and say to our friends, "Let's go get some drinks."

"Thank *god*," says Artie, not bothering to lower his voice, leading the way out of the aisle. "I love being a person who goes to the ballet, but I hate *being* at the ballet."

"I don't know how those girls do it, it looks like *such* hard work. I can barely do my mile a day." Jane pulls a cigarette out of an old-school case and lights it with a match.

We burst out onto the street, fresh, icy air and dusty smog draping around us. It's not until we're out there that I realize how claustrophobic I felt inside. Out here there's a chaotic din I can get lost in. It's New Year's Day, and since Christmas was only a week ago, the streets are still strung with twinkling lights and everyone in London is in that postholiday haze where mulled wine seems like a perfectly fine way to welcome the early afternoon.

I've never had the classic Christmas holiday, since I was raised by a woman who didn't seem to understand the concept of childhood, much less indulge the idea of magic that's necessary to keep an eight-year-old girl excited with visions of sugarplums. This year was the most festive I've ever been. On Christmas Eve, Jordan and I went to Jane's house, where she and her partner, Emily, made an elaborate—and very English—meal of beef Wellington, roasted root vegetables, buttery potatoes, and trifle for dessert. Artie was there with his brand-new girlfriend, Julia, whom he has already dumped for being too *intellectually plebian*.

We went through about a case of wine and spent the night

taking turns switching out the records on her vintage Victrola. It was a cozy scene of cashmere and pinot noir, and actually roasting chestnuts on a roaring fire. Something I've only heard in the song. I felt like I was in a Christmas movie for a few minutes.

Jordan and I woke up miraculously bright-eyed the next morning, if tired. He made pancakes and coffee, I made mimosas, and we curled up to watch *The Shop Around the Corner*. Later in the afternoon we went to a pub where a live Irish band was playing festive music and drinking as much as the rest of us. We drank pints of Guinness and ate fried food and—well, let's just say I'm not surprised no one knows I'm a ballerina. I have packed on a healthy ten pounds. I look a little prettier, actually, the unfamiliar weight adding a softness to my features I've never seen. I've been about fifteen pounds *underweight* my entire life. For the holiday season, it feels nice to indulge and even to see myself this way, but I have a feeling that once the lights are taken down and Jordan starts talking about weekends in Mallorca, I'm going to feel differently about the new ratio between my waist and my hips.

"Can you imagine being a ballerina?" asks Artie. "I feel like your whole life just winds up being about sacrifice. I mean, life is for buttered bread and perfect crème brûlée! And wine as—as luscious as velvet. Life is *not* for anorexia and discipline. Maybe a little recreational anorexia, but ugh, discipline."

"You poets drive me mental," says Jane. "'Wine as luscious as velvet.' Jesus Christ." She drags on her cigarette. "Not that I don't agree, but what a pretentious fuck you are."

I glance at her cigarette case and think she's also a bit of a pretentious fuck. Not that I don't like her. I do. But it's sort of the Le Creuset pot calling the Alessi kettle *hot*.

Artie bumps her with his shoulder indulgently and takes a cigarette from her case.

I look at Jordan. His expression means *You still haven't told them about your old life?*

I smile and give a slight shake of the head. He smiles back.

It's true, I haven't. I've artfully dodged any questions about my past, managing not to admit my seedy Louisiana upbringing, my gold-digging mother, or my lifetime in ballet slippers.

My phone buzzes in my clutch and I take it out to see a text from Sylvie and a missed call from an unsaved and unfamiliar number. I ignore the random call and focus on the text from Sylvie, my closest friend and the person with whom I've shared the most secrets and the most contention. If it weren't for the fact that we've hooked up, I'd say she's like a sister.

I open the message.

Happy New Year's! Only a few more shows of Nutcracker! I wish you were here—the new principal they hired to replace you is insane. She's such a diva. I swear she won't last the year.

I laugh reading it and then put it away, saying to Jane and Artie, "You know, I used to be a ballerina."

A gust of cold air.

"Shut up. When you were a kid?" asks Artie.

"Oh my god, of course you were, look at you with that absurd waifish body of yours."

She should have seen me in New York.

"No, not only as a kid. I only left the ballet about five months ago."

"Seven months," corrects Jordan kindly.

"Seven?" I ask. "Huh."

I take a drag of Jane's cigarette.

She takes it back and says, "How do we not know this? We've all been attached at the hip ever since you two moved to London, and yet *this* didn't come out? I feel betrayed."

Artie is gaping at me. "I feel betrayed. And guilty for saying how much I hate the ballet."

I laugh. "It's fine."

"Why did you quit?"

I feel Jordan's protective energy waft over me. "She's just on a break. I think she'll go back when she's ready."

Artie and Jane have a hundred more questions as we walk down a cobblestone street lit by gas lamps, meandering in the lawless way we often do until we stumble upon some great little cocktail club or speakeasy.

Jane and I clutch each other and giggle as we try to stay upright in our stilettos. Since leaving the stage and joining the audience, I have learned that they always overpour—and overcharge for—wine at the theater. And then I drink way too much.

Tonight, it's a cabaret that we find.

"Oh, I've heard of this place! Let's go in here," I say. "I've been dying to go."

It's true, but I'm also feeling the heat rise in my cheeks as their questions threaten truths and feelings to rise up and take me over, and a cabaret is exactly the sort of distraction that can save me.

I'm absolutely right. As soon as we step through the doors of Josephine's, we are taken away to the rich, decadent world of America's Jazz Age. My vintage fur coat and beaded Oscar de la Renta dress are perfectly in theme, and I wish—for not the first time lately—that I really could travel in time.

My mind starts to wander and I desperately regain control of it. We need drinks. Stat. I still have a headache from last night's cocktails, but I don't care. I just need to feel less.

Jordan leans toward me. "You okay? We can always go back to our place."

"I'm fine," I say, with the biting tone I can't seem to leave out of my voice lately. I smile to lessen the impact, but I don't feel like it works. He gives me an affectionate squeeze anyway.

"What would you like?" asks Jordan, impervious.

"Something strong. Sazerac."

He hesitates, but he never tells me what to do, so he orders one for me. I notice he gets it made with the highest-quality whiskey they sell, trying to save me from tomorrow's hangover.

And then I hear my name. "Jocelyn?"

I turn to see the source, suddenly remembering with blistering clarity how I had heard of this club.

"David," I say, with an impossibly warm smile, masking the fact that I could not be less excited to see him.

"Oh my god, you look absolutely gorgeous," he says, coming to me and putting an arm around me. "I love how you look so good with some weight on you. I can never pull off having extra pounds on me."

Christ.

I have to admit that David, though a total bitch, is a strikingly beautiful dancer. I know him from my old company in New York, North American Ballet. He and I have never been particularly close. He's a gossip who *loves* good drama and gravitates toward it, bailing on anyone the second they might need him. I don't need friends like that.

I shouldn't be surprised to see David here in London. I did see when we were looking up which *Nutcracker* show to watch that he was guesting for the season. He's English, and they love having him back here. I purposely avoided his *Nutcracker* show, but I have terrible fucking luck.

"I took some time off," I say, accepting my drink from Jordan and letting the plume of absinthe in the glass rise and sting my nostrils as I sip.

"Well, girl, you definitely look better with tits."

I want to be clever, but instead, I am struck silent and uncreative as I wince a nasty smile at him and roll my eyes. He's unfazed and turns to Jordan.

"Is this Jordan?" he gushes, holding out his hand. "I think we may have crossed paths once or twice. You're the artist Jocelyn left her hard-won career for?"

There's something about the way he asks this question like he and I were ever close. Jordan is an artist, an extraordinary painter, who has managed to catch global attention lately. As Artie said in his most recent write-up on him for the *Guardian*, "Despite the maddening crowd's constant insistence that things like *paintings* are dying at the altar of modernity, Jordan Morales manages to keep our attention."

But there's also something about the way David says *artist* that makes it sound like he's saying, *You're the guy with the fingerpaints, right?*

"Nice to meet you, David." Jordan never takes the bait. "I've heard a lot about you."

They hold each other's gaze for a moment, David seeming to glean that whatever Jordan's heard, it's not all good.

"Yes, yes." David snaps his fingers at the bartender, who reluctantly comes over and takes his order. "Bottle of Krug."

No *please*, no *thank you*, no *sorry for snapping my fingers at you like a dogcatcher in an old movie*. I forgot how obnoxious David can be.

The bartender nods. I look apologetically at her, but she looks at me like I'm part of the problem. And I am. Just by my proximity to him, I'm guilty.

Jordan looks irritated, and I know it's on my behalf. He knows that running into another dancer from New York is the last thing I want right now. And it really is.

I just know David is going to text everyone in NAB about how I've gained a bunch of weight and how I'm just hanging around London with some guy, throwing my life away.

"I'm here with some friends you should meet," says David to me now, fully bounced back from the moment of discomfort. "Come over and join our table."

The club is clearly on an intermission between acts, and there's a deeply thrumming exotica beat coming out of every hidden speaker in the place.

I look across the dark room and see the group he points out. To my surprise, I recognize one of the women.

But I turn away, not wanting her to spot me. I accept a glass of champagne from David. I have two drinks now, and somehow it still doesn't seem like enough.

My phone buzzes and I assume it's Sylvie again. I pull it out and see it's an unknown number. I ignore it and put it away.

The girl does see me and as soon as she does, she heads over to us.

"Arabella," bursts David. "Meet Jocelyn Banks."

"Jocelyn." She leans in, and we do the obligatory double air kiss. She smells of booze but also like she just bathed in rose petals. "Yes, yes. I already know this gorgeous creature, David. This is who I was telling you about tonight! I was telling David, I said there's a girl from New York that I've been watching at open classes for a few months who is just *fantastic*." Her words are drenched in a strong, sexy Spanish accent. She smiles big. With her magazine-worthy, messy black hair, petite stature, and buttery olive skin, she's like a green-eyed Penélope Cruz, especially in her role as Maria Elena in *Vicky Cristina Barcelona*.

"Oh my god! I should have put two and two together. I knew Jocelyn was in town somewhere. I guess I just didn't think she'd be out impressing people with her prowess. Silly me!" David practically shouts. "Well, you two *need* to exchange numbers." He turns to me. "Jocelyn, Arabella is a principal at the Royal National Ballet here. She danced in *The Nutcracker* tonight."

"I was just there," I say. "It was great." I try to place her in the show. "Oh, you were the Snow Queen, weren't you?"

She looks so different offstage with her voluminous hair.

"Yes, I was."

"You were wonderful," I say, feeling a stab of jealousy. I'm usually the one wrapping up a show and grabbing drinks nearby, feeling like a star among the normal people when I do.

"And you got out of the theater quick, too," I notice. The Snow Queen is a gorgeous pas de deux before the snow scene where the girl's ribbon came undone.

"Of course! I'm actually lucky I wasn't the Sugarplum tonight so I didn't have to stay until the end and I could get out quicker to hang with this *guapo* creature before he goes back to New York." She smiles and kisses David.

"I swear, Arabella will be your best friend. She's absolutely crazy, though!" David gives her a pinch.

I smile at Arabella. I'm taken aback a bit that she's been talking about me, as we've never actually spoken. We've really only smiled politely at each other in the open ballet class that I've been taking twice a week over the past couple of months. I do it to stay in semi-shape, just in case the urge to dance again overtakes me.

Arabella is good. Very good. It's not surprising she's a principal.

But she's been watching me for months? Is that weird? It feels like she would have said something. I mean, it's not like she seems to be very shy or anything.

I shake it off. I'm the one being weird. It's a ballet class. We all watch each other.

I've been out of my world too long, and now the oddness of it is starting to sneak up on me.

"So great to meet you, Arabella. Yeah, let's definitely go for drinks or something one day after class."

"Of course, darling! Ah, one moment . . ." She then gives us all an apologetic look and holds up her phone, which is ringing. "Now, excuse me, I have to take this. My donor."

David leans into me and whispers, "The donor shit is *crazy* here, by the way. If you do start dancing again, just be prepared for that." He pulls back and then says, at a normal volume, "Not that it looks like you'll be returning to the stage anytime soon. You look perfectly happy in this new role of yours."

I squint at him. "New role?"

He shrugs. "Trophy girlfriend. He's the talent, you're the pretty little thing. I like it, no judgment. I think it suits you."

He winks, and I do believe he means it, but that doesn't mean it's any less obnoxious.

I watch Arabella on the phone. She's interesting. One of those people who just draws you in the second you meet. For better or worse. She seems to have a fire burning just beneath the surface.

I have a feeling Arabella could get me into all kinds of trouble.

My phone buzzes again. The same unknown number. They also left a voicemail. I ignore it again.

There's a screech of feedback and a large, buxom woman in glimmering sequins takes the stage with a bedazzled microphone.

She looks like a curvier version of Velma Kelly from *Chicago*. The bobbed black hair, the eternal smirk.

"Ladies and gentlemen, welcome to the bewitching, beguiling, and be*sexing* Josephine's!"

There's a sudden wave of applause and catcalls.

"Now, I know you could all look at my beautiful tits—I mean *face*—all night long, but of course, I'm a generous soul, so I'll be sharing the stage this evening with some absolute *babes* tonight. And every once in a while"—she directs her eye contact over toward our group—"I'm able to convince my friends to come up and strut what their mamas wish they'd never given them. David, any interest tonight?"

She puts on a pouty face as a spotlight soars over to David.

He smiles. He loves the attention, I know he does, but he acts demure.

"I'm with my friends," he says, elbow on the bar, giving her that kind of self-impressed smile that means he simply needs to be begged.

"Oh, he's with his friends," she says, pouting even more, and even stomping her foot as she bats her eyelashes on the crowd. "What do we think, is that a good excuse?"

Everyone starts to boo, and the emcee grins at David.

"You're so bad," he says to her.

"Come on, Davey, one little dance."

He looks at me. "I'll do it if she does it with me."

The emcee's heavily blackened eyelashes flit to me. "Do we have another dancer in the house this evening?"

Heat rises fast in my cheeks as the spotlight moves onto me, too.

I almost spit out my cocktail. "What?"

"Come on, babe, let's show them what real dancers do," says David.

"*What real dancers do*? What is this, *Step Up*?"

"Come on!" He starts to pull at me.

"Dav—" I look at the stage area. "No. No way. Ballet is not cabaret."

"Oh my god, do it!" says Jane.

"You have to," says Artie. "Do it for the experience."

Artie's a writer, so he writes everything off as being *for the experience*, no matter how negative it is.

"Hey there, handsome," says David.

I roll my eyes. Artie, who is also open to any kind of *experience*, gives a flirtatious flick of his perfectly groomed hair to David.

"You can dangle your beautiful friend in front of me all you want," says David, winking at Artie over my shoulder, "but you can't distract me. We're *dancing*."

I let out an exasperated sigh and say, "This is ridiculous."

David takes this as a relent, and says, "We'll do it!"

The room cheers, dumbly, though they have no idea—just like I don't have any idea—what is about to happen.

David goes off to whisper something to the hostess. She grins and nods, turning the Rolex on his wrist toward her. I turn completely from the whole scene.

Jordan turns to me. "You don't have to do it," he says.

I swig from my Sazerac and look up to the ceiling.

"All right, ladies and sluts, in the boudoir tonight we have a few special guests. David Thornton, a dancer with the North American Ballet in New York City." She pauses and claps long manicured fingers along with all the catcalls and whooping from the audience. "Don't worry, he's a proper Englishman. Well, sort of—he's from South London."

Laughter fills the room. She drifts over in my direction and my heart starts to pound. I never get stage fright when I dance, but the second someone puts a microphone in front of my face, I tend to start bumbling.

"But we *also* have an elegant, gorgeous, absolute *swan* of a ballerina as well. Jocelyn Banks!"

More applause, but less, because unlike David, I am not standing and hamming it up with a little bow and curtsy.

"And I don't know where you're from, love, from where do you hail?"

The diamond-encrusted microphone lands in front of my lips.

I hate admitting where I'm from.

"Louisiana."

"Ooh, New Orleans? I absolutely *love* New Orleans."

There are a few cheers. I am not from New Orleans, but in order to avoid having to explain how many bad neighborhoods you'd have to drive through to get to the one I'm from, I say, "I bet New Orleans loves you, too."

This does the trick. Not-Velma-Kelly does a flattered little frown and places a hand over her cleavage-covered heart. "Aw, what a *sweetheart*." She looks at me. "Even if you are American. Ha!"

She cackles loudly and drifts back to her spot on the stage.

"We're going to bring these two lovely specimens up onstage tonight to perform a sexy little dance for you all—would you like that?"

I'm torn. Part of me is mortified at the idea of stepping up in front of all these people and dancing something unrehearsed.

But another part of me is *itching* to be in front of an audience. To stretch my limbs and do what I'm great at. Watching the dancers in *The Nutcracker* tonight made me go almost out of my skin.

The crowd urges us on.

Jordan puts a hand on my waist. It's meant as a reminder that I can do whatever I want. I slip out of his light grasp, the limelight-addicted half of me winning out.

I slam the last of my champagne and slink up to the stage and take David's outstretched hand.

He whispers into my ear. "We got this, babe. Just let loose a little."

I nod, feeling high on the spontaneity and frozen with the uncertainty. It's not like we're jazz dancers and can whip out a routine. I remember David doing something like this at a major donor's Christmas party. He threw another ballerina in the air, caught her gracefully, and then spun her around. Everyone went wild. But *that* was five seconds.

I take a deep breath. It would be more embarrassing to walk away now.

I kick off my high heels, left only with stockinged feet. There's more cheering. That one was for the foot crowd, I guess.

The room darkens and the spotlight tightens in on the two of us as we take up position. "Little Red Rooster" by Howlin' Wolf starts up. I feel the muscles twitch in my cheeks as I almost want to smile at the sound of the first few beats of music I recognize. David turns to face me, winking. Erik Note, an award-winning choreographer, did a piece to this for a gala a couple of years ago. David and I were first cast.

Nerves and energy race around my bones like ribbons, my blood rushing hot, my muscles strong and well trained. I can tell they have not forgotten.

It's like riding a bike. Except I'm pretty sure I have forgotten how to ride a bike.

Ballet I could never forget.

I slowly start to raise my leg to the side, going higher and higher to the beat of the music, glad I'm wearing a nice thong beneath my dress, as it is *definitely* showing through my sheer stockings.

Once my toe is above my head, David takes hold of my pointed foot and I pivot my body to face him. He lowers with control down to one knee so I can slide my leg across his shoulder. I bend my knee to secure my balance and he slowly stands, me straddled across his shoulder. His hips move to the beat and my arms sensually move through the lyrics as if moving through muddy water.

And from there we're off.

I stretch and bend like a willow in the wind; his movements are tight and sure. When I step into his hand's grasp, it is as stable as a marble stair, and when I drape over his outstretched arm, I am as fluid as velvet in a Renaissance painting.

My body is out of practice, but the basics are there. I've been dancing since I was a child, my bones and my muscles formed around dance. My hamstrings are tighter than usual and I'm sure David is working a little harder than usual to lift me, but it doesn't show. I know it doesn't.

We slip a little at the final moment as my bare feet don't allow me to spin quite like a ballet slipper, but no one minds and neither do we. Everyone is high on the drug of watching real professionals do what they do well.

I'm uncertain about a lot in my life. I second-guess myself. I say stupid things to baristas and I can never quite decide whether or not I can really pull off hats the way some people can, but dance? Dance I am sure of. Ballet I am good at. There is no question, and I never doubt that. I've never been able to afford that kind of doubt.

I laugh at the sound of the last note and fall into David's arms, both of us shedding the personality of the characters we have just briefly inhabited. I was a coquette. He was a stallion.

Now we're back to being what we really are. Me, a traumatized ex-ballerina with a fear of inferiority, and him, a slightly femme, extremely horned-up playboy queen.

The whole room has erupted into applause and whistling and cheering. My cheeks are flushed from the exertion and the attention and the stage lights. I forgot how warm they can be.

I return to Jane and Artie and Jordan. Arabella is nearby, too, but still on the phone.

Jane and Artie start gushing. Jane is smoking another cigarette, her black curtain bangs resting on her slightly dimming eyelashes. "You're amazing, incredible, I've never seen anything like it."

Artie seems almost offended. "I find it *shocking* that you didn't tell us you could *do* this. My god, woman, we were at *The Nutcracker* tonight and it only barely came up! What other secrets are you hiding from us?"

CHAPTER TWO

A few hours later Jordan and I stumble into our building laughing. I am high on it all. I can't believe something as stupid as dancing at that club made me feel like myself again.

Like a dancer.

As we wait for the elevator Jordan grabs my hand and squeezes. I look at him and squeeze back. I feel good right now. Not irritated with him. Not unhappy. Not lost. I started feeling like this a month ago and keep trying to ignore it, which just makes me act bitchy to him a lot.

Maybe things will get better.

He pulls me into the elevator and as soon as the doors close, he grabs my waist and scoops me to him while hungrily kissing my neck. His body feels strong against mine. He's so mellow in his daily life, so I absolutely *love it* when he takes control. His stubble gently tickles my neck and I lean my head back and moan. He moves up to my ear and whispers, "I need to be inside you."

Ecstasy runs through me. I put my hands in his hair and move his head so his lips are on mine. "I want you," I whisper back.

He slides his hand up my legs, wrapping the string of my thong around his fingers and pulling hungrily at me. I move closer to him, intoxicated, as he pulls the thong down in an impressively fast and seamless motion and I step lightly, as if choreographed, out of the sliver of lace.

He touches me, reacting to how wet I am, saying gruffly into my ear, "Fuck, Jocelyn."

He tastes so good. Touching him is as exciting as the very first time, but so much more satisfying still, now that he knows all the little spots on me that make me go crazy. Now that I recognize his natural scent and anticipate the way his hands feel in my hair and the way the hardness of his stomach feels against mine.

The elevator stops in time, stopping us. It's a good thing, too, because I don't think we would have waited. We hurry down the little hall to our flat, both of us suppressing laughter as we pass our judgmental, rude neighbor, Janice.

Once past her, I can't help but explode with a snort.

"Shh!" he says, gently clapping a hand over my mouth and an arm around my shoulder, him laughing just as hard as I am.

He gets the big brass key into the lock, and we stumble in like a new couple in a rom-com instead of what we are, which is almost a year into domestic bliss.

We run through our small apartment, barely able to get to the bedroom fast enough. I'm pulling at his belt while he's unbuttoning his shirt and the straps of my dress are hanging off my shoulders, exposing my breasts.

He pushes me onto the bed with just the right amount of force, and stands there for a moment to take me in.

"God, you're beautiful. And so fucking *hot*."

With this, he climbs on top of me, groaning into my neck with hunger.

I moan against the warmth of his skin, his shirt fully off now. He goes lower, taking my nipple in his teeth, where he gently flicks it with his tongue.

"Oh god," I whisper, "please more."

He moves his mouth to my other breast but continues to tease the first one gently between his fingers. I arch my back and inadvertently push my breast further into his mouth. He growls in pleasure.

My phone rings on the floor where I dropped it. I glance over at it: it's another unknown number, so it can wait. I moan and turn my attention back to Jordan, whose tongue is still teasing my nipples. His hands move my dress down to my waist and his mouth follows, lifting up my hips and sliding the dress further down still. His mouth is warm on my skin. Between the euphoric feeling and the chill in the air, I shiver. He pulls the dress off completely, and once he's between my legs I feel as if I could finish immediately. But I want to wait for him. Do it with him, together. I want to please him. So I push him back.

"Stand up," I whisper, pushing him gently and going to my knees. His belt is already undone, as is the top button of his trousers. I look up at him with hooded eyes and pull the zipper down. His pants fall to his ankles and his black Calvin Klein boxer briefs are stretched tight against his hard cock. I start to move them down, never taking my eyes off him, making him wait just long enough before putting my mouth around him, both of us letting out a sound of relief as I do.

My mind wanders, but not far, as I think how a guy like him doesn't need a big dick to be hot. Some guys do—some guys *only* have that kind of thing going for them. But Jordan is deeply sexy. The fact that he's endowed like the hero of an old bodice-ripping paperback romance is just icing on the cake.

I get him close and then stop, wanting this to last. He lies down on the bed, pulling me by my hand, then my wrist, then my arm, closer and closer to him until his mouth is on mine. He moves me beneath him, moves himself above me.

We start slow. I raise my hips up gently at first as he pushes into me. We move together, our eyes locked. I can feel him getting harder and harder inside of me.

God, he looks so hot when he's sex-drunk.

I wrap my legs around him, pulling him deeper and deeper until I can feel that he's ready and I can hardly take any more waiting. I thrust my hips up again, harder this time, and he grabs my waist, holding me there. We pause and take each other in, both loving this moment more every time we come to it. We're like puzzle pieces fitting together perfectly. We start to move again. His breathing and mine both becoming heavier, more serious. My thoughts become more concentrated and yet more abstract and synesthetic—which is exactly how I feel when I dance.

I pull him down to me now, his forehead to mine, our temperatures both now risen high despite the cold air leaking through the old windows.

"Jocelyn," he whispers. "Are you ready?"

"Yes, yes, please."

I groan as we finish together, bodies entwined.

As we lie together after in the soft glow of streetlights from outside, I hear my phone buzz over and over.

"Ugh, one second. This number has been calling me over and over, let me just answer."

He lets me go, still holding me by the thigh, running his fingers up and down me.

"Hello?" I say into my phone, smiling at Jordan.

"Hello, Jocelyn Banks?"

"May I ask who's calling?"

"This is Joel Carson. I'm . . . I'm a friend of your mother's."

I sit up fast.

"Yes?" I say, suddenly panicked. My nakedness now feeling completely inappropriate, leaving me too vulnerable.

"I need to speak with you. Are you somewhere private?"

"What happened?"

He takes a moment before saying, "She had a terrible accident last night."

"What do you mean, accident?"

My heart rate skyrockets as I push Jordan off of me. As my mind starts to catch up with my nervous system, my hands begin to shake with the sudden surge of adrenaline. I've bitten the side of my tongue and I can taste blood.

"She was driving down L'Enfant around two in the morning last night and it seems like something went wrong with the car. She veered off the road and hit a tree."

"Is she okay?"

Of course she's not. If she was, she'd be calling.

"She's in the hospital. She's . . . it's not looking good, Jocelyn. I'm so sorry to call and have to tell you this."

My stomach feels like it's filled with acid.

"Is she . . . going to die?" The words sting like an open electrical wire has just been placed on my tongue.

Jordan is sitting up beside me, looking steady and concerned.

Joel takes a long beat before saying, "I think you should try to get here as soon as possible, if you can."

"I can't, I can't, I've got—no, I mean, fuck!" I'm scrambling, angry, misfiring it toward Joel when he didn't do anything wrong. "Sorry," I say.

"Don't apologize." We're both silent for a long moment before he goes on. "I'll text you the details, okay? I'm so sorry, Jocelyn."

I hang up without saying anything else, holding the phone in my hand and staring at the wall across from me.

"It's okay, baby, it's okay," says Jordan, trying to touch me.

"Stop it," I say, swatting his hand away.

I walk over to the window and look down to the street.

I close my eyes but instantly regret it.

My mom.

A crash.

I gasp and inhale sharply, but it feels shallow.

CHAPTER THREE

Well, maybe this whole thing was a fucking mistake!" I shout, slamming my open palm on the butcher block in our tiny galley kitchen.

"Jocelyn, can you please look at me? You're not even looking at me!"

I turn, eyebrows up, arms crossed, tongue pressed between my top and bottom teeth. I light a cigarette. I don't usually smoke, or I didn't used to, but lately I have been. I'm blaming it on Europe, but the truth is it's probably because I'm miserable inside and it's the only thing that makes me feel like I have control. Even though it makes me feel awful. What I started to feel a month ago, the insidious grieving of my lost career, has turned into rage since the phone call from Joel a week ago. I focus it all on Jordan all the time. And knowing that this is what I'm doing is not enough, apparently, to stop me.

Jordan and I have been fighting for a week straight. He tried to get me to go to my mom, and I didn't want to go. Then, last night, we got the call that my mother had died.

It was expected. She was on life support and had no signs of improvement in the last few days. I didn't really feel anything when I got the news, and Jordan trying to care for me and tell me to *feel* my feelings made me mad. Like he was trying to get me to feel something I don't feel.

My mom was a bitch. Most of my life. Why would I be upset?

We keep making up and then something small will set me off again, and we start fighting. We'll wake up in the morning and everything will be fine, but then he'll ask me to close the window because I'm letting all the hot air out, and I'll explode. We're sometimes meanest to those we love most, taking advantage that the love will always be there. All the anger I feel toward my mom I have turned toward him.

"I'm looking at you," I say. "Better?"

He looks so hurt. "Baby, you've been drinking tonight, and you're going through a lot right now. I get that. But please don't say this whole thing was a mistake."

"I don't know what the fuck I'm doing here! I was a fucking *ballerina*. Do you have any idea how hard that is?"

"Yes, I—"

"No, no, seriously, do you have a clue? Since I was *seven years old* I spent every single day trying to force my body to do things it didn't want to do. You grew up driving to the beach for the weekend or whatever, eating ice cream and pizza."

I hate myself. I'm weaponizing a memory shared with me, minimizing it and using it as an example of how provincial his life has been compared to mine. What's worse is that I know that memory is one of the last times he spent with his father before he divorced his mom.

"I didn't grow up with that shit," I say, doubling down. "I was in the studio *killing myself* for ballet. And then—and *then*, Jordan? I actually *got* the career that it was all for. I got it. I was living my dream. And then you come along and now it's all just . . ." I ash the cigarette onto the ground. "Fucking dust."

"I didn't ask you to do that. Can we—"

"You're a fucking idiot."

A small smile plays at the corner of his lips. He used to be able to smile like that and any anger I had would just evaporate.

Not tonight.

"What are you fucking smiling at?" I seethe.

"It's just . . . you're clearly not mad at me. This isn't about me or ballet."

"Oh, fuck you."

I turn, my back to him again. I bite the filter of the cigarette and work on getting the bottle of wine open.

"Jocelyn, please don't say *fuck you* to me. Don't stomp around here calling me an idiot and saying *fuck you*. I get it, you're mad. You're upset. You just found out—"

"I can say whatever I want," I say, my syllables muddy from the object in my mouth. His calm, sweet way of treating me makes me want to scream at him more. I want him to stop being so nice so I have something to yell at.

"Yeah, but could you not?" he implores.

"You're treating me like I'm a fucking child. Or like I'm sick or dying or—ugh!" I struggle with the bottle and finally it pops open. "Every time I look at you, you're staring at me, you watch me like I'm a—a—fuck, I don't know, it's like you're waiting for me to explode. I feel like you want me to, you want me to break so you can clean me up."

He's not even acting like I'm a child. I'm *acting* like a child, and I'm afraid he knows it. I know he knows it.

I march out of the kitchen and into the living room.

There's a light blue velvet sofa and a coffee table full of magazines and books we're both halfway through. We used to light candles and pour wine, entangle our legs, and read together.

Massive canvases lean against every wall. And above the old, gorgeous mantel, there is a painting of me. Not that you'd know it if Jordan didn't tell you, since his style is abstract.

It's all done in tones of white, some with a tint of blue, some with a tint of red, some purple. He said the lines were *gestural* and that this painting is what it looks like to him when I dance. There's an elegance and grace to it.

I love it. Or I did. Now I hate everything.

He stands across the room, leaning against the doorframe, still halfway between the kitchen and the living room.

"What?" I ask.

"This is just getting to be too much." His lips form a tight line.

I pause, stunned. It feels like a searing hot poker going through my chest.

"What's that supposed to mean?" I say, instead of finding contrition.

"It's like this every night lately."

"It doesn't have to be," I say, like he's the crazy one. "You're the one who can't stop doing . . ." I gesture at him. "Whatever this is."

"Honey, your mom died. You think that has nothing to do with all this? That I'm suddenly some monster making your life harder, instead of the fact that maybe you're just not okay right now and things are harder because of it? Your mom died. It's hard."

I say nothing for a moment, unwilling to burst into tears, insistent upon staying on my angry, seething high horse. Then I say, "Yeah? I mean, I know that?"

He's patient. "I think you might be feeling some guilt for not going to the hospital. I think it's time to acknowledge what happened and start trying to address the pain instead of pretending—"

"What the fuck, Jordan. I hated my mom," I say, angrily. "Or do you not remember that because you don't listen?"

It's actually impressive what a raging bitch I'm being. Some part of me inside is still sane and normal, hearing myself like I'm someone else. *I* would dump me, I mean, Jesus.

Even in my state, I can hear how ungodly nasty I'm being.

"Even if you hated her, it doesn't mean it's not painful. There are still feelings there, baby."

"Don't fucking *baby* me."

"I think maybe we should find a therapist to help you work through—"

"Oh my *god*, Jordan. Sometimes it's not as simple as just, oh, someone died, now everyone's sad about it. You don't even know what things used to be like. It was awful. Horrible. She was a villain. And now she's dead and I never—"

I almost say, *And I never got to tell her how angry I am at her*, but I know it'll prove his point, so I stop.

"Jocelyn."

"And this *isn't* about her, though I know that's an awful convenient thing for you to blame all this on," I insist, suddenly finding a way to redirect. "It's about the fact that suddenly I have no life! No independence! All I do is walk around with you as your arm candy. Hanging with *your* friends. Living *your* life."

"That's not fair, Jocelyn. I didn't make you quit ballet. I said we could make the long-distance thing work for a bit until I could come to you. I never once said you needed to uproot for me. You wanted to do that. I've also been encouraging you to reach out to the ballet companies here. You can have your own life. I love having you around, and I also love when you do your own thing. There's no crisis here." His voice remains calm and steady. There's no way he can win with me right now, because even this makes me furious.

"Whatever," I snap.

I don't even recognize myself right now. I'm completely shut down. Any love or affection I have for Jordan has vanished. Or, if it's still there, it's hiding. The kinder he is, the more annoyed I feel by him. He's giving me unconditional love. The kind people usually get from their parents growing up. The kind people talk about getting in their relationships. When people really love you, they're with you during the hard times. You're supposed to be able to yell and scream at them and have a fit and *be* wrong. You're supposed to know that they love you no matter what. It's so far from what I grew up with in my own home that it's almost laughable.

If I wanted to be loved, I had to go to my grandmother's house. Mimi is still alive, but she's not present. Her dementia got worse about a year ago, around when I got together with Jordan. My mom had her in a memory care facility. I don't even talk to her anymore, which makes me feel even worse and guiltier.

The problem is, when I do FaceTime her, there's always an aide there. I understand why, but it makes me feel chaperoned and I have trouble being myself. I feel embarrassed in front of the person monitoring. Afraid to ask Mimi if she remembers me or remembers her own life.

No wonder I'm such a mess. My life has crumbled.

On top of everything, I know that Jordan's right. I know he's right even *in* my rage. I know I gave it all up for him, that he didn't ask me to. He's not even taking all the credit he deserves. When I said I was quitting, he told me he'd sooner give up the opportunity in London than let me leave the NAB. So, I did it behind his back and didn't give him a chance to stop me.

It was supposed to be spontaneous. It was supposed to be romantic. Now it just seems like self-sabotage.

"Jocelyn, can we work on this? Together? Do you think we can do this? I want to. If you want me, I'm not going anywhere. But ever since your mom's accident, you have torn me and us apart every single night. And now that she's passed away I don't think it's going to get better."

"Now who's being dramatic?" I roll my eyes.

He's right. Again.

"Jocelyn. Please."

I bite the tip of my tongue hard. My mind is starting to tangle with the fact that his words are threatening to access the things inside that I'm not yet ready to access. It's like he's jimmied the lock open and I know that if the door opens, all hell will spill out. I'm not ready to deal, so I stuff the lock to stop him.

I say the words that will crush him.

"Jordan, I'm done."

I'm cool as a poisonous apple. No warmth in my tone. No regret in my eyes. No uncertainty in my words.

The blood rushes out of his face.

"Don't say that. Don't say that unless you mean it. We swore we would never play games, Jocelyn. If you're saying this, I believe you."

My back is stiff and my glass nearly empty already. "Jordan, just go to bed. I'll be gone by the morning."

I can see I have hurt him. He looks like I just told him I'd murdered his dog and I'd done it for fun.

He gives a small shake of the head and comes over to me. He kisses me on top of the head. "Please come to bed, Jocelyn. If you go, I know you mean it. I don't want that. But I can't fight for us every day and every night."

"Go!" I scream it with such unexpected vigor that I see it shock him even more than it shocks me. "Get the fuck away from me."

I hate myself. I can't stop. I feel possessed.

"I'll give you some space. Jocelyn, please don't go. I'll be right in there. You don't need to apologize or anything, just come in when you're ready."

And then he leaves. He goes to our room. He doesn't fight for me any further.

All I really want is for him to get angry with me. To yell, too. To hold me and not let go until I can cry. Cry for my mother. I hated her, yes, but she is—was—still my mother and I abandoned her. I wanted her to know how it felt to be abandoned. I just didn't anticipate she wouldn't recover.

I know what it would feel like to crawl in there beside him. Into our linen sheets beneath our fluffy comforter. The twinkle lights he let me wrap around the brass headboard would glow behind us. If I wanted to apologize, he would hear it. If I curled up against him and told him I loved him and I was sorry, he would hear it. I could promise to get help, to talk to someone. I could even tell him he was right.

But instead, I get out my phone and type out a text.

Can I stay over?

CHAPTER FOUR

Davidanswers after only a few minutes.

> **Sorry hon, I'm already back in NY. Text
> Arabella she will help you, one hundred
> percent. Kisses.**

He gives me her number.

I hesitate for a long time before deciding what to do. I hardly know this girl. She's essentially a stranger to me.

And yet, in a weird way I feel I know her better than Jane or Artie, who I am now categorizing as Jordan's friends.

She's from my world; they are from Jordan's.

I take a deep breath. Maybe it's time I return to my world.

I grab a few pairs of pointe shoes, some ballet things, and a few other essentials and throw them in my old Longchamp backpack. I don't want to bring too much and invite the old *what are you doing, moving in?* joke.

I decide not to take a car and instead walk to her place. It's freezing and wet outside. I feel like a sponge soaking up icy water as I walk through the streets.

What have I done? Why am I ruining things with Jordan? Why can't I *control* myself?

It's almost a half-hour walk, and in that time I sober up considerably and feel even worse and weirder than I did before. Part of me wants to turn around already, go back to Jordan and apologize. But a bigger part of me is urging me onward. To Arabella. Back to ballet. Away from being just someone's girlfriend. Away from being some man's *pretty little thing*.

I text her when I arrive and she comes out of her own window and hangs over the railing. "You beautiful fucking thing, it's *frigid* out there, come on up here where it's warm, darling!"

There really are certain things you can only say and sound cool when you do so in a sexy accent. If I had said exactly that, with my own American accent—which is the kind of neutral you only get when you're covering up a poor southern twang—I would have sounded like a complete idiot.

I climb the three flights of steps to get to her floor and find her holding the door open with her body at a forty-five-degree angle. Her toe is balancing the door to keep it open, and her attention is inside the flat, where she is screaming at someone in Spanish.

At first, I think I've made a mistake in coming. If she's having a fight with her own boyfriend or something, I certainly don't need to come in reeling from my own and add fuel to their fire. As I don't know Arabella all that well, I don't even know if she *has* a boyfriend, but if I had to guess, I'd guess she has several.

She turns to me, smiling big. "Welcome, *cariño*."

"Thanks so much for helping me out," I say. "My boyfriend and I had a fight, and—"

"You don't even need to tell me," she says. "My place is open for you anytime you want." She uses her toes to lift up the mat in front of the door, where there is a key hidden. "This is always here. Always, all my friends know, it's an open-door policy."

"That's so nice," I say. Something in me doesn't quite trust it, but I know I'm probably just being paranoid.

"So come in, *vamos*, come!"

"Thanks so much for answering so late, too," I say, walking through the door and leaning to give her a hug when I see her arm open to me. In her other hand is a dirty martini.

"Don't even worry!" She grabs me by the chin and plants a plump kiss on my lips. "We only got back from dinner an hour ago. Sorry I didn't hang around the club the other night—I always seem to have drama to deal with." She laughs.

Once in her apartment, I see that there are several girls in the living room lying around like cats. They're all pretty and petite, their ages hard to tell, but they look like they're all around twenty to twenty-three. They *all* look like ballerinas.

A sexy, warm, slinky song hums from the record player.

"Martini?" asks Arabella.

I really shouldn't. What I *should* do is go home and make things better with Jordan. What I *should* do is get some sleep and wake up tomorrow clearheaded to make some decisions about my future. What I *should* do is stop smoking and drinking and eating fried fish drenched in malt vinegar, and start reaching out about auditions.

"Sure," I say anyway, as usual lately, completely ignoring my internal compass. "I like the music."

"Manu Chao," she says, swinging her hips. She's kind of amazing. She has tight curves and moves her body with the sex appeal of an erotic dancer, but I've seen her in class and I know she also has perfect ballerina form. It might seem like a given, but not every ballet dancer can go out to a club and dance and still look hot.

Arabella certainly can.

"Twist or dirty?" she asks.

"Dirty," I say.

"Good girl," she says with a wink, but then she frowns when she sees my expression.

"Sorry to hear about you and your man. But don't all men just seem to either cause heartache or headaches?" She stirs my martini in a mixing glass with a long, twirly spoon.

"I guess so," I say. "Actually, no. I don't think they all seem like that."

"Well, those are the ones I like, I guess," she laughs.

She finishes making the martini and hands it to me, and I say, "Thanks. Cheers."

Then she gestures back to the living room. "These are the girls, by the way. Anastasia"—she leans in to me—"and you *must* pronounce it that way, *Anna-stah-jia.*"

"It is correct pronunciation," Anastasia says, her Russian accent strong. She is leaning with her elbows on her knees, with legs spread wide as she leans over the coffee table. It's only then that I register that they're using playing cards to cut lines of coke.

"That's Cynthia; she's American like you."

"I am from Colombia!" she insists.

"Originally maybe, but you're American, darling. You grew up in Texas."

Cynthia laughs. "Fuck you."

"And that's Nadia and Nina," she says last, pointing to two gorgeous blondes, and I realize then that they are identical twins. In the ballet world the girls so often look similar that it's easy to overlook actual relatives. Jordan once admitted, with shame, that he couldn't tell which one I was when he saw me dancing one time.

"Would you like some?" asks one of the blondes with a delicate English accent, gesturing at the drugs.

"Oh, no, I'm fine," I say, starting to make an excuse before remembering I don't need one.

"So," says Arabella, leading me to a vintage chaise in the corner. "Come sit with me."

Before she can talk to me, she is drawn in by another yelling match with Cynthia, and I see now that it's all in good fun. Yelling is just their shared love language. I wonder if they're together.

Behind the chaise is a long narrow table of pillar candles, all melted to different levels, dripping onto a silk scarf that's been thrown over the wood surface. On the wall is an old French *Lolita* movie poster that says, COMMENT A-T-ON OSÉ FAIRE UN FILM DE *LOLITA*? Which, I think, means *How dare we make a film out of* Lolita?

I look around some more. I can see the kitchen from here. Copper pots and pans, a vase of fresh black dahlias, a French market bag spilling heads of garlic and shallots and onions out onto the wooden counter. I wonder if she cooks, or if it's simply a perfectly curated show.

I want to see her bedroom. I bet it's a gorgeous mess.

This whole apartment is like being in an Anthropologie campaign that got taken over by Alessandro Michele.

"Hello? Jocelyn?" Arabella snaps her fingers to get my attention. She pronounces my name *Jozzleen*.

"Oh, sorry. I was just looking around your flat. I love it."

"My god, wait!" She sloshes her martini and doesn't even care that it gets on the tiger skin rug beneath our feet. "You need a place to live? This breakup with your Jordan, did it leave you without a place to live?"

Well, when you put it that way. "I guess I do need to find a place. Maybe just for a while?"

"You could live here! I have another room, I never use it. It's got the best light in the place, sometimes I just go in and lie on the floor. I'll show you later. But tell me, when are you going back to ballet? Was it that stupid Jordan stopping you? Men can be such boors."

"No—how did you know I—well, I want to go back to ballet. It's on my list of things to figure out. Like, as soon as possible."

"I could probably set up an audition? Not that you need me to. I googled you after the first class. Found you were a principal at NAB. *Impresionante.*"

"Wait," I say, practically inhaling my sip of briny gin. "That's so nice, but I couldn't ask you to do that."

I'm unseated by this offer. Ballerinas are a lot of things, but *nice to each other* isn't famously one of them. There are so few spots to succeed, we can't afford to boost each other up.

"Don't be silly! You're not asking me. I'm offering."

"To be honest"—the truth spilling out of me after the draining evening and too much booze—"I find it kind of weird that you'd help me like that. Most ballerinas are not—"

She bursts into laughter. "I love how you say it how it is," she says. "You can trust me or not. I understand. But listen, it's because—well, you've seen me dance. I'm amazing!" She shrugs her shoulders happily. "I don't need to be competitive. Helping a girl out who just got stomped on by some asshole is far more my style, *cariño*. I don't like to push girls down."

There's something so charming about her that keeps the words from seeming like blatantly off-putting narcissism. There's something about her that I do trust. But I'm still hesitant. I stall.

"Do you all dance at the Royal National Ballet?" I ask the rest of the girls.

"*Claro*, of course!" answers Arabella.

The girls have started snorting the lines, so they aren't really listening.

"When I first saw you at open class," I say, "I did think you were too good to just be freelancing. Why do you go? Aren't you already busy enough?"

She lights a cigarette. These Europeans.

"I'll tell you why," she says. "It's a deal I have with my donor. He lets me do whatever I want. Doesn't matter what I eat or drink or who I fuck or *don't* fuck. As long as I keep myself in pristine shape. Ariana Kingsley is the best retired ballerina and now the best coach there is, her *little weekly class* is a tradition in London. Any girl who wishes to advance further faster, she takes Ariana's class. I just do it to . . ." She snaps her fingers, hunting for the lost word. ". . . *supplement* my other rehearsals so that everyone stays off my back."

"Got it."

"So what do you think?" she asks.

I think for a moment. I'm too lost to not accept help. "I would love to take you up on that offer. I should never have left New York. I should never have left ballet."

"Oh, please, *cariño*, you did it for love! You did it because you are alive on *Earth* and you were having some free will! What is so wrong with that?" She shrugs and makes a face like this is the most obvious thing in the world.

And once she does, it makes me realize how badly I want to

think like that. To stop putting the weight of the world behind every decision. To allow myself to be young, dumb, and free.

"Let me show you the room!" she says.

And then she jumps up like a flicked potato chip and yanks me up, too.

I down the rest of my drink and follow her.

I pass the bathroom, which has a pink-orange glow from the reflection of more candles bouncing off coral wallpaper. I see her room, and it's every bit the gauzy, dimly lit mess I thought it might be.

She pushes open the door across the hallway, showing me the spare room, and I gasp when I see it. The warm streetlights outside pour through the rippling old glass windows, casting golden rectangles onto the dusty wood floors. The walls are covered in aesthetically peeling turquoise wallpaper.

"You just let this sit empty?"

"I never wanted to let someone I didn't like come in to live here," she says. "But I like you. And I think you need me. You can just pay me what you can afford. Then I'll get you a new spot at my company and I'll *know* you can afford the rent."

I laugh out loud at the frankness in her words, but I shake my head a little.

She pushes me a little too hard with her cigarette-clamping fingers. "That's what it is! I know what your problem is, *cariño*, you don't let people take care of you! Of course! This is what your problem is, I see it all now. This Jordan, and—yes, I see it all very clearly—*what?*" she shrieks out into the hall after hearing her name called from the other room. "I'll be right back, these fucking girls, you want to talk about needing . . ."

Her words fade as she disappears back down the hall.

I stand there in the empty room, letting her words ring

through my ears, watching the smoke she left behind as it swirls and rises in the light.

Is she right? Do I have trouble needing people?

I don't know. I don't feel like the trouble is that I can't accept help so much as I never *need* help. I've always done it all myself, and—oh my god, she's right.

This strange, explosive little Spanish girl whom I barely know and who barely knows me has completely accurately figured me out.

And what had I *just* been thinking earlier? I'd been thinking how much I wish I had an adult. Someone to just . . . fucking . . . *figure it out* with. In the past few months Mimi has been worse than usual, and I haven't even tried to talk to her.

Tomorrow is Monday. What I've been dreading all weekend. I have a call with the friend of my mother's, Joel, someone who *is* back home figuring things out. I don't know why. I don't really know him or how he knows my mother. Knew. Knew my mother.

I don't know anything. I just don't want to think about it.

That night, after the other girls leave, Arabella pours us each a small glass of *vermut* and opens a bottle of Pellegrino to bring to the bedroom.

She offers me something to sleep in, as she herself takes off her clothes completely and slips into a threadbare white T-shirt.

"You need something sexy tonight," she says. She pulls out a silk button-down. "Vintage Versace. My last donor bought it for me. I fucking *hate* Versace, you can keep it if you want."

I slip it on and am stunned by how soft the silk is on my warm skin.

I take a sip of my vermouth and get into the bed. "Oh my *god*," I say. "This bed!"

"It's the Palais from Kluft," she says. "Another gift from my donor." She sits down on her knees on the bed and puts on a pouty, baby-girl face. "'Arabella needs her best sleep if she wants to dance well for everybody, doesn't she?'"

I have no idea what Kluft or a Palais is, but I smile anyway. "Well, you can't really deny that. When I was in school for dance, we would sleep as much as possible so that we wouldn't eat too much or do anything else that could be bad for us. It would have been a lot easier with something like this."

"A few hours of sleep in this bed is like a full night's sleep anywhere else."

I'm feeling drowsy already. She dims the lights by shouting in Spanish at an unseen robot, and then gets into the king-sized bed with me.

She looks pretty even with all the makeup gone. There's still a smudging of black eyeliner rimming her eyes, but it looks intentional. Unlike how, on me, it would look like I was just released from the hospital.

"I don't know what happened to you in your past," says Arabella as she shuts her eyes, "but you're going to be okay, Jocelyn Banks."

Jozzleen Bonx.

And she drifts off to sleep. I should feel too awkward to sleep lying next to this woman I've just met, but it's the most relaxed I've been all week. The chaos is more soothing than the comfort.

It's not long before I'm asleep, too, my dreams coming as a dark montage of things I've tried to forget.

CHAPTER FIVE

EIGHTEEN YEARS AGO

Mimi's house was always cool. Summers in Tristesse, Louisiana, reached highs of over one hundred degrees. My house was always sweltering. The walls were hot. The floors were hot. When you turned on the shower, the water was hot. Fans blew constantly, but all they were doing was exhaling heavy, hot sighs. In the dead of summer, I would often wake up in the middle of the night with a pounding heart and pulsing skin, and go to the bathroom where I would take handfuls of water and paste it over my body so that the fans in my room would waft over my wet skin and make me cooler.

But Mimi's house was always cool. Her backyard was lush with dewy grass intermittently being sprayed by sprinklers on timers. Things could *grow* in her garden. She tried to help me plant some flowers in ours once, but they died so fast I'd barely cleaned the soil off my hands before they were gone.

It was on a hot day in August, a few weeks before school started up again. I was seven years old, getting ready to start second grade. I felt very grown-up, finally being well into the *grades* instead of just kindergarten.

I was lying on the floor in front of Mimi's box-shaped TV, eating a homemade raspberry-lemonade popsicle, watching *Some Like It Hot*. I was considering putting my bathing suit on and going out back to play in the sprinklers with Benny, Mimi's sweet old mutt. My plan was interrupted at the sound of tires and squeaking brakes outside.

My heart sank as I realized it must be my mom.

I pretended not to hear her come in, even though the screen door slamming behind her was unmistakable, and even though I was tucked away in the back den where I could hear but not be seen.

"Oh, hi, honey," said Mimi, "close the door, will you? The air-conditioning."

My mom shut the front door. "Mom, we need to talk."

"Come on in, I was just making an Arnold Palmer. Would you like one?"

I strained my ears. I was always eavesdropping, even though I almost never heard anything interesting. The number of stairwells I'd perched at the top of and corners I'd hidden behind. I think I was always hoping that I'd overhear some kind of secret about myself. Some *when do we tell her she's a princess*–type thing.

"Thanks," said my mom, presumably accepting the cold drink. "Listen, I got your message. I appreciate you offering, but it's not going to happen."

There was a thick pause.

"Brandy, the schools are better here. I'm up early every day, I can make her breakfast, I can make sure she gets there on time. Your schedule is so inconsistent, you deserve to sleep in, all those late nights you work at the bar."

"But she's *my* daughter, Mom. You think I'm just going to miss her childhood so I can sleep in?"

"Is it worth her education going down the pipes? Those schools near you, honey, they just don't have the—"

"Mom, please. Just respect what I'm saying! Jesus."

My mom always started off calm, but her fuse was short. Especially with Mimi, which I could never understand, because to me, Mimi was perfect.

Were they arguing about whether or not I'd get to *live* with Mimi?

My mind went wild with imagination. I was already mentally decorating the bedroom I always slept in—which had a canopy bed and a desk with tons of secret drawers. There was a table with a skirt around it where I could hide or read. The sheets were always cool and soft. And mornings at Mimi's, I was always given real food—no Toaster Scrambles or Eggo waffles. I was given fresh scrambled eggs and pancakes topped with butter and thick, amber maple syrup.

"Sometimes you have to do what is best for your child. I'm not saying you can't come see her—"

"Of course you're fucking not, are you *joking*? She's my daughter, you don't get to tell me whether or not I can see her!"

"That's what I just said, honey. Will you please just consider it?"

"Absolutely not. And by the way, I *am* doing what's best for her. I'm giving her as many opportunities as possible."

"What, dragging her all over the country to those auditions? Brandy, that's not opportunity. You're trotting her out like some dog, trying to win best in show."

"Wow. I mean, *really*, Mom? You say that like we didn't almost get the Gerber commercial. And just last week, the people at the audition said she'd be perfect if she could just calm down a little and gain a bit more poise."

"And now you're going to start taking her to these ballet classes, I know. But is that healthy for her? My god, those girls work themselves to death and for what, to retire by twenty-five?"

"It's not a career, Mom, it's just to help her gain some more, you know, grace. To make her a little more elegant."

"You'll take her to classes where they'll whip her into elegance instead of just providing her with a better education. Your priorities are—"

"Okay, you know what? We have to go. She has a ballet class today at two, and I nearly killed myself to get her in with Mrs. O'Hara."

"Mrs. O'Hara? The one who runs that fancy place in town here? How are you affording that?"

There's another heavy pause. "I know her husband."

Yet another pause, and the sound of a heavy-bottomed glass being set down on the wood of the kitchen table.

"Don't even start—"

"Brandy, this is no life for that little girl."

"Just butt out! Fucking hell." The last part came bellowing down the hallway as my mom approached the den.

The popsicle, which I'd stopped paying attention to, was now melting all the way down my hand and arm.

"Oh, for fuck's sake. Go get cleaned up—now. We have to go."

"I want to live with Mimi," I said, as she yanked me up.

"Shut *up*," whisper-screamed my mom as her own mother rounded the corner into the room.

"Listen to her, Brandy, she's not being paid to say it, you know." She gave a frustrated laugh.

"Bathroom—now. Get it all off. And change into these," she said, thrusting some fabric into my chest. I hesitated, and she said, *"Now."*

I scurried off, using soap and warm water to get the sticky juice off my skin, and then looked at the clothes I'd been handed. I was momentarily confused, but then through the door I heard my mom say, "The tights go *under* the leotard, Jocelyn."

I nodded, even though she couldn't see me, and then took off my jean shorts and floral T-shirt and slithered into the stockings. Next, I put on the thing I'd just learned was called a *leotard*, and looked at myself in the mirror and grinned.

As soon as that compressing fabric was on me, I felt something new. I loved the way it held me. I loved how slinky and powerful it made me feel. I felt like a wild animal, finally in the right skin.

And I looked like a ballerina. I knew them from cartoons and movies and things. I *loved* what I saw in the mirror.

When I came out of the bathroom, Mimi and my mom—who had clearly still been arguing—both looked at me with unfamiliar looks on their faces.

"Come here, Jocelyn, you're missing one thing. Ballerinas wear their hair up." Mimi quickly but softly pulled my hair off my neck and twisted it up into a knot.

"Are you excited for ballet, Jocelyn?" she whispered.

I nodded, not sure that I was, necessarily, but knowing for sure that I was enjoying the outfit.

"Jocelyn, let's go," said my mom. "Put on your sneakers and let's go."

I pulled on my white sneakers—now less white and more gray and black from all the scuffs—and went out into the hot summer heat.

The Camry's air-conditioning system had been *on the fritz*, as my mom called it, so it was incredibly hot in the car. My mom turned it on and lowered the windows, which did almost nothing to alleviate the oppressive air, and pulled out of the driveway.

"Think about it, Brandy!" yelled Mimi after us, her hands on her hips.

"Un-fucking-believable," muttered my mom, then cranked up the song "Rio" by Duran Duran, which was playing from one of her CDs. She loved that song. I hoped it made her feel better.

We walked into the ballet studio and I felt the same thing I'd felt when I saw myself in the mirror—an utter *right*ness. My heart was pounding hard, as if I was about to get on a roller coaster. There were lots of other girls there, all of whom were dressed like me but in plenty of other colors. I made a mental note to ask my mom for the purple set.

A woman walked over to us. "You must be Brandy and Jocelyn Banks, is that right?"

"Yes," said my mom.

"It's so nice to meet you, Brandy. And this must be Jocelyn." She crouched down to talk to me, and I noticed she moved with more youth and flexibility than most grown-ups I knew. Even my mom groaned when she crouched down like that, and she was a lot younger than all my friends' moms.

"Yes," I said, holding out a hand to shake hers. "Pleased to meet you."

"What nice manners," she said, shaking my hand. "I'm Mrs. O'Hara. Have you ever danced before?"

"All the time," I said, wanting to elaborate about how much I loved music and dancing. "I love Duran Duran and—"

"That's not what she means, honey," said my mom. "No, this is her first class."

"Okay," said Mrs. O'Hara, now surveying me. She stood and said to my mom, "She's got just the right build. If she's got any talent, she'll do very well."

"A big *if*, right?" joked my mom.

Mrs. O'Hara did not laugh, and my mom's smile faded.

"Okay, that's all we need from you, Mom. You filled out all the necessary paperwork when you were here yesterday, correct?"

"Yes."

"Then you can go. Class lets out at three thirty, please be timely."

Mrs. O'Hara started to lead me away from my mom, who I could see watching me in about four different mirrors.

I saw her turn and go, then Mrs. O'Hara said, "All right, love, go pick out a tutu from the box over there."

I nodded and then my heart lifted as I realized I'd get to wear an actual *tutu*. I ran over to the box and found the purple one.

"Ladies, please collect a tutu from the box and then take your places. Thank you."

The girls ran over to the box, and I scooted away as fast as I could so no one took the purple one.

"Hey, get in line!" said one of the girls.

The kids at school were always snatching things from each other, always screaming and bullying. But I looked now and saw that these girls had formed a neat little line, each taking one and then going over to stand at the wall. All the walls were mirrored, and there was a bar like a stair rail going across the middle.

I got in the back of the line, bouncing a little on my tiptoes as I watched what color each girl chose.

Two ahead of me was the girl in all lavender. She would probably take it because it matched. I hated her for it already.

And then she didn't. She took a sparkly black one.

So if the girl in front of me didn't choose it . . .

She didn't. She picked white.

I got up to the trunk and reached in for the purple tutu. I clutched it to my chest and then looked around for an empty spot.

"Jocelyn, let's put you here, okay?" Mrs. O'Hara put a gentle hand on my back and led me. She had me stand between two girls who smiled politely at me. "For today, just try to follow along. Copy what the other girls do. I'll take those shoes of yours."

I took off my shoes.

"Good girl," she said, and then, "now you can have these."

She held out a pair of pig-pink ballet slippers with cascading ribbons.

"Really?" I asked, excited.

She laughed. "That's right. Now go on."

Mrs. O'Hara walked off with my shoes held delicately from her index and middle finger, set them down by the front door, and then clapped her hands together and raised her voice to say, "Ladies, first position, please!"

The girls all seemed to move as one, suddenly going silent and rigid. What was *first position*?

I noticed the girl in front of me had her feet splayed out heel to heel and her hands *just so*. I maneuvered myself until my hands and feet did the same.

"Now second," said the instructor.

The girls spread their feet apart and put their arms out. I copied.

"And *third*!"

This one was like first. But one arm out in front of me and one to the side.

"Fourth," she hollered.

This one was more complicated, a space between the legs and feet but toes going in opposite directions. I did it and glanced at the teacher for approval.

"And *fifth*," she said, not giving it to me.

The girls' hands went in the air, feet slid together. Right heel to left toe. Left toe to right heel.

My heart pounded.

I was in *love*. I could hardly contain myself. I wanted to run around and jump on things, swing from the bar and watch myself in the mirror in my cute outfit. But I knew I was supposed to be calm and *poised*, a word my mom had taught me after I didn't get the last audition.

This was so *cool*. I felt glamorous and fancy and—oh, I mean, I was just beyond words.

For the rest of class, I copied what all the other girls did. I'd always been a fast learner. In P.E., I always picked up the physical games and things faster than everyone else. I remembered every little note Mrs. O'Hara gave; when she said to shift our shoulder blades down and lift our chins high, the other girls forgot to keep things where they belonged when they shifted from position to position, but I remembered. It was like "The House That Jack Built"—each note and instruction layering onto the last one, and me remembering each and every one. It was a skill of mine, clearly.

At the end of class, I met some of the other girls. They'd all been taking Mrs. O'Hara's class since they were four or five. I was behind already, but I didn't mind. Usually, I felt embarrassed when I didn't have something the kids around me had, but I was too happy just *being* there to feel bad or weird about anything.

When my mom came to pick me up, Mrs. O'Hara walked right over and started talking to her. Fear gripped me—was she going to tell me I was too late? I wasn't good enough? That I should have joined her class two years ago if I wanted any sort of chance at being allowed to keep taking it?

I ran over and heard the tail end of what she was saying.

"—truly exceptional. She's got a natural gift, I'm telling you."

"Oh, this is just to get her to calm down, learn some manners, get a little more poised."

My ears pinged the way they always did when I'd recently learned a word and heard it being used.

"To look at it that way would be a mistake, in my opinion," said Mrs. O'Hara. Both adults were ignoring my presence. "She has a talent, and I think she enjoyed it. It would be a mistake to look at this as something supplemental. I think she should begin classes twice a week to catch up with the other girls, and I don't think it'll take long for her to surpass them."

"Oh, I don't know . . . to be quite honest, Mrs. O'Hara, we just can't afford it."

Mrs. O'Hara turned to look at me. I had idly propped one of my legs up on the rail and was bending to meet my nose to my knee.

"I'll tell you what, come in tomorrow and we'll see what we can work out," said Mrs. O'Hara, turning back to my mother.

"I also don't know if—"

"My husband said you thought she might be a prodigy. After he met you at the fundraiser last week, he spoke very highly of you. It's the only reason I allowed her into my very full class. But it seems you were not exaggerating."

"Right. Well—"

"Three o'clock." She then turned and walked away, raising her voice at another girl. "Maria, get your mouth off the floor, absolutely not."

I took my foot down and ran to my mom. "I loved it, Mom, I loved it! Please let me keep coming. Please? *Please*."

"Time to go, come on."

"You met her husband at a—fun . . . a fun raiser? What is that?"

She glanced behind her and wrenched me out of the studio and toward the car.

"It doesn't matter, honey. Did you really like that class?"

I felt the sudden, unexpected urge to cry. My eyes welled with tears, and I nodded. "I loved it, Mommy! It was so fun, I felt like a fairy." I spun around in a circle.

She looked conflicted, and then squeezed my hand. "Into the car. We can think about it."

"Mommy, it's the only thing I've ever liked, *ever*! Ow!"

My skin burned on the hot back seat.

"Ballet costs money, Jocelyn, it doesn't *make* money. That's not really what we're going for right now."

I didn't quite understand her meaning, but instead I kicked the back of the seat and made a *humph* sound.

"Jocelyn, do not kick the back of the seat."

I was tempted to do it again, as I often was when she told me *not* to do something, but for the first time, I had something I really wanted. And I was not willing to risk losing it.

"Sorry," I said, in a small voice.

A few minutes later, once we were on the road we always took home, my mom asked, "Did you mean it when you said you wanted to live with Mimi?"

I almost nodded and blurted out *yeah*. Instead, I considered. My mom did not want me to live with Mimi. I wanted to make my mom happy so she'd let me keep doing ballet. That meant there was only one thing to say.

"No, Mommy, I was just saying that to be nice. I want to live with you."

Her eyes landed on the rearview mirror and met mine. She smiled a sad smile. "Really?"

I nodded. And then, after a moment, said, "And I want to do ballet."

CHAPTER SIX

I step out onto Arabella's chilly balcony a few minutes before eight a.m. with my black coffee to take the call from Joel Carson, my mom's friend, the one who's taken over the bulk of responsibility for all the logistics back home since my mom died.

It's overcast and gray, as it so often is in London. My phone rings exactly at eight. My heart plunges as I answer.

"Hello?"

"Jocelyn? Hi, honey, how you holdin' up?"

It's my third time talking to him on the phone and it's only ever bad news. I've actually never even met him. All our correspondence the last week has been via text, and he's one of those older guys who texts with proper punctuation, which always makes the conversation seem weird and serious. But his tone on the phone is completely different. He sounds present and kind of cool.

"I'm okay. How about you?"

"I'm good, I'm good. So, you have a few minutes to catch up about all the stuff going on with your mom's estate?"

I know what he means by *estate*, but it sounds like a laughable exaggeration of what is really just a two-bedroom shithole in sweaty Louisiana.

"Yep, I have time," I say.

Joel was named executor of my mom's . . . estate, which was fine with me, because I wouldn't know the first thing about trying to handle any of this stuff. When he asked if I wanted to have a funeral, I said no. My mom didn't know enough people. Not enough people who'd still admit to knowing her—all the men she had affairs with didn't count. Although, since I didn't know about Joel, I wonder how many other people I didn't know about.

I also don't know what Joel's deal is. I assume he's a lawyer or something who she slept with somewhere along the way who happened to be one of the good ones.

Joel tells me that, since I said I don't want anything from the house, it will all be sold or donated. He said that the house was listed for sale and they were hopeful it would sell quickly. He said her car had been irreparable after the accident.

My mind flashes with a horrible imagining of what her final moments might have been like. A car accident feels so dark and sudden and frightening. Did she feel anything after? When they took her to the hospital, did she know? Her heart was still beating, barely, but was she aware? Would she have heard me if I had gone to her?

My breath becomes shallow.

I clear my mind.

"Just do whatever with the car. It doesn't matter. I don't need anything from the house or anything else. You have my permission to do whatever you think is best with everything left."

He seems to sense my unease and gives me a minute before continuing on.

"Your mom had a life insurance policy," he begins, my hope lifting just a little, "and that was just enough to handle her debt and the fees for the cremation."

I breathe in deeply. "Okay. So it's net neutral, basically."

"Yes, except . . . for Mimi."

"What about Mimi?" I ask stupidly.

"Her care home is several thousand dollars a month, and though there's enough payment for this month, after that . . . there aren't any more funds."

I start to panic. "What about the sale of the house?"

Shameful as it is, I never thought about the cost of Mimi's care. I had assumed Mimi had savings that paid for it.

"To be honest, it needs a lot of work and most of the sale price is going to the mortgage. Anything it makes, of course, is going to you, but I wouldn't expect it to cover more than a couple months and that's it."

My body goes hot. "What happens then?"

He hesitates. "That's what we have to figure out."

I feel like I'm falling. My eyes catch on Arabella's pack of Sobranie cigarettes and matches inside. I open the door, grab them, and light one. My friend Sylvie and I used to share cigarettes on my old fire escape and talk about everything in our lives. A lot of what I did was talk about how much I hated my mom. And how much I love Mimi.

"Well . . . what are our options?" I ask.

He tells me exactly how much the care home costs per month. "Your grandmother needs intensive memory care. And your mom"—he gives a fond laugh—"she wouldn't settle for any less than the best facility."

"Uh . . . wow, that's . . . that's really expensive."

"I know, honey. I'm sorry."

"Okay." I blink down at my feet. "That's really how much my mom was paying a month?" I ask, astounded.

"Yes," he says. "She worked hard for the money to pay for it. She didn't want your grandmother in a depressing place. She told me that."

"Yes."

"You could move her to another facility, though that could be costly as well, and if you want her to receive the same quality of care, then I imagine the price will stay around the same."

"How did you know my mom?" I ask suddenly.

He hesitates, and then laughs, taken off guard. "Kind of a funny story, actually. We have the same therapist. We met in the waiting room. I was kind of a mess when I met her and she was just this great, funny, strong woman who came into my life. I was actually at a wine bar with her when I met my husband. She walked right up to him and told him I thought he was cute. The rest is history, as they say."

I drag on the cigarette, feeling a little dizzy from it. Or is it from the surprise of this new information?

My mom was in *therapy*? That doesn't seem like her at all. Is there a chance she was trying to change? To grow?

I suppose this is the kind of story that I would have heard at her funeral. In theory. Somehow, I sort of thought no one would show up. No one would have anything to say. How many other stories about my mom like this are out there?

To Joel, it sounds like she was . . . well, *normal*. It feels impossible to believe it, but there's a chance other people saw her differently than I did.

Of course, thinking otherwise is ridiculously juvenile. People don't exist in a vacuum.

There's something about Joel that seems so normal and cool. And capable. And grown-up. I can't reconcile that with the fact that my mom and he even got along. And that he's gay, no less, so presumably she didn't just get him into bed.

The concept that my mom was more than I knew is far too much for me to consider right now. At this hour. When it's this cold out. When I'm about to audition. When it's so recent. When I hated her as much as I did.

So, I sweep it away under the rug like I have been doing with every other emotion related to my mom. Or at least the ones I seem to have a modicum of control over.

My chest stings. I glance inside and see Arabella is gesturing at the door. Her hair is swept back in a bun and she has her dance bag with the ribbons from her pointe shoes cascading out.

"Listen, Joel, I have to go. Thank you so much for all your help. And thanks for talking so late your time—I know the time difference made it difficult to set up a call."

"Don't give it another thought. We'll talk soon when there's more information to go off of. You take care of yourself, that's what Brandy would want."

I say goodbye and then get off the call and go inside, where Arabella is checking her makeup in one of the many mirrors.

"Sorry, I had one of your cigarettes," I say.

"What's mine is yours, darling. *Mi cáncer de pulmón es su cáncer de pulmón.*" I get the gist of what she says and smile politely.

"Come on. They said you could take class this morning. You can borrow some of my ballet warm-ups. I keep most of it at the theater in my dressing room."

I follow her out the door thankful that what I grabbed the night before from Jordan's were those pointe shoes, ballet shoes, and some leotards and tights. My heart is pounding at the idea of dancing again. I didn't think Arabella would call immediately. I thought I had a few days at least. But I'll take what I get right now.

Open classes are one thing, but dancing with a company—that's a whole other level. Especially when, suddenly, my whole life and Mimi's seem to depend on it. My thoughts swirl sickly as I do mental calculations. Even if I get taken on to dance with the Royal National Ballet—and that's a *big* if, even with my talent and experience—then with Mimi's bills, I will still be scraping together the money to eat and live.

And on top of all of this, I pushed away Jordan. Jordan, who would at least be able to keep me calm in this storm. Plus, he's about to do a show that his agent says will make him a millionaire by next tax season. Maybe I should go back to him.

I cringe as I realize I just thought that. Oh my *god*, what's wrong with me?

There's always a latent fear lying beneath my skin. A fear that I am my mom. That I'm just one bad day—or one young retirement—away from drowning financially, living in whatever shithole I can afford, sleeping with anyone and everyone who might be able to get me further in life.

I am not my mother. I am not Brandy Banks.

It's good I'm not with Jordan. I need to be able to stand on my own. I *have* to figure things out without someone else to depend on.

I can't lean on him. And right now . . . I really can't. The fact that I can't—and even that I'm having to lean so hard on this stranger, Arabella—really scares me.

Arabella links her arm through mine. "I'm sure they're going to love you," she says. "The only thing is . . . you're going to need a donor."

"A donor?"

She reels, looking astonished. "You don't have donors in the U.S.?"

"I mean, we do, but no one really talks about it. And I never even met mine. The company always emphasized the importance of donors. And we were frequently told to behave well because of the donors, but they were kind of like an out-of-sight boss for me personally. But that really didn't have anything to do with other dancers. Some formed close relationships and enjoyed perks. But I—well, I guess I was lucky and just got to focus on dancing."

She nods slowly as we keep walking. "Well . . . it's a bit different here. I'll tell you that."

"Different how?" I had stupidly assumed with all the government funding for the arts in England and Europe that it wasn't much of a thing here.

She exhales. "It's a whole game. It's a whole part of the job."

What I know for a fact about donors is that they essentially invest in dancers. The more we succeed, the more they do. It's like the stock market, only instead of numbers, it's us. It's our bodies. Our careers. Our lives.

I take a deep breath. To my donor in New York, I was a tax write-off. But I've heard horror stories about the experience for some girls. Not only do you feel a bit like a puppy being paraded to find an owner, but some feel they are treated like a high-end escort. Especially when it's a man. I take the hair tie from my wrist and pull my hair up off my neck and shoulders and immediately feel myself cool down. I've suddenly become very hot despite the chill outside. I tie it up in a messy bun.

"If I'm honest with you," says Arabella conspiratorially, "I kind of love the game. There are still very strict rules about donors and dancers. You're obviously not allowed to sleep together and it's meant to be all very protected. But that doesn't mean you can't find a few benefits from the whole thing. My donor is named Cadence Montgomery—her family like *invested* in Harrods or something like this, and *dios mío* is she rich!"

She practically screams the last word and I laugh. "How rich?"

"So rich. And she takes me to all these events where there are other rich men! I haven't paid for a meal in two years. I had a boyfriend paying my rent until last week. Which is why the extra room."

"What happened?"

She rolls her eyes. "It was kind of a fucked-up story actually. His wife is a quite important political figure. I'll stay quiet to protect her anonymity," she says, putting a finger to her lips playfully. "And when she found out he was sleeping with me, they apparently had this huge fight, the fight turned to lovemaking, and then it turned out that the whole thing brought the spark of spicy stuff back into their love life. They would talk about me in bed; she would say, *Tell me what you did with Arabella*." She says this part in a bad English accent. "So eventually, they got the idea—maybe she did, maybe he did, I don't know—that they should invite in the real thing. Me!"

"They . . . she found out he was cheating with you and then she invited you to, what, a threesome?"

"Not just one," she says, "we did it for a few months actually. But then it got messy."

"I see," I say, not used to feeling like the prude in the room. "Well, at least they didn't kink-shame themselves."

She smiles again. "I'll introduce you to some people. We'll get you sorted out."

A half hour later we walk up to a pale pink door in a building that must be hundreds of years old. She pulls it open and warm heat breathes out onto us.

"Follow me, new girl," she says.

CHAPTER SEVEN

So, there are two company classes here," says Arabella as we walk toward a security desk. "They split us up into a men's and women's class sometimes like we're horny teenagers or something. But we're going to take the class with the men today. You will stand out more."

She smiles and cocks her head at the man at the security desk.

"All set," he says, smiling sheepishly back at her and looking back down at his book.

I follow her to an elevator and we go up to floor two.

"You'll love Charlie," she goes on. "Charlie is the director. Charles Haydn-Cole. He's fabulous and has such a good sense of things. He discovered Victoria Haley, you know."

"Ah," I say, finally with some recognition.

Of course I know Charles Haydn-Cole, as he's the director, but I actually *know* know Victoria. She is a stunning dancer who rose to principal here and then started acting, which led to movies, especially the dark adaptation of *The Red Shoes* she did, and now never dances with companies anymore unless it's some sort of *one night only* deal. "I've met her."

Arabella leads me out of the elevator and to the principal dressing rooms.

"You didn't! Ugh, I've always wanted to. We've been like passing ships, I never get to meet her."

"She was fine," I say as we change, not even touching the truth, which is that she was a bitch with a drug problem.

We leave our normal-people things behind and I follow her back to the elevator as a ballerina.

"Yeah, I've heard she's a bit of a diva, but I can't help but admire her. I love a good bitch, you know?"

I laugh. "Then you'd love her."

"The studios are on floors five and six, and we'll be on floor six today."

She gives a bit of a devilish grin.

"What?" I ask, feeling like I'm about to walk in on a surprise party.

"I think you're going to like the studio, that's all. It's a bit of a flex."

The elevator doors open up and I can see immediately that she's right. It's fucking gorgeous.

Outside and downstairs, the building was gorgeous in the old European way. Hallowed with age, a patina over all the glamorous silk wallpapers and intricate corners of the architecture. But up here, it's completely different. It's amazing that it's even the same building.

The big studio has soft blond wood floors underneath the smooth gray vinyl marley flooring that keeps dancers from slipping. There are soaring mirrors that reach the high ceilings. And on two entire sides of the room, there are massive round windows braced by steel designs. Through the massive windows, golden sunlight spills across the floor, and outside there is what must be the best view in London.

"Wow," I say.

"Told you so," she says.

The clean, stark environment doesn't take away from the cozy, lived-in feel of the floors below. Instead, somehow, it just feels even homier. I could honestly cry. I am so completely certain I am in the right place.

A pang of missing Jordan glints through me as I suppress my first instinct, which is to take a picture of the space and text it to him as an aspiration for our future home.

I still haven't heard from him. I thought I would. Maybe I still will. I didn't really want to break up. I was just being crazy. Being *me* right now, which is completely unhinged. But instead, he's actually let me go. I must have really been too much.

Okay, okay, enough thinking about Jordan.

I clear my mind as meditatively as possible and follow Arabella across the studio. We come up to one of the girls who was there the night before.

"Hey, guys," she says, popping up like a tight rubber band as we approach.

She and Arabella kiss briefly right on the lips, and I wonder again if she has a relationship with her, or if this is just how they are.

"Jocelyn, right?" she asks.

"Yeah, and you're . . . Cynthia?"

"Yes, good job!" She gives me two air kisses. "The other American."

This part she says with an eye roll as she looks back to Arabella.

"Hang here a minute," Arabella says. "I'm going to see if there are any good spots at the barre."

"You know the guys don't care as much about spots at the barre as we do," says Cynthia.

"I know, but I still have to ask!"

Cynthia, who has one leg stretched up on the ballet barre, says, "Fair enough, fair enough," as Arabella walks away. Then to me, as she lowers her leg, "I'll keep you company."

"I appreciate that," I say.

"It's so great you got an opportunity to take class so quickly. Arabella said you were a principal at NAB?"

"Yep," I say, stretching my own legs.

"That's a pretty big deal. Why did you leave?"

I search for a short answer. While I do, she watches me and then says, "Ah, for love, then."

I blush. "Yep."

"Someone in the company?"

"No. An artist."

"Ah, very sexy," she says.

"So you're taken," she says. "That's good, that's at least one ballerina who won't sleep with Luca, then."

"Luca?"

She laughs. "Luca is"—she points—"that."

Across the studio is a guy who is so ridiculously fucking hot that it almost seems like a joke.

"Jesus," I say.

"I know. Italian. Luca Salerno. He literally looks like a Roman statue of, like, a . . . warrior or something, I don't know."

"He's straight?" Guys that good-looking never are.

"Yep," she says. "And I'm not. But even so, I think that is one of the sexiest guys I've ever met. If not *the*."

"What's his deal?" I ask, stretching my calves.

"His deal is that he's super fucking nice, he's very, very talented, and every woman loves him. But I mean, rightfully so. He always says he's looking for love, which is very nice and romantic. That doesn't stop him from sleeping with any of the many, many girls who throw themselves at him."

"And he's not a dick?" I ask.

"Not at all. Somehow, no one has ever gotten mad at him. It's like he's such a specimen that we've all just accepted that he can belong to none of us. It's like, oh, you're new, well, only a matter of time until you go through the initiation of fucking Luca."

I laugh. "Wow. He's like a unicorn."

"He is," she says. "But we don't have to worry about that with you, it sounds like you're in love."

"Actually, we just broke up."

"Oh, no. Sorry."

I shrug, which doesn't match my genuine feelings on the matter. "It's okay. But I have no intention of sleeping with anyone right now. I'm kind of off the whole love thing."

"Sex doesn't have to be love," she says.

"I'm off sex, too," I say. "I think I should just focus on my career right now. You know?"

I feel a set of eyes on me and see that Luca, who's stretching, is looking at me.

He smiles and gives a charming, neutral wave. Oh, man. I can see how he does it.

I wave back.

Cynthia sees the interaction and rolls her eyes. "God, another one bites the dust."

"No, I'll be fine," I say. "I'm really not going to do anything like that."

There's a pause, then she says, "If you say so. Anyways, we can definitely take your mind off your breakup. You came here at just the right time. There are so many girls out right now. Two out on maternity leave and five injured."

"Five injured? Jesus."

She shrugs. "That's what happens when you do a run of about a hundred *Nutcracker* shows and only get a few days off after."

"Damn. Well, the ones out on maternity leave will surely be back soon, right?"

"Hell no, they get a year leave here. This is Europe, girl. None of that one-month-paid-time-off shit like in America." She glances across the studio. "Anyway, good luck. Arabella's waving you over, looks like she found you a good spot."

"Thanks," I say, then leave to meet Arabella.

"Did she get you to talk about your life in less than a minute?" she asks as soon as I'm in earshot.

"Wh—yes," I say. "How did you know?"

"She has a gift. She's one of those people. Everyone tells her everything."

As the class starts, I take a deep breath and try to relax. My nerves are out of control, which is *crazy* because I've never been nervous when it comes to dancing. Then again, since I was about seven years old, I never took a break. Now I have taken a break, and it's like I'm afraid I've broken a magic spell that was holding my talent together.

The ballet mistress is named Sarika Khatri, and she's one of those former ballerinas who have aged into a next-level form of poise that makes their whole presence seem angelic. She doesn't seem to walk or step so much as glide. Her voice is soft and gentle but bright as glass, as if she did nothing but drink chamomile tea for her entire existence.

I don't take her temperate presence at face value, though, knowing that all ballerinas have a hard edge inside them. You have to—we go through too much to be soft. We are soft-petaled roses, but we have thorns.

I inhale deeply and place one hand on the barre and feet in first position to begin the ritual that is ballet class. The music begins for pliés and I smile a real smile for the first time in a long time. I feel home.

CHAPTER EIGHT

Over the next few days, class goes well. It's just a ballet class, at the end of the day, and I should have trusted my body more to remember what it's doing. It's just the same as it was when I was little, only now I've done it a million times. It's the same basic routine, the same foundation. When I was seven and began dancing, we started ballet class beginning at the barre, then center, then jumps. And it's the same today. I've just gotten better at it.

It's been interesting staying with Arabella, who's been letting me borrow all her clothes and ballet stuff. I went to Boots and got all my own basics and some makeup. A toothbrush, some floss, boring CeraVe face wash and lotion, which is what I use anyway. I know I need to go by Jordan's and get my things, but I am dreading it.

So I've just thrown myself into ballet. It's been easy, as Arabella is like a completely different person during the workweek. It's all Epsom salt baths and yin yoga before bed, soothing piano music playing from the speakers, cups of tea and green juices in the morning delivered fresh from a place down the road.

It's kind of a nice change.

By Thursday, though, the director still hasn't come by to see me dance, and I'm starting to freak out a little. Arabella tells me not to worry, that there's no way Sarika isn't telling him how great I am. On Friday, just as the barres are taken away and we begin to work in the center, Charlie Haydn-Cole appears.

He's a tall, thin man with a dark complexion and a shock of bleached natural hair. He's in a turquoise suit I recognize as one of Virgil Abloh's designs for Off-White from a few years ago. Not what I had expected, since ballet—especially in England—is famed for being a bit on the traditional side. Which usually calls to mind boring white men with too much power and money.

After class, I'm discouraged again when Charlie disappears quickly. But Sarika tells me to meet him in his office.

Arabella and I head to her dressing room to change.

"This is it!" she says, grabbing me by the arms as the elevator doors close. "I know he's going to hire you. I just know it."

"I hope so." I look upward at my reflection in the mirrored ceiling.

The elevator dings as we arrive on floor two. We hurry to the dressing room, and I put on my street clothes.

"Wait, wait, let me check you," she says, holding my arms and standing back to take me in. "You look fucking perfect."

I smile. "Thank you."

She leans in and kisses me on the lips before saying, "Go get 'em, tiger!"

I giggle from her silly American phrase and I feel dazed from the kiss—clearly that's just how she is with her friends—and then start to head out.

"I'll wait outside for you!" she calls down the hall.

"Okay!" I wave. I feel like I'm being dropped off on my first day of school.

I get into the elevator and take it one more flight up.

It takes only a few seconds, and I'm out on another hallway upstairs, so similar to the one downstairs that it's spooky.

I look for his office, find it, and his assistant points me through, and then I rap gently on the door.

There's no answer, and I hesitate another moment before knocking again, more loudly this time.

Still nothing, then the door swings open.

Charlie takes expensive-looking headphones off and says, "I thought I heard something. Come in, come in."

I do, and sit in the chair he offers. He moves to his side of the desk and sits in his own.

"Sorry to interrupt," I say. "Sarika said you wanted to see me?"

"Yes, yes, I apologize, I had a quick casting emergency to sort. Water?"

"Yes, please."

"Sparkling or still?" He stands and crosses to a small black refrigerator hidden behind a wooden cabinet door.

"Uh, sparkling," I say.

He pulls out two San Pellegrinos and hands me one.

"I was just listening to the new orchestra's most recent recording. We're doing a new *Swan Lake* soon. I think it's going to be exceptional. I really do. Okay, where were we?"

He claps his hands together.

He's got such a strong, present energy. His scattered nature makes him seem less like he can't stay focused and more like he thinks in a million directions at once. He's like jazz, as a man.

"Jocelyn," he says, centering on me. "It is so lovely to meet you.

I've heard phenomenal things about you in the last few days. Forgive me for only getting a chance to sit in for a bit today, but I've seen you dance quite a few times in New York."

"Oh, thank you so much. I'm honored. It's wonderful to meet you as well."

The fact that he's seen me dance in New York gives me a huge surge of relief. I was afraid that the classes wouldn't show my talent enough.

"I have good news and bad news," he says.

My brief moment of relief is squashed by plummeting fear. Already, my mind is whirring with questions. Where to go from here, what connections do I have? Do I call my old director? If I leave London, am I going to lose Jordan for good? Have I already?

"Okay," I say, calmly, as if my mind isn't on its own miserable roller coaster.

"I know you're coming from a principal position at the NAB, but I don't have that position available. Also, it's clear you've had a bit of a time-off, and you'll need to work to get back into performance shape."

His face is just as pleasant as ever, as he is seemingly unaware that he's delivering news that is making me queasy.

"However, that being said," he goes on, "I would like to offer you a soloist position, starting immediately."

My insides run cool as the roller coaster comes to a screeching halt. Is this really happening?

"Really?" I ask, breathless.

"Absolutely. We're down quite a few dancers and we start *Swan Lake* in two weeks, so you'll jump right in. At the same time, we'll begin rehearsals for the run of *Manon* in the spring. And hopefully we'll have a donor arranged for you by then. Will that work for you?"

"Yes!" I burst out. "Thank you so much!"

The mention of a donor rings a small alarm bell in the back of my mind. I resist asking more about it and think of Mimi. I need a donor. I need to get back on my feet. I need to get more than on my feet. I need a good donor.

"Great, well, welcome to the team," he says, standing. It's the international in-office gesture of *We're done here*.

He sends me to meet with the company manager and sign a contract. I get the usual rundown of company life. Then I'm free to go—leaving today as a soloist with the Royal National Ballet.

I can hardly contain my excitement. I can hardly breathe. Talk about being in the right place at the right time! I decide to skip the elevator, too excited to meet up with Arabella, and head for the stairwell.

Rushing down the stairs two at a time, I run smack into Luca. Like a hero in a Marvel movie, he grabs me as I fall backward, nearly hitting my head.

"Careful, *bella*," he says, in a gorgeous Italian accent.

"Thanks." I smile, blushing at him and righting myself.

He winks, I die a little at how incredibly fucking hot he is, and then I resume existing on planet Earth.

I burst outside and see Arabella across the narrow street having an Aperol Spritz and reading *Feel Free* by Zadie Smith. Girl has untold depths.

"Let me guess—soloist?" she asks, as soon as I sit down.

"Yes! God, you're good."

"I make it my business to have an understanding of what's going on at all times. It makes the most sense. Charlie's brilliant. He couldn't possibly turn you away. You're Jocelyn Fucking Banks."

A server comes over with a spritz for me. "Thank you," I say to him. Then to her, I point at the drink. "How?"

"I told him to bring one over as soon as you joined me. Come on, darling, child's play. Cheers!"

I clink glasses with her and take a deep sip of the bright, icy cold drink. It tastes better than anything I can remember.

"I have him make it with Dom Pérignon and Campari," she says.

"God, really? No wonder it's so good."

"Just a taste of the good life, love," she says, leaning forward. "Now get ready, because tomorrow we are getting your things out of that flat of Jordan's, and you're starting your new life."

CHAPTER NINE

Arabella insists on coming with me to get my things from Jordan's flat. I appreciate her coming, as I feel a little afraid I'll collapse in a puddle and refuse to leave if I'm on my own.

I've been looking for a good time to go over there, and I know that tonight he has a show at Whitechapel Gallery, so he won't be home. I was supposed to be at this show with him. We'd planned to go to this restaurant called Brick Lane after the show for Indian food.

I try to stop thinking about it as I turn the ancient key in the doorknob and let us in.

All around the place, I see our ghosts. Me, standing at the kitchen sink rinsing out wineglasses when he came up behind me and kissed my neck and we let the water run. The times on the couch when we fell asleep watching some old Buñuel movie. The shower with its low pressure that we never minded because we were so often in there together, skin to skin, keeping each other warm.

The way my heels used to be in a pile by the door from kicking them off after arriving home late at night. Or the way my lipstick would leave a print on the rocks glass. Or—wait.

"Oh my god," I say, feeling suddenly weak in the knees.

"What is it?" asks Arabella.

There are shoes by the door. There is a glass with lipstick. But they're not mine.

I tell Arabella that those things aren't mine and she immediately picks up the glass from the coffee table and throws it into the empty fireplace.

"Arabella!"

"What? Fuck him!"

"No, no, just—we're not breaking things, just let me think."

"Fine, okay, I'm sorry, darling, I'm sorry, men just make me so *fucking mad*! How dare he move on so quickly without you? And who knows how many women? Is it worse if it is just one?"

"Okay, you're making it worse now, I'm not even there yet."

She does a zip-lip gesture. "I'm done. *Lo siento, lo siento.*"

"Todo bien," I say with an eye roll. "Let's just get my stuff and get the hell out of here."

I go to the bedroom and get my big black Samsonite suitcase and throw all my clothes and dance wear into it without being neat. In the bathroom, I throw all my perfume and makeup and everything into the Longchamp backpack I brought, freezing when I see a toothbrush by the sink that isn't mine and that isn't Jordan's.

There are a few pairs of shoes of mine in the closet, which I indicate to Arabella, and she puts them into an old leather bag I've had my whole life. She finds my Canada Goose jacket and shoves it in.

And that's pretty much all there is to get.

I look around.

"Aw, no, not these sad eyes," says Arabella, coming over to me and swiping hair out of my lashes. "No, baby, no sadness."

Tears fill my eyes as I shut them hard, thinking of the women's shoes by the door. He's moved on.

"It's just . . . we weren't here for long. In this flat. But somehow, I had thought I really might have this place to come home to. I lived out of a suitcase as a kid and now I am again. As a child I was either at my mom's house or at my grandmother's house. Then ballet."

"It's the life we chose, right?"

"Yeah, but. Still. For how long?"

She laughs, which surprises me. "Look, baby." She holds my face in her hands. "One day, you're going to have a home with all your kids or dogs or birds or whatever you want then—"

"Birds?" I laugh, the tears properly coming now.

"Who knows? But then you're going to remember this time of running around, and you're going to miss it. Try to miss it now. Maybe you can love it that way."

I don't have time to process just how profound and deeply comforting that thought is, because we both suddenly jerk our heads toward the sound of a key in the lock of the front door.

"Shit," says Arabella, who jumps to action, throwing the bags and suitcase in the closet and then stuffing me in, too, following and shutting the door just in time.

I brace myself, looking through the slats, unsure just how I'll feel seeing Jordan. Especially now, after realizing he's moved on to another girl already.

But it's not Jordan.

It's a woman.

Arabella puts a supportive hand on my bare thigh. The faint hairs stand on end and I stay frozen.

The woman looks around for a moment and then pulls out her phone. After a few rings, she says, "Okay, where the hell are they? Your place is a mess."

He's on speaker, so I hear Jordan say, "Fuck you! It's not usually a mess. It's ever since you've been around."

"Whatever." She laughs. "Asshole. Okay, where?"

"They're in the bedroom in a velvet box full of tie stays and things like that. Emerald and gold, and they're probably just loose in there."

She comes into the bedroom, and Arabella and I go even more still. Jesus, this is like a movie.

I know from the description that she's looking for the cuff links he was given by the gallery owner. He told me more than once to remind him to wear them tonight for the show. Looks like he forgot, as anticipated.

Also, I know where they are. They're by the front door in the key dish. I put them there a couple of weeks ago so we wouldn't forget.

"Oh, wait," he says. "They're in the key thing by the door. I forgot. Jocelyn put them there."

The woman pauses. "We're saying her name now?"

There is silence on the other end of the phone. "Just grab them."

She leaves and goes toward the front door. "Holy shit, these are so hideous."

"Tell me about it," he says. "Listen, I gotta go."

"You're so lucky I love you," she says. "I did not feel like coming all the way over here, it's *very* out of my way."

He laughs. "I love you, too. Now get your ass here, I don't think I can do this without you."

Arabella's hand tightens on my leg as the woman leaves, locking the door behind her.

It's over. It's really over. I can't come back from this, even if he wanted to. My mom just died, for fuck's sake, we break up, and he's already with someone new? And they're saying *I love you?* Was he cheating on me? Is she an ex?

My mind reels.

We wait a moment, making sure she's really gone, and then we burst out of the closet.

"Why did she have to be hot?" I ask. What I really mean is . . . did he really just say *I love you* to someone?

"It would be worse if she were ugly," says Arabella.

"How's that?"

"Because then it would be love. Come on, let's get your things and get the hell out of this place."

Arabella's right, I think. But it doesn't mean it doesn't hurt.

Whoever that was, she was tall and thin with a sleek blond bob, olive skin, and plush, puffy lips painted with bright red lipstick. And even through the slats I could see that she had long black lashes as thick and pigmented as any mascara ad.

And they said they loved each other.

They *love* each other? Already?

It doesn't make me feel better, but it must be an ex or someone he used to have something with. Otherwise that's *way* too fast to fall in love.

Or . . . is it? Once *Romeo and Juliet* closed last year, and he surprised me by showing up, he and I were only together a week or so before we decided to move to London. Not only that, but I'd been willing to give up everything for him.

I had *thought* that was because we were special. Soulmates. But maybe this is just what he does. Maybe this is what everyone feels like when they're with him.

It's hard to suddenly see him through this new light, but . . . what other explanation is there?

When I say all of that to Arabella, both of us stuffed into the back of a taxi with all my things, she says, "I don't know, does he have a sister or something?"

There's a moment of hope. "Wait, he does have a sister," I say. Then I remember. "But she's got long black hair and last time she FaceTimed she was much heavier than that girl was. She was pregnant, but still."

"She might have bleached her hair?" says Arabella encouragingly.

The taxi driver glances back in the mirror and then I see him give a small shake of the head, not for my benefit. He probably hears things like this all the time. Scorned women trying to rationalize away the fact that whatever dumb man is just not that into her.

"She also lives in California and has another young kid and she's married. That woman, on top of not looking like her, was not wearing a ring."

"You're like Sherlock Holmes," says Arabella. "I guess that makes me Whatsit."

I snort. "Whatsit?"

She's not making a joke. She furrows her brow. "Yes, Sherlock and Whatsit. You know, that line? 'Elementary, my dear Whatsit.'"

I don't know if it's the intensity of the other emotions rolling around inside me, but when she says that, I start laughing and I cannot stop.

She starts laughing, too. "Is that not right?"

I shake my head, still unable to speak for laughing. "Wat—it's *Watson*!"

"Shut up, you're kidding me. My whole life I thought it was the silly name Whatsit."

When I finally catch my breath, the crushing fear and frenzy of what I just did and heard hits me. Jordan. That woman.

I'm not like that political wife Arabella told me about, the one who found it sexy to imagine her husband with another woman. Have I had a threesome? Yes. But do it with the person I'm in love with? I could never. It would kill me.

I shut my eyes.

"Are you okay?" asks Arabella, seeing me.

"Yeah, sorry." I fight the tears that want to pour out of me. "Just a hard breakup." I bite my tongue and then add, "Something big better be coming. Or the fucking universe hates me."

"Oh, something big will come. I promise you that."

She laughs and then looks out the window. I think she's making a sex joke, but there's something just a little bit off about the way she said it.

CHAPTER TEN

"What do you say we go out to dinner? Hm? We can go forget about stupid men."

Arabella and I have just gotten back to her apartment—or, I guess, our apartment.

"It's my treat," she adds, sweetening the deal.

"No, that's okay," I say.

I'm not sure why I say no. I like Arabella. I guess I just want to be alone.

"You sure?" she asks.

I nod. "I'm just going to go for a walk, I think," I say.

She looks concerned, but says, "Okay. Bring your phone with you, *sí?*"

"Will do."

The late evening sun is warm on my cheeks as I walk down the unfamiliar streets. My mind is so preoccupied that I don't even listen to music or anything. I have too many thoughts to sort through. They're so tangled and discordant, it's like listening to a hundred concertos at the same time and being asked to dance with it.

I don't even mean to do it, but after winding around, street after street, I find myself around the corner from Jordan's show.

I feel like one of those psycho stalkers from a melodramatic TV show as I stand there, looking on at the gallery in the near distance. There are dramatic up-lights outside, and there is an energetic buzz around the place.

I move closer. The show looks like a massive success. I'm so happy for him, but miserable for myself as I resist the compulsion to run inside and wrap my arms around him. I would undoubtedly burst into tears.

People come and go, and I feel sick knowing that this place is off-limits to me, when only days ago, I was more than entitled to be there.

What the fuck was I thinking breaking up with Jordan? My feelings for him haven't changed. They never change. It's just that when I'm mad, I can't see straight. I can't think straight. I can't do anything right.

I'm close enough to see inside now, through the big picture windows that line one wall of the building. I gasp when Jordan comes into view, walking around a corner with a group of wealthy-looking people who listen to whatever he's saying with rapt attention.

He looks so good. He looks nervous, but happy. He's wearing the suit I helped him pick out, but his shoes are new. For some reason, this makes me feel unseated. Like he's already moved on and the shoes are the evidence.

Speak of the devil, the blonde arrives. She hands him a glass of champagne, says something evidently *hilarious*, judging by the round of laughter from her little audience, and then leaves again, patting Jordan on the shoulder as she goes.

Okay, it's time to go. I'm just a weird stalker out here in the dimming twilight, literally staring through a window at my ex-boyfriend and his new girlfriend.

As much as I would love to get arrested for something like this, I know I have to go.

I walk down the block and stop at a lively-looking restaurant with large, open windows and a busy patio. I walk up to the hostess and say, "Just one," and she offers me a seat at the bar.

There's only one open seat, and it's toward the end of the bar, beside an attractive man in the corner who probably sat there because he wanted to be left alone.

I sit on the stool and accept the menu handed to me by the hostess.

"Sorry," I say, when my elbow touches his.

"No problem," he says. His voice is low, a little gruff.

I order a glass of wine and say that I need a second for food.

"The mussels are phenomenal," he says, so quietly that at first I don't realize he's talking to me.

"Oh—oh, are they?"

"Yes," he says. "Highly recommend them. Their seafood is all fresh."

"Okay, maybe I'll try those."

When the bartender comes back over, I order the mussels and hand back the menu.

"Thanks," I say to the man.

He says nothing, just gives a small *no problem* shake of the head.

I go to use my phone, feeling a little nervous beside this man and wanting to hide behind it.

But it's dead.

Damn.

I put it away and sit there, feeling weirdly awkward as I try to figure out what to do with my hands and gaze.

I hear a small chuckle beside me and I turn to see that the man is laughing. At, I'm pretty sure, me.

"Are you laughing at me?" I ask.

"People your age are so lost without your phones."

My mouth falls open in surprise at his candor. "Okay, well, if I had known I was going to be out dining alone, I would have brought something to read or something."

He nods, eating another mussel and then taking a sip of his own wine.

I let out a *tsk* sound and then try again to occupy myself in a nonawkward way.

But again, I hear him beside me.

"Okay, well, what is it you do when you dine alone, laugh at the people around you and just . . . I mean . . ."

I narrow my eyes at him and for the first time, his lock on mine. They're gorgeous, steely gray. The laugh lines around his eyes make him all the more attractive.

"I'm Max," he says, holding out a hand.

I hesitate. Then say, "Jocelyn," as I put my hand in his. I can tell now that his accent is English, but there's a hint of something else. I'm no expert, though, so it's probably just that he's from the North or something.

He releases after a moment and says, "So what were you doing that you find yourself dining alone? Surely you didn't get stood up."

I think that was a compliment.

"No. More pathetic, actually. My ex-boyfriend's got an art show at the gallery down the block. I went for a walk and just sort of ended up outside. I know that probably sounds psycho."

He shrugs, and I appreciate when he doesn't get on the psycho-ex-girlfriend bandwagon with me.

"Did you go in?"

"No, I just stood out there. Like a creep."

"Why did you break up?"

"I don't know, actually."

My mussels arrive then, and I thank the bartender and start eating.

"You must know," he pushes.

"You really want to hear this?" I ask. "Is this how hard up people your age are since they won't just go on their phones like normal people?"

He laughs. "I deserved that. Sure. Tell me."

And then somehow, though I can hardly parse through it myself, I find myself telling him the truth. The whole truth.

I don't just monologue at him. He asks questions.

The conversation goes on and the dinner crowd is thinning around us, the last few of our mussels going cold. Our drinks keep being refilled by the bartender, due to the flick of an eyebrow from Max.

He's really, really hot. He's not *older* older, but he's probably in his forties. I think about how I've never slept with a man in his forties, and then wonder why my brain is going there.

"It sounds like you still love him," he says, when I finish telling him the whole sorry tale. "But it sounds like he probably still loves you, too. I imagine he'll be there when you go crawling back."

I laugh. "Wow, rude."

He gives a casual shrug. "Am I wrong?"

"No. I mean, you're not wrong that I'll go crawling back at some point. Probably. Whether or not he'll still be there, I have no idea."

"I'm sure he will."

"But what about Blondie over there?" I ask.

He waves a hand. "Men are idiots. He probably just called up someone he had from his past and asked her to come round to distract himself from what he's really feeling, which is misery over losing you."

"I think I was pretty awful."

"All women are awful at times," he says. "So are all men. Love isn't about that. Love is about being there anyway."

"My, you're sage," I say. "Who knew. I thought you were just an asshole."

I'm afraid this jab is too far, but he just smiles and says, "I deserve that, too."

"So what about you?" I ask. "Who do you love?"

He tears a piece of bread from the hunk on his plate. "My wife."

Something in me depresses. He's not wearing a ring, so I had foolishly thought maybe he wasn't married. But of course he is. He's gorgeous and has an air of wealth I can't help but notice.

I am my mother's daughter.

"That's nice," I say.

"It should be," he says. "We're not in the best place these days."

"No?"

The bar is close to empty now. Just an old man drinking solo at the end of the bar, a couple on a date in a far corner, and two girls outside on the patio with a dalmatian at their feet.

"She doesn't love me anymore. She wants a divorce. I'm not surprised, it's been a long time coming. We haven't told anyone yet. Not her family or mine. Or the"—he gestures dismissively—"press."

"The press?"

"They care about her, not me," he clarifies. "But they'll assume it's my fault anyway. Which is fine."

"I'm sorry," I say.

"S'alright. I don't know if I love her the way I want to love someone anyhow. We've been together a long time. I think it's all habit at this point."

"That's depressing."

"Tell me about it."

"Well. I'm sure you won't have any trouble finding someone new, when you want it."

His gray eyes land on mine as he scans me, reading between the lines. I hadn't meant to be so flirtatious, but I couldn't help it.

I've had a little bit of wine, he's beautiful, and the other option is wallowing in my devastation.

"Neither will you," he says.

I bite my bottom lip briefly, wetting it with my tongue. I clear my throat and sip my wine.

It's one of those moments that doesn't need to be acknowledged head-on for us both to know what's happening.

After a long silence, I say, "You know what always seems to happen in movies?"

"What's that?"

"Strangers meet and get a hotel room to go fuck. I've never done that. Do you think it really happens?"

Holy shit, I'm feeling bold apparently.

He furrows his brow, and says, "I don't think it does. Or at least, not to me."

My chest feels light, my legs weak.

"That's a shame," I say. "It would be nice if life were more like the movies."

He holds up his hand to the bartender, and then gestures at both of our plates, handing over a card.

"What are you doing?" I ask.

"Buying you dinner first."

My heart trills at his words. "Before . . ."

"That's up to you."

After he pays, I take the last few sips of my wine and lead the way out of the restaurant.

This is crazy. Are we really about to do this?

It's always been very, very against my personal code to sleep with a married man. Lots of girls in the world don't care. They go on their sexual journeys, feeling like they're entitled to whatever they want.

I think, besides the obvious, that it's morally fucked, I personally object to it after seeing my mom do it. I mean, not *literally* seeing her do it, but knowing that she did. It felt like it got her nowhere good.

But this man is getting divorced. He sounds like the wronged party. And it's a one-night stand. I'll never see him again.

He doesn't even know I'm a ballerina. I don't know what he does. I don't know who his wife is. We don't know each other's last names. We can't hurt each other. This can just be a dream we both have, one time, one night, together.

We walk until we find a hotel, neither of us saying a word, but the energy between us buzzing hot.

When we go in, he tells me to go to the bar and order us some drinks, handing me some cash. He then goes up to the lobby desk.

It's a fucking nice hotel. The kind of thing that looked like a Disney princess castle to me as a kid. It's warmly lit with crystal chandeliers, the décor would make Marie Antoinette feel at home, and the cocktails at the bar all cost twenty-five dollars or more.

I get us both dry gin martinis with a twist. Even if he's not a martini person, I figure he probably won't mind. At its best, a martini is a delicate exploration. At its laziest, it's a huge shot.

He finds me at the bar, putting a hand on my lower back and asking, "Ready?"

I nod and we go to the elevator with our cocktails, his hand still on the small of my back gently leading me, both of us clearly nervous but eager.

We go to the top floor of the hotel and he takes us to the end of a long, ornately carpeted hallway, to room 2000.

He opens the door and my jaw falls open.

It's an extremely glamorous, opulent room.

It's a luxurious oasis, a lavish retreat from the hustle and bustle of the city outside. The foyer is adorned with ornate, gilded accents that glimmer in the soft light of the crystal chandeliers. The walls are draped in plush, deep-hued fabrics, and the floors are lined with sumptuous carpets that cushion each step.

The room itself is expansive, with soaring ceilings and massive windows that would let in a flood of natural light during the daytime. The furnishings are decadent and indulgent, with plush velvet sofas and armchairs, intricately carved wooden tables, and massive, ornate mirrors that reflect the opulence of the space.

I go to the bedroom, where a grand four-poster bed dominates the room. It's draped in swaths of silk and satiny linens that whisper against the skin when I touch them. The bed is flanked by intricately carved side tables, each topped with a glittering crystal lamp that casts a warm, amber glow across the space.

The bathroom is a marvel of modern design, with gleaming marble floors and counters, an enormous Jacuzzi tub, and a spacious glass-enclosed shower that's big enough for two. Soft, fluffy towels and plush robes are neatly arranged on heated racks, ready to envelop guests in their soft embrace. Overall, the room exudes a sense of timeless elegance and indulgence, offering an escape from the ordinary and an opportunity to revel in the luxury of the space.

My life with Jordan was not glamorous. It was beautiful, but it wasn't this. I've never really had this. It happens sometimes that I attend a gala for my company, something like that. But this is not my usual. It impresses me.

He walks up behind me and we both sip from our martinis. It's awkward, but in a way that amuses me. I laugh.

"Now look who's laughing," he says.

This cracks me up further, and that makes him laugh.

When we finally start to catch our breath, I say, "I can't believe we're here right now."

"No? It was your idea, wasn't it?" He sets down his martini and takes a step toward me.

"Yes," I say, as I take a deep breath and set my drink down as well.

And then I feel my smile fade as our eyes lock. His gaze drops to my lips and I step toward him fast, just as he reaches out to pull me toward him.

We crash into each other, into an urgent kiss. His strangeness intoxicates me further.

As we kiss, I feel like I'm in a dream. It's a strange feeling, like I'm watching myself from a distance, but at the same time, I'm completely present in the moment. His lips are soft and warm, and they fit perfectly against mine. I can feel the heat between us, and I sense that we both want more.

Our hands race over each other's bodies, my fingers frantically unbuttoning his shirt, his hand pulling up my lacy top, eventually pulling it over my head. My hair cascades over my face and he pushes it out of the way.

I let out a sound of desire as he kisses me again, letting his now-unbuttoned shirt fall to the ground.

He presses against me and I feel his hardness against my lower abdomen.

"Fuck," I say.

Effortlessly, he unsnaps my bra. He then picks me up and carries me to the bed, throwing me down on it. "God, your body is beautiful."

"I'm a ballerina," I say, my voice practically a whine of desire.

"Really? In London?"

"Yes." I breathe heavily, lowering his mouth to my breast. He envelops it, his tongue warmly thrashing against my nipple. My hands run through his hair as I say, "Bite me."

He does it, just a little past gently, and it feels good.

I kind of want to be dirty and a bit rough. I'm sure it's a reflection of how dark and fucked up everything around me has been lately, and that any therapist worth their salt would have a field day with me. But I don't care what the reasons are.

"Harder," I say.

He obeys, then moving to my other breast and doing the same to me there.

"Harder." I breathe heavily and push my breast into his mouth, as much as I can. "I want you to leave a bite mark around my tit."

He groans happily and bites me hard. I gasp. It's really fucking hard, but I like the pain of it.

A moment later I pull him up and climb on top of him, taking in his incredible physique, my wetness against him. I undo his belt and step off the bed to pull off my own leggings, leaving them in a heap on the floor with his pants.

I pull off my thong and then tear off his briefs.

"Jesus Christ," I say, seeing his dick. "It's fucking huge."

I give a laugh, and so does he, but it quickly gives way as I climb back on top of him. He reaches his fingers up to my mouth, and I wet them. He then pulls them away and lubricates the head of his penis before I envelop him.

He's so hard and big that I have to go slowly, but soon the desire takes me over and I find myself moving on top of him with hunger.

I bend over him and bite his jaw lightly, then kiss his neck. He groans softly against me.

"Jocelyn, god, you're so . . . *shit*." He goes breathless as I hit him with a new angle.

He flips me over on my back and I let out constant moans as I watch his incredible body move powerfully against mine.

When I get close, I tell him, and when I do, he tells me that he is, too.

We finish at the same time, him pulling out just in time.

Afterward, we lie beside each other catching our breath.

"That was the best sex I've had in—" he starts.

I interrupt him by covering his lips with my fingers. "Just say it's the best you ever had."

He bites the tips of my fingers and when I pull them away, he says, "I didn't want to say that. I wanted to seem cooler than that. That was the best sex I've ever had."

"Me too," I lie. It was fucking amazing, I want more. But the best sex I've ever had was with Jordan.

"Liar," he says.

"What?" I feign innocence.

"It's okay," he says. "Maybe this time it'll be the best you ever had."

And with that, he lowers his mouth to my body again, kissing me from my neck to my tit, to my stomach, and then lower, lower . . .

His mouth on my clit, I moan as we begin again.

CHAPTER ELEVEN

Y ou're not supposed to know about the black book," says Mary
    Simon.

Arabella gives her a devilish look and sips on her Chablis. I sip
on mine and look between them. "What black book?"

Mary throws back her head in a laugh. She reminds me of
Kristin Scott Thomas with her posh, gentle accent and piercing
blue eyes. She's probably in her sixties, but you get the feeling by
looking at her that she's gotten more and more beautiful and
glamorous with every passing year.

Somehow, Arabella finagled a last-minute meeting with Mary
Simon. She says this *never* happens.

"Darling, I love you, but you must stop telling everyone about
it. You could really get me into trouble."

"Nobody would dare! You're Mary Simon. They *cower* in your
presence."

She laughs again and shakes her head. "You're such a flatterer.

Excuse me"—she flags down the bartender—"could we get an order of that—what's that special popcorn you have?"

"The black truffle and Parmigiano-Reggiano, ma'am?"

"Yes, yes, that's the one, we'll have one of those to share, please, thank you, Tommy. And another round for us."

I exchange a look with Arabella. It's going well.

Mary Simon is the director of Major Gifts, which means basically that she's the link between me and the donor who could change my life.

The black book is a binder full of headshots of dancers who need sponsoring. Below the headshot is a brief bio on the dancer's career. The book is given to a potential donor or a preexisting donor that the company feels will be willing to raise their donation level. Usually, they are encouraged to pick two or three dancers they like and are invited to a rehearsal to watch them and have a brief introduction after. From there, a donor decides whom to sponsor.

I knew of part of this process, having been sponsored before, but I didn't know about the book. I didn't realize we were all being shopped for and chosen like that.

The part of the process I knew before was when the donors came to watch. We would get alerted that a potential donor was coming to rehearsal, as it is always company policy for any guests to be announced.

But since talking to Arabella, I've learned that donors are usually pushed and guided on which dancer to sponsor. If the company wants the dancer sponsored as soon as possible, they won't give the potential donor the book, but rather Mary Simon will email a picture and rave about the wonderful up-and-coming ballerina that the sponsor is being given an opportunity to support.

Without a donor, you just cannot rise through the ranks. It's a system I don't agree with, but if I want to dance and succeed again, I have to deal.

I do feel sort of like a product being sold. Like a horse being auctioned off to the richest fat cat with the most illegal cigars and the nicest sports car.

I push the thought out of my mind. The point of all this is that I want—I *need*—to dance again. And this is how it works. After all, Botticelli was sponsored by the Medici family. Penny Chenery had sponsors for Secretariat. People invested in Apple.

Why shouldn't I accept a little support?

When Arabella and Mary go off on a tangent about the last Fashion Week in Paris where they crossed paths, I look desperately for a corner of the conversation where I can edge in and prove that I, too, am interesting and charming. It's hard to do as over and over, my mind wanders to memories of the night before with Max.

We left without exchanging information. Just crossing through the lobby, both of us a little more rumpled than we were a few hours before. We went our separate ways, never to see each other again.

I take the last sip of my wine and replace it with the new one in front of me. I look around the bar, which is floor-to-ceiling chestnut wood. There are glowing golden lights and the tables are small, which leads to a lot of cozy conversations. Everyone has bowls of nuts or olives and cocktails or wine or beer, and there's a roaring fire in a fireplace in the center of it all. It's January in London, which means that the winds are wicked and wet, and it's been so long since we all saw the sun that we might not recognize it next time it shows up.

When the conversation finally turns to toxic men, I perk up.

"Do you know Sebastian Alvarez?" I ask Mary.

Her eyes widen. "Oh my god, you were dancing with the NAB when that scandal happened, weren't you?"

"Yes," I say. "Sylvie Carter is my best friend."

"Oh, give me the scoop," she says, leaning in.

Arabella mouths something behind her. I figure out that she's saying *She loves gossip* and giving me an approving thumbs-up.

"Well," I say, smiling, "it all started when Sylvie and I went over to his town house after a boozy brunch at the Waverly Inn."

I tell her the whole tale of last year's biggest ballet scandal, leaving out the parts that make me look like an idiot and the parts that Sylvie wouldn't want thrown around. But I'm honest about what a dick he is. I have the fleeting thought that talking shit about someone in the ballet world might not be smart, but if you're not allowed to discredit a misogynist's lies, then what are you allowed to do?

By the end, Mary is practically on the floor with the shock of it all.

"I knew I didn't like him," she says. "I saw him once at the Ivy and I just didn't like the way he leered at my daughter. He's got eyes like a shark."

"Yeah, people never seem to notice that second row of teeth he's got," I say with a cheeky grin.

Now I'm the one making Mary laugh.

The night is clearly winding down a few minutes later as the popcorn bowl runs down to the unpopped kernels and our drinks empty. Arabella looks delighted with how the night has gone, but we're both tense—are we going to get some sort of signal that Mary is willing to move my name up the waitlist?

"Well." Mary rounds on me while texting something on her phone. "I need to get going, but let's quickly chat about you." Her tone has changed.

"I like you. I can tell you've got a spark to you. I haven't seen you dance lately, though I did see you perform in Vienna a couple of years ago. You're good. And you seem to have a good head on your shoulders. I can tell you're not a wild card, which makes you a good investment and easier sell. And after the whole Alvarez fiasco, I'm certain you won't find yourself with another man abusing his power."

"Absolutely not," I say. My heart is lifting me into an even straighter posture.

"I'll tell you what," she starts. "Are you familiar with the Cavendishes? Clementine and Alistair Cavendish?"

"Um . . ."

Arabella nearly chokes on her last drop of wine. "The Cavendishes?" she bursts out. She has a look of shock on her face but quickly regains composure and says, "Of course Jocelyn is. Everyone knows them. Are you sure the Cavendishes are right for Jocelyn?"

Something is being communicated between them that I am not meant to understand.

"I think it would be a good match," says Mary. "They aren't sponsoring any dancer at the moment. As you know." Mary turns her attention back to me. "After losing Victoria Haley to Hollywood, Clementine has been extremely selective about whom to next sponsor." She narrows her eyes. "I'm going to recommend that she have a meeting with you. I was with her in Vienna, I know she's familiar with your work."

"That would be—" I try not to sputter desperately. "That would be incredible."

"To be completely honest with you, they're the only donors in the city I can see being willing to take on a new dancer. There are very few spots at the best of times, but lately, even fewer.

"Are you free this weekend?"

"Yes, of course I am, I'll make the time."

"Good answer." Her phone lights up and she glances at it. "My car is here. Keep your phone handy, I'll message you the second I get word on her availability. Arabella, please behave."

They double-air-kiss and hug, Arabella groaning, "But behaving is no fun, Mary."

Mary smiles indulgently. "Thank you for introducing me to this star." She moves on to me: "Jocelyn, I'll be in touch."

She does the air kiss and hug with me.

"I'm so glad to have met you. This was so fun," I say.

And then, off she goes.

Once she's through the door, Arabella and I turn to each other.

"I think she likes me, right?" I ask, insecure.

Arabella pauses a beat too long while eyeing me. I get a bit of a chill from it, but then she quickly gushes, "Oh my god, of course she does, what is there not to like?"

"I have very shallow nail beds," I joke.

She shoves me playfully. "Cheers, doll, you're in the good graces of one of the most powerful women in the arts."

I clink glasses with her. "Thanks to you."

"Thanks to me," she agrees. "God, the Cavendishes? You don't have any idea who they are, I take it?"

"Not the foggiest."

"Well, they're basically new old-money. Alistair's family made their fortune in America's prohibition era. They shipped gin in through Boston or something like that. His family was in Ireland, but he's properly English, raised here and everything. He's fucking gorgeous, an absolute silver fox. Or getting there, anyway; he's in his late forties. He spends money like Jay Gatsby. Like it might go away at any moment. If he takes you out for drinks, you'll wind up underground at some secret place—like a *real* speakeasy, not the Instagram-era kind where everyone on the Internet knows about it. I mean, he knows where the real fun is."

"Well, you definitely seem to know a lot about him!" I laugh. "Has he taken you out for drinks or something?"

"You silly girl, of course not! But I have friends who have gone." She winks.

I laugh again, becoming a bit giddy. "Okay, okay. What about his wife?"

"She's one of those distant relatives of the royal family in some way. She's related to Princess Diana in some cousin-once-removed kind of way. But her maiden name was Spencer."

"Jesus, really?"

"Really. But her family didn't have much money, just a lot of land. I mean, she did grow up in what is basically a castle out in the countryside. She's a true blue blood. There was an article in *Vanity Fair* about her when she was in her twenties—she was a *socialite*. Isn't that glam?"

"Very glam."

I scrape the bottom of the popcorn bowl for any stray pieces.

"You better be careful," says Arabella. "You're not on a hiatus anymore."

I'm not sure what she means at first, but then I realize she's talking about the popcorn.

I don't respond, but rebelliously eat a piece anyway.

"I'm sorry if that sounded rude," she says, "I'm just looking out for you."

It's sort of an apology. But in the way that means *I'm sorry if that hurt your feelings* and not *I'm sorry.*

"It's fine," I say.

She taps her head and says, *"Como una cabra,"* then rolls her eyes. "Now, shall we get out of here? I have an incredible bottle of champagne at home. We should celebrate that you're going to meet the fucking Cavendishes."

"That sounds good," I say. "Ugh, it's freezing."

"I have an idea," she says, giving me a mischievous look.

Chapter Twelve

"Your turn." Arabella steps out of the water and into her silk robe. She then perches on the edge of the tub while I slide into the hot water. We're both wearing a hair mask and a face mask. She lights a cigarette; the steam and smoke swirl together and loud French pop music is coming out of the speaker. I sink into the big tub and feel utterly relaxed.

"Okay, lift your leg. I'm going to shave you," she says.

Look, I know. This bitch is crazy. But I kind of fucking love it. Her chaotic energy is exactly what I need right now. I've never had a girls' night like this; it feels like it's from the movies.

She's using a terrifying-looking straight razor to shave my legs, one that she says is the same used on the men of the royal family.

"Nothing gets closer," she says, when I ask her. "Okay, now stand up, it's time to do the rest."

"The rest?"

She gestures, and I realize what she means. "You're fucking kidding me."

"Oh, please. Have you ever gotten a wax?"

"Of course, but—"

"It's the same thing, only better! You're welcome, by the way!"

I shake my head but start to stand, hesitating still, because I can't believe she means it. "Seriously?" I ask.

She shifts the cigarette to the corner of her mouth and sits with legs spread wide, like she's offering a shoe polish. "Go on."

I stand up. "This is so weird."

"It's a bit sensual, isn't it?" she says. "A nice intimacy to have with friends. Leg on the edge, please."

I breathe in deeply. "Why do women do this?" I ask. "Why do we feel we have to be completely hairless?"

"No, no," she says. "It's nothing like that. It's just that we need to do what makes *us* feel as sexy and confident as possible. Head to toe. It may be just your secret, but people can tell when you're at your best even beneath your clothes. Even if no one ever sees. Although they'd be so lucky."

I bite my lip and look down. I agree. I love the feeling of just-shaved legs, and I do feel sexier. But this is so weird. But also, kind of . . . hot in a weird way. Which makes me feel crazier. Like suddenly *I'm* the one who's being weird.

"Nearly through," she says. "You have such a nice pussy."

She says it so matter-of-factly that I'm taken aback. I laugh. "Thank you?"

She looks up at me. "Do you ever have sex with women?"

The tone of everything suddenly changes a little, and the blood begins rushing hot to my thighs. "Sometimes," I say.

She smiles at me from her position by my knees. "Maybe it would help you to forget about that man."

I raise an eyebrow and smile. "Maybe it would."

She sets down the razor with painfully slow caution as I find myself suddenly wanting her, wishing she wouldn't take her time.

But she does. She stands up and puts the cigarette out, stepping back against the door, her big, messy bun falling out in tendrils around her ears.

"Turn on the shower," she says.

I do as she instructs.

Her robe falls to the floor. She's still damp from her bath. This whole time, her nude body was just hiding away, only barely out of sight.

I see that she has a landing strip, identical to the one she's given me. She also has perfect, round breasts that are bigger than I thought they were. She hides them well in her leotards. Some girls are just blessed with the kind that can hide away or be shown off like this.

She steps into the clawfoot tub, which has a showerhead on the wall above, and turns me around so my hair stays out of the water. "Let me rinse the mask off your face. Keep your hair out of it. Let the conditioner sit a little longer."

I smile. "Only a girl would say something like that."

She bites her lip and I let the water run over my face. She uses her fingers to get off the rest of the cream and then says, "Okay," when it's gone.

She reaches out of the shower and grabs her glass of champagne and hands me mine. We drink them, and then she takes the glasses, puts them down, and puts her mouth on mine.

Her mouth is cold at first, from the drink, but as our tongues meet, soft and delicate but urgent, we create a heat between us.

It's been a while since I've done something like this. With Jordan, it was love. It was different. It was deep. It was meaningful.

But there's something about sex just for the sake of sex that is its own kind of special.

My hands run over her body as it grows warmer and wetter from the steam. We're about the same height, so when she moves even closer, our breasts press against each other's, her hard nipples matching up with mine.

I let out a moan as her lips travel down the side of my neck. One hand is on my jaw, the other on my waist.

The water dampens her hair and I undo her hair tie.

She says, "Only a girl could do that without tying it all in knots."

She kisses me and I can't believe how good she tastes. The champagne and cigarettes and the lip stain from earlier have all somehow combined into something so delicious that I find myself desperately wanting more, *more*, *more*.

Her hand travels between my legs. She groans. "It feels even better than it looks," she says. "You're so warm and wet. Oh . . . yes, baby. I just felt you get tighter. You're so sexy, *fuck*."

She says this last part into my mouth as her tongue licks my lips and mine finds hers.

Her fingers feel so good. I start to breathe more heavily and she says, "I wonder if you taste as good as you feel."

She drops to her knees while I stay standing, sinking into the still-full tub beneath us. It's draining through the hole in the side, but staying filled almost to the brim.

Her mouth on my clit has me immediately let out a cry of desperate, greedy desire. The heat of it, the accuracy of her aim. The softness of her lips.

I get close, put my hand on the back of her neck as I grind her closer, closer into me, and then . . .

The wave of pleasure washes over me.

"Now, come here," she says, pulling me down into the water with her.

I kiss her and she tastes like me, which is strangely intoxicating. I touch her and she lets out a deep, carnal sound of pleasure. We cannot get enough of each other, and we're both drenched in water and each other. The sound of Film Noir's "Prends la pierre" plays out of the speaker, seeming to set the tempo and tone of our connections. She climbs on top of me in the water and slides her leg beneath mine, so that our landing strips are right up against each other.

It feels amazing, and I'm still tingling from finishing as hard as I did. This time I slide my fingers into her. She cries out for more. I thrust harder, then she looks me in the eye and says, "More than two, more than two, give me your fist."

I don't hesitate, though I've never done it before. My hand is small, but it's enough. After only a moment of me fisting her, she lets out a deep scream and calls out something in Spanish that I don't understand. I don't need to in order to know what it means.

We both catch our breath, her leaning back against the side of the tub.

When we can both breathe, she looks at me and then laughs and splashes me. "What a fucking mess!"

Both of us shampoo and condition, then rinse off and get out. "Don't worry about the water," she says, as I step through the one inch of pooled water on the tile. "I'll clean it up."

"I'll get some towels for it," I say, opening the door, both of us walking out of the steam and into the hallway in fluffy white towels around our heads and bodies.

"I think the steam was really good for that hair mask," she's saying, when her face falls. I look where her gaze has landed. It's Cynthia.

"Oh, fuck," says Arabella. "Thia, what are you doing here?"

Cynthia starts spewing out angry Spanish, and I feel suddenly very guilty and very weird. I thought it was just a little fun. Just a little distraction from Jordan. But now I have a sinking feeling that I don't think Jordan would think of it like that, just as I don't think Cynthia is either. I slip into my bare room and curl up on the air mattress.

What the hell am I doing?

CHAPTER THIRTEEN

FOURTEEN YEARS AGO

*Y*ou can rely on the old man's money, you can rely on the old man's
money!"

I scream-sang along with the lyrics to the Hall & Oates song
"Rich Girl" with my best friend, Sadie. We were both dressed in
outfits curated from items in my mom's closet. She wasn't home,
and usually when it was past seven on a weekend night, she
wouldn't be home all night.

Sadie was sleeping over, and her parents had taken us to the
grocery store to pick out some junk food before dropping us off. I
may have lied and told them my mom was home.

We picked out Sno-Caps and Sour Patch Kids and this micro-
wavable popcorn with a packet of butter (flavoring) and a two-liter
of the Christmas version of Sprite. We had plans to watch *Moulin
Rouge!*, which I was not allowed to watch, but which Sadie had a
copy of and said was her favorite movie.

Sadie's dad used to work in Hollywood, she'd told me, doing
music for movies. So where I was used to listening to what was on

the radio, Sadie had playlist upon playlist of music I'd never heard of that was so much better and so much fun. Also she was allowed to watch and listen to whatever, because her parents trusted her with "art," apparently. Anyway, that was what Sadie said.

"You could get along if you try to be strong——" I sang, but then stopped when I heard something mixing in with the deafening music.

I turned on my heel and saw my mom standing in the doorway with her hands on her hips and her eyes so angry they were practically red.

I smacked Sadie on the shoulder and silenced the music.

The air filled with the emptiness and I said, "Hi, Mom."

"What the *fuck* is going on here?"

I felt slapped by the words, but Sadie didn't shiver. She was a rated-R-movie and there's-always-dessert-in-the-house kind of kid. Nothing seemed to freak her out.

"Are those—my bras?" asked my mom, furious.

Sadie and I looked down at the drooping satin fabric on our flat chests.

I looked up and then noticed a man walking up the staircase. My mom turned to him.

"I'm going to head out," he said.

"What? Roger, no—"

But he was already walking down the steps again. My mom gave me a look filled with hate and then went after him, whoever he was.

Sadie and I looked at each other.

"Holy shit," said Sadie. "Your mom looked like she was about to go full *Kill Bill*."

I didn't get the reference, but shrugged and said, "Hurry, let's get this stuff off."

We hurried out of my mom's lingerie, both of us down to the leotards we had on underneath. Sadie was in my ballet class, and we had spent most of the evening so far dancing around.

We ran to put my mom's stuff away and then scrambled back to my room, where I started anxiously cleaning up the mess of two eleven-year-olds left to their own devices.

Sadie didn't miss a beat, rushing with me to make things neat again.

My mom reappeared in the doorway. "What were you *thinking*?" she asked.

"I—we were just practicing and then we were playing," I said. "We—her—Sadie's parents said she could have a sleepover."

"No, no. Absolutely not. After this? No way. Was that song supposed to be funny?"

I screwed up my face. "Huh?"

She shook her head and breathed in deeply, like she couldn't believe how dumb I could be.

"Sadie, go call your parents, have them pick you up."

Sadie, eyes wide, shuffled off to the phone to go call, and I cowered in my mom's presence by myself.

I was told to wait outside with Sadie until her parents arrived, and neither of us said a word until her parents' minivan pulled up and Sadie said, "Well . . . bye."

I dreaded going back inside. I didn't know who that man was or what was going on, but my mom was clearly pissed.

I found her in the kitchen with a trash bag, throwing out all the junk food Sadie's parents had bought us.

"Mom, no!" I said, tears starting, as if she were throwing out my old stuffed animals or something. Which I could also see her doing.

"You can't eat this shit, are you kidding me? I'm out there

finding you opportunities and you're back here doing this? What's anyone going to want with you when you can't fit through the doorway and your skin is all covered in pimples and your fat rolls are all lumpy under your leotard?"

I looked at the trash bag. I had never made a connection between food and appearance like that before. Not consciously.

"Do you know who that man was?" she asked, pointing at the doorway, where presumably he had exited. "That was Roger Harris! He has a cousin who works at one of the best ballet schools in the country. And you ruined that for yourself!"

My stomach churned.

"I'm sorry," I said quietly.

"*Sorry* my fat ass. You have to stop eating this crap—I can tell when you come back from Mimi's and she's been stuffing you with chocolate chip cookies and popcorn all goddamn weekend. You get this little roll of fat right on the edge of your leotard. See? You can see it now!"

I looked down and saw where the top of my tights ended around my stomach. "I just thought that's because it was tight. And because it's skin."

"Why do you think it's so tight, Jocelyn Rose? Jesus Christ."

She inhaled deeply and leaned against the counter.

"You have that," I said.

"I have what?"

I started to second-guess my words. "Never mind."

"I have what?" She launched off the counter and turned to me.

"The skin thing. Your clothes are tight, too."

She raised her eyebrows and bit her tongue. "It's a little different, Jocelyn. And I'm not the one who decided she so desperately needed to become a fucking prima ballerina. You know how expensive this whole thing is?"

"No," I said, honestly.

"No. Exactly. Go put on your sneakers, we're going to the club."

"What? Now?"

"Now. Let's go."

The club is a health club. We go and I run on the treadmill or use the light weight machines. But never like this. Never as punishment. Never on a Friday night.

I thought I was going to have a fun girls' night and instead, I'm going to the gym.

"Now!" she screamed.

Ten minutes later we were in the car. Ten minutes after that, we were at the gym.

I was on the treadmill, running, and my mom was at the counter, talking to some guy.

After half an hour of running, my mom came over with the guy and said, "Honey," in a sweet, girlish voice, "this is Mateo. He's a personal trainer, and he has just agreed to take you on as a client!"

She opened her mouth wide like this was the best surprise ever.

"Hi, Jocelyn. We'll keep you in shape no problem."

He sounded like a moron.

"Okay, honey, back on the treadmill. I'm going to go discuss payment options with Mateo."

The two of them left, going in the direction of the locker rooms. I ran and ran.

CHAPTER FOURTEEN

I put an outfit on the bed for you, wear it, it's perfect for the Holiday Club." Arabella says this to me, then, "Cynthia! Calm down, fucking hell!"

Cynthia is clearly still not over the other night. I don't really blame her. I tried to apologize as I hadn't really understood they were *together* together, but she waved me off. I hear her saying, "You want to talk, let's talk, but chill the fuck out. She has a meeting with the Cavendishes—she can't be dealing with all this shit before that."

Cynthia's rage pauses as she looks at me. "The Cavendishes? Clementine and Alistair?"

I nod.

Cynthia gives Arabella a meaningful look. Maybe Cynthia is one of the friends Arabella mentioned the other night.

"I'm going to get ready," I say.

"Go," says Arabella. The two of them start yelling again in Spanish.

I go into Arabella's room. I see the outfit she's picked out.

It's a nude bodice dress from Dolce & Gabbana. The shoes are strappy, also nude, Stuart Weitzman. Beside it is a dark camel coat, wool and oversized. It's as if she's setting me up to say, I am a blank slate. I can be anything.

Which she probably is. And which I am. I have to be. Arabella is a bit like a fairy godmother to me right now. I don't know what I'd do without her.

I blow-dry my hair—Cynthia and Arabella yelling so loudly I can hear them over the speaker *and* the blow-dryer. I do my makeup in a simple way that matches the look. I do just a light layer of mascara on my top lashes, brush Urban Decay's Space Cowboy eyeshadow on my lids, and line and dress my lips in a dark nude.

I look in the massive mirror she has against her bedroom wall. I look fucking good. I've already lost a few pounds thanks to being back in the studio every day and Arabella's somewhat batshit rule of no food in the apartment. There's even a little flush in my cheeks that makes me look healthy and glowing. Thanks for that, too, Arabella.

It's time for me to go, and so I walk out into the living room and see that Arabella and Cynthia are now crowding around a phone screen cackling at some video.

Guess they made up, then?

"You look gorgeous!" says Arabella. "Remember, focus on Clementine. Ballet is her thing. She's obsessed with it and goes all the time. And she loves New York, so talk about New York with her, too."

Cynthia says nothing but "Good luck."

"Uh—yeah, thank you," I say, then wave and leave.

As Mary promised, there is a car waiting for me. A glossy black car with completely opaque windows.

The driver gets out and comes to the back passenger side. "For the Cavendish dinner?" he asks, his accent *very* posh English. He sounds like Batman's butler.

"Yes, Jocelyn Banks."

"Right this way, miss."

He opens the back door and my jaw drops. It's a nice, nice, nice car. Every surface gleams; the leather seats are as soft as butter.

The driver gets in his seat and says, "Ready, miss?"

"Um—yes! Thanks. Yeah."

I'm a nervous wreck.

He glances at me before saying, "There are champagne splits in the middle console, miss."

I look where he indicates, and then open the narrow door to see six small bottles of Moët & Chandon. On a ribbon on the neck, there is a tiny gold cone I know is for putting in the top of the bottle so you can drink straight out of it without it backing up and exploding all over.

"Thank you," I say.

I'm not sure if it's the smartest thing to have champagne from the car they sent to pick me up—what if it's some kind of test?

But I could do with some liquid courage and I always get about twenty-five percent more charming after a drink or two.

I think it before I remember that it's something my mom used to say about herself.

I pop open the bottle. I deserve it.

It tastes incredible. I can't help but smile as I look out the window at the night lights of London from this absolutely over-the-top car. Where I'm drinking one of my favorite champagnes.

A wave of nerves comes over me again as I remember that I have to go impress two complete strangers. Two complete, *powerful* strangers.

I'm just starting to think maybe the champagne *was* a test when the car slows in front of a gorgeous, grand building that looks like a hotel, but which has no sign out front.

"Here we are, miss."

I'm taken to the top floor of the building in a tiny, gold elevator by a man in white gloves and a perfectly pressed, perfectly clean uniform.

The elevator opens on a glamorous, very modern, very beautiful restaurant. A woman with crossed hands is waiting for me as the doors open. She is in an all-cream linen outfit.

"Ms. Banks?" she asks.

"Uh—yeah, yes. Sorry."

A man, also in cream linen, appears and hands the woman a small glass of something pale and pink.

She in turn offers it to me. "This is an aperitif that we recommend to those of our guests who will be imbibing alcohol with their meal."

I take it, my heart pounding. This place is so soothing and relaxed, and yet I feel nothing but my nerves.

"I'll lead you to the table. Please feel free to sip as we walk."

As I follow her, I think about the local "nice" restaurant in my hometown. It was called Shister's, which was obviously mercilessly mocked by every child, teenager, and adult. When we'd arrive at Shister's, the hostess there would take a break from texting on her phone to demand to know how many of you there were, and then she would take however many menus needed—always covered in something sticky—and slap them down on a dirty table before saying something like, *Svedka will be right over to take your order.*

This is . . . a lot different.

The floor is a pale pink carpet, and the windows are floor to ceiling. The ceilings are low, but it lends an intimate, interesting feel to the place. I realize that every color is nude, cream, or this very soft salmon. Even the guests' outfits. Thank God I let Arabella dress me. If I'd been on my own, I probably would have worn something like a maraschino-red satin dress. It would have looked absurd here. Like spilled blood on a white sand beach.

As we round a corner, I see the table she is leading me to. There is only one occupant, and he is unmistakable. Even among all the wealthy diners here, his wealth just emanates off of him differently.

Max looks up and sees the hostess and me.

"What the fuck?" I say under my breath.

CHAPTER FIFTEEN

Max stands, buttoning his blazer.

He cuts an imposing figure, his features chiseled, his eyes piercing. I feel a shiver go down my spine as those eyes land on mine.

"Jocelyn," says Alistair, in a deep, husky voice. "A pleasure to finally meet you. Alistair Cavendish."

I'm so confused. This is Max. As in, Max, the one-night stand I was supposed to have and forget. I mean, the forgetting wasn't going that well—I've thought about that night every hour since it happened—but I wasn't supposed to see him again. And why is he saying he's Alistair?

He holds out a hand and I take it, his strong grip making my own feel weak.

He gives me a glance that indicates that the hostess is still there and listening. I'm supposed to go along with this.

"Likewise, Mr. Cavendish," I say, winging it. "Thank you for agreeing to meet with me."

"Of course. I always like to meet the new young talent in town. Please, sit."

I can hear that hint of something besides English in his accent, and I remember what Arabella told me about his past and how his family made its money.

I do as I'm told, and pretend to look at the menu, but really I'm looking at him through my lashes. I suddenly feel very bare. Completely exposed.

He is dressed in a suit so completely, startlingly well fitting that it must have been made from scratch just for him. His crisp white shirt is unbuttoned at the neck and I see a glimpse of his collarbone.

I stutter, "Is—is your wife joining us?"

"Yes. I apologize for her tardiness, she's not usually late. I haven't checked my phone, I can't stand being so attached to it." He pulls out his phone anyway, but is interrupted by a small squeak.

The hostess, who still hasn't left.

Alistair and I both turn to her.

"I'm so sorry, Mr. Cavendish, I forgot to tell you that Mrs. Cavendish won't be joining you this evening. I'm so sorry, sir."

He holds her gaze with such intense impassivity that I feel a crushing secondhand embarrassment.

"I'm so sorry, Mr. Cavendish. She said you weren't answering your phone, I—I simply forgot, sir."

She then bows her head in apology.

He nods once slowly before saying, "That'll be all, Francesca."

She whispers another apology before heading off, and I feel so bad for her I almost want to go with her and tell her it's all right.

My cheeks flush. I look down at the menu, feeling an awful, weird rush of embarrassment for my very existence. Even though

I'm where I'm supposed to be, doing what I'm supposed to be doing.

Finally, we're alone. I put down my menu and hiss, "What the fuck is going on?"

He shuts his eyes impatiently. "I lied about my name."

"Well, duh."

"I never use my real name when I meet strangers," he says. "I'm not the only Alistair in the city, but I am the only one in the social pages. It's just best to keep the attention off of me."

"I see."

"I've given my real name before and seen it in the headlines the next day alongside a slew of lies. It's just easier."

"Got it."

"I'm sorry about all this," he says, formally.

"It's fine. We didn't know."

There's a long silence as a woman comes over and asks, "Sparkling or still?"

We both say, "Still," then avoid eye contact.

She leaves, comes back, fills our glasses, and then leaves again.

"I apologize," he says. "This sponsorship was supposed to be more for Clementine, not me. I haven't been that involved in the ballet lately."

He looks at me, and for the first time I see something less than steely wash over his irises.

"I hope she's all right," I say.

"I'm sure she's fine. Just a busy woman. Hard to pin down."

Our eyes latch for an unexpected moment, and I laugh nervously and then can't think of anything to say.

"To be completely honest with you, I'm not sure why we're bringing on another dancer, Ms. Banks. Clementine hardly has time for a dinner, much less a sponsorship."

This is so awkward. Talking business with a man who wasn't supposed to exist after the other night.

"Back in New York I barely even saw my donor. Honestly, I'm no trouble. I'm very good and—" I laugh again. "Sorry, I sound like a puppy hoping to be adopted."

"Dad not around much when you were growing up?"

I feel like I missed a step. "Sorry?"

A server approaches the table, hands behind her back.

"Good evening, and welcome. Have we had a chance to look over the wine list?"

"Do you have a preference?" he asks me.

"Oh—anything."

This isn't quite true, but I assume he's not going to order a box of Franzia, so I'm sure it's fine.

"We'll take a bottle of that Chablis, thank you, Mauritia."

"Thank you, Mr. Cavendish." She smiles gently and then walks off.

"As I was saying," he goes on. "I am happy to buy you dinner so that you don't feel as though you wasted your time, but I have to be up-front and tell you that we're simply not in a position to be taking on any more sponsorships. You seem like a nice girl. I don't want to try to fool you. I wish Clementine hadn't agreed to this dinner at all, especially since she couldn't come. It's exactly the problem—she doesn't have time for this right now. I'm sorry."

Well, for one thing, that *isn't* what he was saying, *he* was saying something about me having Daddy issues.

Nevertheless, I feel my heart sink down to the salmon-colored floor. Mary Simon said they were the only donors in town that would be big enough to move me up quickly. My mind begins to immediately reel with the need for new plans. To try a new company, I would need to move somewhere else.

Is my position at my old ballet company still available?

That would mean truly letting go of Jordan. How could we ever bounce back if I move away again?

A moment later, Mauritia reappears with a bottle of white wine. She presents it to us.

"This is the nineteen ninety-six Vincent Dauvissat Chablis Grand Cru 'Les Clos.'"

"Perfect."

Nineteen ninety-*six*? This wine is older than *I* am.

The server opens the bottle and then pours a splash into his glass. He swirls the glass, then sniffs it, then tastes it. "That's excellent, thank you."

She pours our glasses, then places the bottle in a tableside chiller that appears to be temperature regulated.

"It's all such a ridiculous thing, the wine. I know. It's a pretention. But it's also damn good wine."

I nod and say, "Probably better than that shit we drank the other night."

We both take a sip, our eyes catching over the rims of our glasses. I can see amusement in his.

My heart sinks as I realize what's happening here. He's really rejecting me. And he's *slept* with me. The answer must really be no.

"You look deflated," he says when he sets his glass down.

"To be honest, I am," I say, and then much to my bewilderment and fury, tears start to well. I dab at my eyes with the napkin, which feels like a waste of such fine fabric, and then shake my head. "God, I'm so sorry, I never cry. I don't know what's going on."

"You can still stay at this ballet company and wait for another donor to come around, no? Mary Simon gave you a glowing review. So it's really only a matter of time, correct?"

I nod bravely and clear my throat.

I know I don't have time. I have Mimi to think about.

"Of course. I'm sorry. It's not your problem. I can go. This is all so weird."

I almost want to. Part of me wants to flee, run into the street and burst into ugly tears and then drown my sorrows in a bowl of Guinness Dubliner soup. But another part of me wants to stay here. Convince this man, who is clearly very powerful, to second-guess his good business instinct and sponsor me anyway.

"No. Don't go. I at least owe you dinner after all this."

"You bought me dinner first, remember?"

Another flash of amusement, but then he looks serious again.

"Ma—I mean . . . Mr. Cavendish—" I start to say, adrenaline boosting my nerve.

I don't get a chance to finish, as a food runner comes over with a silver tray of oysters on chipped ice.

"From the chef, Mr. Cavendish," says the runner. "These are Gillardeau oysters from Île d'Oléron, sir."

"Thank you, Eugene.

"These are very good," Alistair tells me. "The Gillardeau oysters come with a laser etching on the shell to prevent counterfeiting."

I hesitate. Should I just storm out? Or should I sink into this?

My eyebrows raise as I take one off the ice. I start to put a splash of mignonette on, when his hand touches mine.

I almost gasp at the surprise of his touch and the warmth of it.

"Trust me, try it on its own first," he says. "They're exceptional."

"Okay." I smile and then do as he says.

For me, oysters are nothing but an expensive vehicle for the crisp, tart bite of mignonette or the sinus-searing electricity of fresh horseradish, but I do it anyway.

He does not seem to be the kind of man you want to say *no* to.

I tilt my head back and let the oyster fall into my mouth. My tongue lights up with the bright minerality and soft texture.

"That's delicious," I say, covering my mouth and pretending it was as delicious as he said it would be. Maybe I'm just unsophisticated, but I missed the shallots and vinegar.

He flips over his shell on the ice and I see the engraving he was talking about, then do the same with my empty shell.

"If this were the other night, it would be time to mention how oysters are an aphrodisiac."

Oh my *god*, why did I say that? That's the kind of thing you *think*, you don't *say*. Holy shit, and how inappropriate!

I bite my bottom lip and look at him, ready to apologize, but he has a slight smile at the corner of his lips. Even if there is a slight expression of cringe in the set of his brow.

"You know, oysters used to grow in the Thames. They went extinct." He gives a shake of his head. "Unimaginable now, though I hear they're back."

"That's a much more interesting tidbit than mine," I say.

"I liked yours, too," he says.

It would sound almost flirtatious if his eyes hadn't completely wandered away from our table and into the belly of the restaurant.

We *cannot* be attracted to each other. As good as the other night was. We just cannot. Not now. Not now that I know who he is.

God, this is such a fucking disaster. This is what I get for wishing *out loud* that life were like a movie.

"This menu is amazing. I don't know where to begin."

This is very, very true. Unlike my review of the naked oyster. Most of this menu is in other languages, seeming to be as much in French as it is in Hebrew as it is in an Asian language I'm too ignorant to identify.

"I'm happy to order for you. If you wish."

"Sure," I say, putting down the menu, relieved.

He doesn't ask me what I like. Doesn't ask if I have any dietary restrictions. It reminds me of when I met Jordan for the first time in Vienna and he helped me order off of a long, complicated menu. He had been thoughtful and gentle. Nothing like this man, who exudes power and couldn't seem less interested in something as frivolous as personal taste or a gluten allergy.

Neither of which I seem to have at the moment.

I sniff a little, still affected by my momentary tears. My nerve has decreased, and I don't have the zeal I had a few moments ago to aggressively tell him to sponsor me.

Instead, I reach for my wine, which I didn't really notice or taste, since I was too busy sharing an unexpected glance with Alistair and trying not to weep openly at what is unquestionably a Michelin-starred restaurant.

It's magnificent. So wildly good that I can't believe I didn't notice it at first.

It tastes like how I imagine butter, but also how I imagine the scent of fresh lemon. The weight of it feels like my tongue pressed against someone else's—someone delicious and intoxicating.

"This wine is amazing," I say.

"It's my favorite."

He orders for us, and I don't even understand what he says, so I'm glad I didn't try to wade through the muddy language waters myself.

It's odd to me, letting a man order for me. It's the kind of thing I never do. It brings to mind Kathy Bates's line in *Titanic* when Cal orders for Rose. *You gonna cut her meat for her, too, there, Cal?*

It's not me at all, but there's something that's sort of a relief about it. To take the reins of my life and hand them over to someone else, even just for a meal.

For the next two courses, I try to get up the guts to tell him to sponsor me and I keep getting distracted by his conversation, his mouth around his fork, his hands on his knife, the scent of his cologne wafting toward me.

We make small talk and pretend we haven't tasted each other.

He tells me about the first time he had the wine and asks me about my own indulgences. I tell him I love champagne and that I can't stop smoking, even though I want to.

He doesn't ask me where or how I grew up. He doesn't ask me about ballet. He doesn't tell me about his wife.

And I don't ask.

I try yet again, two glasses in, to tell him to sponsor me, but I'm thrown off when he asks me what brought me to London.

"I moved here with someone," I say, aware of how thin it sounds. "An artist," I add, to beef it up.

"Anyone I might have heard of?"

"Jordan Morales?"

"That's the artist you mentioned?" He thinks, and then says, "Large abstracts?"

I feel a shudder run through me at the idea that he knows Jordan's work. "Yes," I say.

"I had no idea that was who had a show the other night. I would have loved to go. I was just reading that he is one of the best artists to invest in right now."

I don't mention that my friend Artie wrote that article.

"That's what they say," I agree.

"It's possible I already own a piece. I'm not sure."

"How is that possible?"

He looks puzzled for a second and then adds, "I'm not aware of all the stocks I own at this point either. It's an investment. If I'm correct, and I do own one, then it's likely in a free port wrapped in weather- and climate-resistant packaging in order to preserve it."

"Oh," I say. Then, "He'd hate that."

He finishes the last bite of his food and says, "He won't hate it when he's a millionaire with his work being studied around the world because rich assholes like me made it worth more."

I don't know why it is, but I know this is my chance.

"People act like money can't buy you happiness, but I disagree."

"You say this from the perspective of having none, I presume?"

"Well. I did have some. For a while, when I danced in New York. But I grew up with nothing and my mom was miserable."

"No father?"

My hackles rise a little. "Not that I ever met."

He leans back. "So I was right."

"So we're not pretending you didn't ask that earlier?"

This feisty response seems to intrigue him more. I feel my thighs grow unexpectedly warm.

"You think money would solve all your problems. I'll tell you a little secret." He leans in again. "You're probably right."

I scoff.

He lets me hold his gaze and I do so challengingly. "Sponsor me."

It is my instinct to backtrack. To laugh. To say I'm kidding. To look away. But I do none of these things, letting our eyes stay locked.

"How will that benefit me?" he asks.

This is it.

"I'm fucking amazing. You can't put something like me in a

free port and wrap me in plastic. You only get chances like me in the moment. As you well know."

Something changes in his eyes, something unknowable. His intrigue and amusement meet something else, a box somewhere inside him.

I need to shatter that box.

Our last course is placed in front of us.

I've been so enraptured in his gaze that I didn't even notice the server remove our last plates.

"This is the uni with black garlic," says Mauritia, before backing away professionally.

"So what do you say?" I ask.

He hesitates.

"How far are you willing to go for your career?" he asks.

"A question like that from a man like you—that's when most smart women would get up and leave the table."

He raises his eyebrows. "You seem smart."

"I am."

"Then what are you still doing here?"

My heart is huge in my throat. We're closer than we were before, and even though it's a respectful distance, I feel as though I can feel the heat coming from him.

"Sponsor me. Max."

CHAPTER SIXTEEN

When I get back to Arabella's that night, she has moody music playing and the apartment is cast in darkness but for a few red candles burning by the open windows.

I recognize the music as being a Kelsey Lu album called *Blood*.

Arabella is lying face down on the couch completely naked, flipping through a magazine.

I put the key back under the mat and then shut the door behind me, locking it.

"Arabella?"

She rolls over and I see her whole body. She is slow and languid, moving like honey.

"*Jozz-leen*," she says, wetly. "You came back."

"Of course I did." I glance around. "What's going on in here?"

I ask without judgment, but seriously, what the hell is going on? I realize then that maybe she has someone over.

"Nothing is *going on*," she says. "I'm just feeling myself. I did a *little bit* of Molly. And now I'm sort of rolling around. Looking at pictures of beautiful people."

Oh, so exactly what it looks like.

"That's fun," I say.

"You're a beautiful person," she says. "Where were you?" Her long hair hangs over her breasts, barely concealing her nipples.

"I was at dinner. Remember? The Cavendish dinner?"

Her face darkens. "Right. I remember. I forgot."

"Clementine didn't show up," I say, trying to sound normal, going to the fridge and pouring a glass of water. "So it was just Alistair and me."

There is a heavy silence behind me. I turn and see her looking at me.

When I look at her, she smiles and says, "And how was that?"

"It was okay," I say. "He's very intense."

"Intense."

"Yeah. I think it was okay, though."

"He's not going to sponsor you, though. I heard he has so many things going on that he probably has no space for another."

I narrow my eyes at her momentarily, but then take a sip and say, "He might. I think he might."

She shuts her eyes and shakes her head in confusion. "That can't be right."

This is so weird. I know she's on drugs, but still.

She then seems to change her mind about unpuzzling it all, and bursts into a big, incongruent smile. "Come over here!"

She stretches her arms out and puts a leg down on the ground to make space for me.

I put my phone and purse down and go to her.

"You are so beautiful," she says, putting her arms around me.

Her thick dark hair tangles against her face as she presses her lips to my neck. Then she whispers, "I've been thinking about you all night."

My breath quickens at the sudden contact. Her legs are over my lap; my legs are basically bare beneath the airy slip dress.

Her hand runs slowly from where she tucks my hair behind my ear down my neck, down my collarbone, and to my silk-clad breast.

"*Dios mío*, that is so soft. You wouldn't believe," she says with a deep-throated laugh, her lips and teeth now on my clavicle.

"Will you touch me?" she asks, desperate and lethargic. "Please."

She looks at me, her glassy eyes like those of a doe, her puffy lips swollen and the color of maraschino cherries.

I have so much more to think about, but suddenly my mind is empty of anything but desire. I've been *wanting* all night. I wanted Max. Or Alistair. Whatever his name is.

Now Arabella is here, and I want her, too.

I let my lips land on hers and she lets out a relieved moan of satisfaction.

Our tongues touch for the first time, and hers tastes like vermouth. Hot and red, as juicy as a ripe peach. Suddenly I want to consume her desperately.

I put my glass down and push her back onto the couch. My thigh lands between her legs and I can feel that she is dripping wet. I can smell her, too. As psycho as she may be, Arabella smells like she got her pussy at Le Labo.

It makes me feel drunk with desire.

I pull my straps down and lie on top of her, our nipples touching, our breasts pressing together. I shut my eyes and kiss her, unable to resist thinking of Alistair.

I think of the way his mouth looked as he pressed the oyster shell to it. I imagine his five-o'clock shadow against my thighs.

Arabella groans and it brings me back to her. She takes my hand and drags it across her body and down to the wetness between her legs.

"Oh my god," I say into her ear. "You're so wet."

"Everything feels amazing, just touch me."

I play with her clit, putting my fingers inside her and feeling her soft inside. She writhes against me, her warm skin dewy with sweat. It clings to my dress and to my own skin.

"Jocelyn," she says, "you are so beautiful. So fucking beautiful. You're so hot."

I think of Alistair again as I touch her. I think of him touching me. Those hands, the ones that had such a hard grip—I remember them grabbing my waist, my breasts, cupping my jaw and drinking me in.

His hands on my ass, spreading me apart then entering me.

I let out a gasp of desire and she says, "Oh, yeah, baby? Does that turn you on?"

She pulls up the dress and moves aside the panties, her fingers entering me two at a time. The pressure of the width makes me want more as I think about Alistair.

I remember the taste and feel of his dick, hard as marble and hot as sun-soaked silicone. I picture it entering me, too big to be easy, but not so big that it hurts.

"Harder," I whisper, breathless.

"Harder," she responds.

We both press harder on and into each other.

I bury my face in her neck and breathe in her spicy scent. Kelsey Lu's silky voice sings on in the background, mingling with the street sounds.

I hit the right spot on Arabella and I feel her tighten on my fingers.

"Yes, yes," she says. "*Yes*. I'm going to—I'm—"

She climaxes, tightening and pulsing around the rhythmic motion of my hand.

After she finishes, she hurries out from under me, flips me over until I'm on my stomach, and pulls my ass up toward her until her mouth is on my clit.

I let out a primal sound of pleasure as she puts her fingers inside me and she manages to get her tongue around to my clit.

I remember my ass pressed against Alistair's solid-looking frame. I imagine his strong sculpted stomach. I remember how he pulled me back hard again and again on his throbbing dick during round two.

I get close and I tell Arabella. She groans against me, and the vibration of the hum gets me there.

In my mind, Alistair bursts inside me. On Arabella's couch, I reach climax and I yell out in orgasm.

She slaps a hand over my mouth, laughing behind my ear.

"Shut up, you silly girl, we have neighbors."

I laugh when I can breathe again, and we both collapse on the couch, panting.

"You know I was kidding. You can be loud as you want. I don't care."

"I'm sorry if it was—"

She takes my jaw in her hand and says, "I don't care!" She gets up, still fully naked, and goes over to the window. At the top of her lungs, she screams, "I just *came*, motherfucker!"

I crack up, saying *shhh!* but not really meaning it.

We slip into T-shirts and Arabella makes popcorn, and we fall asleep on the couch watching *Sliding Doors*.

I watch the main character's life split in two, all because of one small decision. Where, and how many times, did my life split?

What if I'd never gone to that restaurant in Vienna and met Jordan?

What if I'd gone to a different bar here in London, never met Alistair, when I thought he was Max?

What if my mom hadn't gotten in the car that night, or had left the house a moment later?

It's a dizzying rabbit hole.

I was supposed to go into that bar that night. It's what gave me the courage to tell Alistair to choose me. And in my last wakeful thoughts, I make a promise to the universe that I'll do anything for him to say yes.

CHAPTER SEVENTEEN

It's Sunday afternoon. The matinee show of *Swan Lake* is about to begin.

It's officially the end of my third week back to work. The first two weeks were brutal, learning a slightly different version of *Swan Lake* than the one at NAB, back in New York. Not to mention the ego death of not being the Swan Queen. It has been humbling, to say the least.

The loudspeaker comes on in the soloist dressing room I share with six other girls, letting us know it is our fifteen-minute call to places. I look at myself in the mirror and do a final check of my makeup. The fake eyelashes enhance my dark eyes so much they almost look like a doll's eyes. My lips are perfect little bows. My cheeks a flushed pink.

My mirror in the dressing room looks a bit untidy, but to me it's an organized mess. I know my hairpins are lying underneath my headpiece and that my MAC concealer is beside the water bottle where I mix them a little together to get the right texture for stage. And my lipstick is beside the banana I was munching on as a reminder to touch up my lips after eating it.

My pointe shoes are divided into two piles. Two pairs selected for today's show and ten pairs as backup for the show and our rehearsal week ahead. Two photos are taped up on my mirror. I put them there after my first show back. One of Sylvie and me when we were eighteen in Paris for the first time, both of us in all black, laughing under the Eiffel Tower. The other is of Mimi and me at my very first recital. I'm wearing the ugliest little bright blue tutu and a tiara on top of my head—I can still remember how it pinched. She is giving me a big hug and beaming with pride.

It's my favorite photo. I've had it up in every dressing room since I became a professional ballerina.

In one of the drawers, I have a picture of my mom and me. I've been going back and forth about putting it up. But it just doesn't feel right. Beneath that picture is a picture of Jordan and me. I know I shouldn't look at it. It's like salt on a wound, but I can't help but take it out every now and then.

As I place my headpiece on my slicked-back hair, Arabella comes waltzing into our dressing room.

"Jocelyn!" she coos. "Come out with Cynthia and me tonight, we're going to celebrate your first performance week back with some *deliciosas tapas*."

"Yeah—um, I'd love to, but are you sure . . . Cynthia wants to?" I look around just to make sure she's not in the room. She's already left for the stage.

"*Claro*, of course. Cynthia's not like that; she knows I love everyone. I'm like the female version of Luca, maybe." She laughs. "I don't mean any harm, she knows this."

I think she's flattering herself a little bit, but she's probably not wrong.

"All right," I say, using hairpins to secure my flower headpiece.

I'm dancing a pas de trois this afternoon as one of Prince Siegfried's friends.

"By the way, what are you doing here?" I ask. "You must be exhausted from playing the Swan Queen last night."

Obviously, I'm slightly jealous. Being the principal means you get to focus on only being the principal and not dancing every show. You *get* to be exhausted.

"I'm here for a massage. It's Benjamin on today as the massage therapist and I was not going to miss a chance at those magic hands rubbing me down." She winks. "I must be off. I'll see you tonight!"

Later that evening, Arabella, Cynthia, and I are leaving a Spanish restaurant where we ordered almost everything on the menu. We justified it to our diets by ordering only the proteins and skipping all the carbs. Well, almost all the carbs. We do have a chance to work it off once *Swan Lake* performances start again Tuesday evening.

Arabella and Cynthia both cheerfully deemed every item as subpar, even though I thought everything was exceptional. And I wouldn't have cared if it was bad anyway. I'm just glad to be out and about, a ballerina again, back onstage, the first week of shows complete. The Band-Aid ripped off. Cynthia and I are getting along. She seems to have released her anger at me. Arabella might be right.

I do feel a bit guilty about it happening again with Arabella, but I'm keeping that moment to myself. Cynthia doesn't need to know. It's not my place to tell her. And it's definitely not like I have feelings for Arabella.

We went through two pitchers of sangria, deciding that we deserved it after five straight days of *Swan Lake* performances. It's been a few weeks now since I joined the company, and my body is feeling the pain. Every muscle is tender. Even my fingers are sore from sewing my pointe shoes. When I get up in the mornings and first put weight on my feet, I feel like my metatarsals are going to snap. But honestly, I fucking love it. It's like I forgot how much my body used to work and I missed it.

My mind missed the push.

And I'm pushing myself *hard*. Since I don't have a confirmed donor, I'm desperate to ensure that I am indispensable to the company. Too good to fire.

As a soloist, I'm dancing roles I haven't danced in years, but I don't care. I'm just happy to be out there breathing again. And, incredibly, my body remembers every little movement like it was yesterday. I've pretty much lost all the weight I gained on my hiatus.

We've left the restaurant now and are walking down the sidewalk to the next place, cracking up about the absurdity of most ballet plots.

"I mean, come on," I'm saying, "an evil sorcerer turning princesses into animals. This is high art."

The girls laugh. My phone rings and I take it out of my purse, looking at the unknown number.

Usually when I get a call from a number I don't recognize, I just ignore it. Like everyone, I've had enough spam calls to last a lifetime. But with Mimi's health, I can't help but pick up.

I peel off from the girls and plug one ear as I answer.

"Hello?"

"Jocelyn Banks," says the voice.

I recognize his voice right away. Alistair Cavendish.

I look up to see Arabella is watching me, her gaze over the shoulder of her fur coat.

I hide the expression on my face and turn away from her.

I know I shouldn't have been, but I've been thinking of him constantly. I can't figure out why. I haven't had contact with him and I've been on pins and needles for a couple of weeks wondering if he's going to sponsor me. Yet my mind often wanders to other parts of him.

My unconscious mind has memorized his every mannerism and feature and quirk. Like how his smile's a little crooked in this wry, constantly clever way. And how his blue eyes are more like turquoise and how they have little rings of hazel around the pupil. And how serious his voice sounds. How noticeably well his clothes hang on him, and how clear it is that every stitch has been measured to fit him perfectly. But most of all, I'm fascinated by the way his looks don't match his spirit. One moment, he looks like a villain, the next, he seems gentle and sweet.

And I cannot help but remember how that spectrum of intensity translates in the bedroom.

Look, I get it, I sound straight-up obsessed. And I'm not.

I mean. Not only are there extreme rules about donor-dancer relationships, with consequences such as losing your job, that I can't afford to break, but also he's married, and also I'm not over Jordan, and a million other things. And yet, did I have not one but *two* super-hot sex dreams about him? Yes, I did.

"This is Alistair Cavendish."

"Oh, hi, how are you?"

"I'm well, thank you for asking. I just had dinner with Charlie. We signed the papers. Clementine and I will officially be sponsoring you."

"Officially . . ."

"We're sponsoring you. You can breathe easy."

"Oh my god," I say, actually doing as he says, and breathing deeply. "That's a huge relief. Thank you!"

I say that last part unsure if that's the appropriate response.

Someone zooms past, laying their hand on the horn, and I hear it on the other end of the phone line.

"I'm out in Soho right now, where are you?" I ask because it sounds like he's literally on the same street as me, but it sounds forward. "I just heard the car horn and—"

He hangs up.

Fuck. Fuck, fuck, *fuck*. I'm an idiot. He *just* said he'd sign me and—

There's a tap on my shoulder.

I turn and slip a little in my stiletto. It's Alistair.

I glance back at Arabella and Cynthia, who are now both staring on with looks of shock.

"Hi," I say.

"Hi," he says back. He doesn't seem like the kind of guy who uses that word a lot, so it sounds a little funny on his tongue.

"What are you doing here?"

"I just left Berenjak. Where have you been?"

"We just had tapas." My heart is pounding. Standing with him on the chilly street is very different from sitting across a table from him in a warm restaurant. "I'm sorry, I'm really surprised to see you. It's nice—it's nice to see you."

He looks at the girls staring on. "Let me take you all for a drink."

I look at Arabella again. They're sitting on the low wall behind them and talking, never taking their eyes off of us.

I weigh the professional benefits of accommodating my donor's request versus having a drink with a married man when I'm a little bit buzzed and have been fantasizing about him for days. We had a one-night stand, but I will not repeat that.

Also I'm not alone. I've got Arabella and Cynthia. They can serve as my chaperones.

"I think there's a place around here . . ."

He wets his lips as he furrows his brow and looks around at the nearby restaurants.

It's definitely a bad idea.

"Sure," I say, ignoring that voice in my head.

"Ah, yes, it's right down there. Get your friends. We can walk there. I'll just text my wife to tell her I'll be a little late."

I want to ask him about the divorce. Why is he suddenly acting like he's just . . . happily married?

I don't ask. Instead I just say, "Are you sure that's a good idea?"

He gives me an intense look that makes me back down.

I go over to Cynthia and Arabella.

"So . . . Alistair wants to take us for drinks."

"Don't you mean Mr. Cavendish?" asks Arabella.

I give a self-conscious laugh, and then say, wryly, "Right, well, whoever that guy is." Then, after checking over my shoulder, I lean into them and excitedly whisper, "He said he and Clementine are going to sponsor me! They just signed the papers!"

Arabella stares at me, her face unchanging. Cynthia looks at her, then to me, then back to Alistair.

She then clears her throat and gives me a look that means *He's coming.*

"So what do you ladies say? I feel it would be impolite not to buy you at least a glass of champagne in celebration. Three of the world's best dancers. I'd be a fool not to."

"Sure, we'll come," says Arabella.

Alistair briefly puts a guiding hand on my lower back, and even through my down coat it gives me chills.

We start down the busy road, Arabella talking to Alistair about some bureaucratic thing that happened at the company last year that only just got resolved.

"This place used to be a tube station," he says as he opens the door for us.

Walking in, I revel in the bizarre juxtaposition of the gleaming, familiar tiles set against the sound of lively chatter and the glow of orange, hot pink, and green lights.

"It's *packed*!" I yell to Arabella, who is standing right next to me.

"What?" she yells back.

I shake my head and do a *never mind* hand gesture.

Alistair leans in to speak close to my ear to be heard, but instead I turn the wrong way and my lips graze his. It's like an electric current. When his lips find my ear, he doesn't even seem to raise his voice, but its deep hum resonates through me so that I feel it more than I hear it. "I'll be right back."

He holds up a finger to tell me to wait a second, and he walks away and speaks to a woman with 1940s-styled hair who immediately nods and takes us to a small, intimate table with a Reserved sign on it. She removes it.

On the wall beside it there is an old poster of a foot on the back of a shovel with the quote, GROW YOUR OWN VEGETABLES FOR THEIR SAKE! beneath it.

I sit down, Alistair sits beside me, and the girls sit across from us, Arabella across from me and Cynthia across from him.

A server comes immediately over. He's definitely getting the star treatment.

"Do you know what you'd like to drink?" he asks, and I can hear him better now, but we still have to speak loudly and lean close.

"Uh—champagne?" I ask the server. It's what he said he wanted to get us, so it feels like the best choice.

"We'll just have a bottle," he says. "Dom is fine if you don't have Krug."

The server nods, looking excited about her upcoming tip, and then goes off to retrieve it.

"You're lucky I still like champagne," says Arabella.

He gives a polite smile.

Understanding starts to creep in. They know each other. There's something to their relationship that is more than passing ships at the company.

Who doesn't Alistair know?

He looks good tonight in a black sweater with the sleeves rolled up and a pair of burgundy jeans. He doesn't look stodgy and old-school. It's clear that he's wearing expensive things that are made to look basic, simple, and clean.

He smells like tobacco and red wine in a way that seems curated. I find him intoxicating. As he looks around the room, I study his profile. His jaw is sharp and cutting and I see stubble from a couple of days without shaving. I love stubble. I imagine the stubble grazing and tickling my tits and then I realize I need some water.

As if she reads my mind, the server comes back over with a glass bottle of Evian water and four glasses. She takes them off her tray and sets them down. A moment later, someone else follows with a bottle of Krug and four glasses.

She sets them down, and he asks her, "Do you have the Zalto glasses? Thanks."

She nods, takes away the champagne flutes, and returns with four angular glasses with narrow stems.

Arabella does an exaggerated roll of the eyes and I kick her under the table.

Once it's poured, I take a sip. It's the best champagne I've ever had.

"Jesus, that's delicious," I say.

"I know Arabella thinks I'm a dick for asking for the nice glasses, but it makes a difference. No matter how rich you are, no one wants to spend four hundred quid on a bottle of champagne and then have it taste like piss."

I'm so surprised by his tone, by his colloquial nature, thinking it's so different from how it was a couple weeks ago. Then I realize—he's already had a few drinks. It's him loosened up. We didn't even finish the bottle at dinner the other night.

"So do you all know each other, then?" I ask, when I see Arabella's intense gaze staying on Alistair.

She lights up then.

"*Claro!* Of course we do! His wife is on the board, and I'm close with Clementine. I must have told you that, no?"

"No," I say.

Cynthia looks uncomfortable.

"He tags along with her to all the parties to meet the beautiful women." She winks at him. "He's like a puppy."

He doesn't get defensive, but he narrows his eyes ever so slightly.

I can't help but think he looks even more handsome when he's brooding.

Arabella then picks up her glass and slams the rest of her champagne. It actually hurts to watch her waste it like that.

She slams her hands on the table.

"Well, we've decided to go somewhere else." Her words are neutral, but something about her tone isn't. "And it looks like you're quite cozy here. You two. You'd make a cute couple, you know."

I'm mortified. It's such a weird thing to say. Such a strange power move.

I give her a look that means *What the fuck is wrong with you*. She ignores me.

"I'll be just fine. Thanks," I say, coolly.

"Be careful with that one," she says to me. "He bites."

He leans back, staring daggers at her. If she were a man, I would think Alistair was about two seconds from knocking him out.

I am extremely grateful that I didn't tell her the one-night stand with Max was actually Alistair.

"Bye-bye," Arabella says, grabbing Cynthia's arm as she struggles to get down the rest of her own champagne. She chokes on it and sets it down.

"Thank you," she says.

They turn to leave, but then Arabella turns back and says, "Alistair, this one is going to be a lot of work." She points at me. "She's into girls. But trust me, she's worth it." She glances at me. "Her pussy tastes amazing."

The smile has faded from Cynthia's face and she pulls Arabella away from us, and the two vanish into the crowd.

I have no idea what to say. I am absolutely mortified.

I knew Arabella had something fiery in her. I knew she couldn't be as nice as she seemed. I know she's drunk. But there was something dark in everything that just happened.

I have no words.

I turn to Alistair when I finally get up the guts to look at him. I'm humiliated.

When he finally looks back at me, he says, "I know we're not supposed to say women are psycho anymore. But Arabella . . ."

"She's a fucking psycho. There, I said it for you."

I feel like if I was made to stand up right now, I'd collapse.

But then he smiles, and then he starts to laugh. After a moment, I can't help but start laughing, too.

"So," he says then, "what are you working on at the ballet now?"

"Are we pretending we don't know each other still?" I ask.

"We are in public." He drops his voice.

"Ha, right, well, uh . . . we're performing *Swan Lake* right now. Rehearsals are about to start for *Manon*. Which is a completely new ballet for me. I've watched it a thousand times, but never performed it, so I'm really excited. It's such a gorgeous ballet," I say.

"Yes, I think I've heard of this one. It's about the prostitute?"

"Well, almost, but not quite." I laugh, nervous. "It's more complex and beautiful than that. It's about a young girl who was supposed to go to a convent, falls in love with a handsome student, then gets persuaded by her brother to become the companion of this older guy."

"Hm."

"Yeah. So instead of being with her true love, she goes with the older guy who has promised to take care of her and her brother."

"What's the catch?"

"Well, he'll support her, but . . . in return for her companionship."

"Ah. I see. I assume that's not the happy ending."

"Well. No. She tries to leave the older guy, to go be with the one she loves. When she does, the older man kills her brother and has her arrested as a prostitute."

"Not very good manners."

"No. So she's sent to perish in an American jail, but her true love goes with her and kills the jailer when he forces himself on Manon."

"There's the happy ending."

"Well, no, then Manon dies in her love's arms in the swamps of Louisiana. It's all very tragic."

"That's a much more romantic way of laying out the story," he says.

"I hope you make it to a show." I blush at my own words.

He notices.

"What can I do for you, Jocelyn?"

"Do for me? I don't . . . I don't know what you mean."

"You're my dancer now. You're my Renoir, and I need to give you the right climate. Wrap you in the right materials. Preserve you. So I want you to tell me how to do it. I'm supposed to help you be the best dancer and in return I guess you give me bragging rights. And backstage access."

My insides swirl. "Well, these drinks are a good start."

I meant it to deflate the double-entendre vibe of the conversation, but after saying it, it was obvious I'd made it worse.

I see the slightest, almost invisible flick of his left eyebrow.

"I'm happy to buy you some champagne, but we should talk soon about this sort of behavior. If you're my dancer, I'll want you to stay in peak physical condition. I'm not a dictator, but I don't want you running around London getting trashed like Arabella does."

I feel embarrassed. Too embarrassed to revert to what my normal reaction to something like this would be, where I'd buck at his implication that he can or should control me.

The truth is . . . he can.

Why does that actually feel like such a relief right now?

"I'm not telling you I'll suck all the fun out of life. If you want biweekly massages—from a qualified professional, of course—we can do that. Or cryotherapy. Or normal therapy. Or orchids flown in from Hawaii every four days. Whatever you need."

"Oh . . . I don't . . ."

"Just say the word. I want you to be able to perform at your absolute best. So, whatever that means to you."

My mind starts to reel as I imagine what I could ask for if I were willing to take full advantage.

And . . . am I not?

I always hate movies where the main character rejects help. Where they tear up checks. Where they turn down the great promotion just because of some ethical dilemma. It's not very human. I went from living in a shithole town to living in a shoebox in New York to this. Why wouldn't I let this rich, incredibly sexy guy—no, no, just this platonic donor—treat me.

I think of Mimi. Mimi, who needs care, who is about to be out on the streets. I open my mouth, trying to get up the nerve to tell him the truth—I need help paying for my grandmother's care.

But at the last second, I can't do it.

"This isn't what it was like for me in the States," I say. "My donor was sort of invisible."

"Not me. I want to be involved. I want to take care of you."

There's something soft in his features then. I crumble under his gaze.

"No one's ever taken care of me," I say, and then regret it so instantly I actually slap my hand over my mouth. "Oh my god, sorry, what a weird thing to say. Maybe I'll take you up on the therapy."

His knee touches mine under the table as he moves it, saying,

"So sorry," touching my thigh briefly in apology and ironically doubling down on the mistake.

"Where are you living?"

"Oh, um. I guess with Arabella. I just left my old flat where I lived with my boyfriend."

"Christ, in that lesbian brothel?" he asks.

He's not wrong. There are constantly girls over and they're constantly hooking up. I mean . . . myself included.

"No offense," he adds.

"I'm not actually a lesbian," I say, remembering what Arabella said to him. "I'm just open. When an opportunity arises and I want it, I usually don't stop myself."

"That's none of my business." He drops to a whisper. "And, anyway, I kind of knew that."

"God. You're killing me."

I push away my glass of champagne.

"What are your conditions like? Do you have a good mattress? Can you afford to eat well? These things matter, Jocelyn."

I pause, again thinking of being in bed with him. "I'm sleeping on an air bed at the moment. But I will get a bed soon, I just haven't had time and I've been settling in and—"

"Your body is too important," he says, looking deadly serious. "Do you think Rembrandt was just leaving his paintbrushes in a dirty bucket every night? No."

There's a sternness to his tone that makes me shy away. "No."

"You deserve better." His eyes briefly seem to glance at my lips. It's so quick that I become certain it was my imagination.

"To be honest," I say, my chest heaving with this low rumble of desire. I look up through my lashes. "I am questioning living with her after her little display tonight. I've never seen her do that before."

"I've got a flat near the theater in Bloomsbury. You can stay there. It's got everything you need. Including a doorman, which I doubt you have right now."

"No doorman, no," I say, understating. "I can't—"

"I bought the place a few years ago. Clem and I were—" His eyes cast downward, and I shrink a little at the nickname for his wife, who has hardly come up yet tonight. "Clem and I were going through a rough patch. The housing market was up and down and I bought the place just to have a place to go if I needed it."

"Did you?"

"Sometimes, but she was always the one to storm out, so. It's pretty much been sitting there empty this whole time."

Somehow, knowing that I am part of his fucked-up priorities makes me surge with intrigue again.

"Would you like to see it?" he asks.

"What—now?"

"I assure you, this is only for your health." He says it seriously, and if I hadn't glanced at his face, I wouldn't have noticed the tiny flash of humor in his lips.

"I'm not sure your wife would be okay with you showing it to me right now, and truthfully, I'm not sure I trust myself around you. I still remember when you were Max," I say, honestly, for the first time tonight, being a little bit principled.

"She's the one who told me to prioritize you over everything else. This ballet thing, it's all her thing, really. But she is always begging me to get involved. She says I need a hobby."

"So why did you take me for drinks?" I ask.

"To be quite frank, it was a suggestion of Clementine's. I have a feeling she and Arabella may have arranged our little run-in. She made the dinner reservations with Charlie. I wouldn't be surprised if she made them for the three of you as well."

"Wait—this is starting to sound very manipulated. Is Arabella—I mean, how close are they?"

"Clementine looks at Arabella as someone to care for."

"Like . . . a daughter?"

"I don't know, I never know what my wife is up to."

"Oh, I'm so sorry."

"I should probably go," he says then.

I'm taken aback by the sudden change and say, "Oh—I'm sorry, did—"

"It's nothing you did," he says. "It's just that we need to stay professional. Even though my wife and I are pretty much separated, we're not on bad terms. I don't want a punitive divorce. And she can be vicious. I don't want you to get in trouble for crossing a line with your donor. But trust me, the thoughts have been consuming me."

"I understand. Of course."

We're silent for a long moment, and then he finishes his drink. "Would you like to see the flat?"

CHAPTER EIGHTEEN

ELEVEN YEARS AGO

I got my period at my fourteenth birthday party. No joke, on the *day* of my fourteenth birthday party.

We were at the aquatic center, which was a complex of indoor pools about half an hour's drive from my house. I was in a dark red bikini and we'd gotten my nails painted red to match. I felt very grown-up.

Mimi paid for both when she took me shopping the previous day after ballet class. I was at her house most of the day, and we celebrated my birthday early since I wouldn't see her at my party. She also paid for the Domino's pizza we ordered and said I could drink Sprite. Nothing tasted better than that meal. My mom was at work until nine, so it was just me and Mimi at her house. I sat there eating pizza and drinking Sprite, watching *Singin' in the Rain* and dancing around the living room. Mimi pointed out that I looked like I'd gotten a little taller, and she took me upstairs to mark my height on the doorframe of her closet like we had since I was little.

"You've grown an entire *inch*!" she said with pride.

I smiled, also proud. I wanted nothing more than to grow up and be a glamorous woman. I watched movies where girls in their twenties had their own apartments in New York and L.A. and Paris and London, and just *yearned* for a space that was really my own. Getting taller felt like growing in the right direction.

"You're such a big girl," said Mimi, shaking her head affectionately and leading me back downstairs. "What do you think of making a big batch of chocolate chip cookies and you can take it home with you."

I was elated. I went downstairs with her and she let me lick the batter off the wand of the KitchenAid, saying not to eat too much raw cookie dough or I'd make myself sick for my party.

I draped myself over the couch and watched Gene Kelly woo Debbie Reynolds, licking the cookie dough and feeling like the luckiest girl in the world.

At home, I *never* got food like this. Sometimes we'd have pasta or veggie burgers, but it was never junk food. To be fair, Mimi didn't usually do this kind of thing either, only for special occasions like my birthday. Or if I was really sad or something.

The smell of cookies started wafting through the house, which was filled with the sound of washing dishes, my old movie, and the pitter-patter of rain that could be heard through the open windows. I was warm inside and out. But it was almost nine, and that meant my mom would soon be there to take me back to our house. Our dark, decidedly unlovely home with its thrifted couch and loud fans.

She arrived a little while later, late, which was fine with me as usual.

"Is that cookies?" was the first thing she said.

My mood plummeted. She didn't say it cheerfully. She said it like Mimi and I were both about to be in trouble.

"It's her birthday, Brandy, for crying out loud."

Mimi's tone was exhausted and low, but I could hear her voice in the kitchen from where I sat in the living room.

I hid the whisk attachment I'd been relishing, and waited to be found. I stared at the screen, alive with Technicolor.

"She can't be having this shit, Ma, have you seen her? She's getting big."

"She is not getting big," she whispered sharply back. The house was too small for an angry whisper to go unheard.

"Jocelyn!" my mom hollered for me. I considered pretending not to hear her, but again, if you can hear a whisper . . .

"Coming," I said.

"Now!"

I went into the kitchen, where my mom gestured at me, as if I were the muddy mess brought in by the dog's paws.

"Do you see?" she asked. "She's getting"—she dropped to a whisper—"big."

"I am, I grew an inch," I said.

My mom lifted her arms and let them fall down to her thighs with the jingle of her keys. "Do you know what happens if we let her get out of control?" she asked Mimi.

"Honey, why don't you go get your things together? Don't forget your new bathing suit!" Mimi directed all this at me, and I knew she just wanted me out of the room.

I could never disobey Mimi, so I left with a nod. But I could also never resist hearing what adults were talking about, so I gathered my things in the blink of an eye and then hid on the staircase to listen.

"—waste of money," my mom was saying. "I've got an opportunity for her to possibly get a scholarship to a prestigious ballet school. They're not gonna want her if she's a fourteen-year-old with love handles."

"Love handles? Honestly, what is the matter with you? I don't know that this is the healthiest thing for her. Maybe she shouldn't be doing ballet."

"She loves ballet. More than anything."

"Does she?"

"Yes!"

There was a long pause, then the sound of a dish being put away, and the cabinet shutting. Mimi said, "I remember another little girl who very badly wanted to be a ballerina."

Another pause. "Every little girl wants to be a ballerina. But unlike you, I'm not going to treat her childhood dream like something silly. Is it better that I grew up to be this, Ma? A half-employed bartender with a chip on her shoulder?"

"The rest of your life was on you; it wasn't up to me. All I knew was that I didn't want you running around worrying about your body when you were just a little girl."

"I'm not having this conversation again. That girl"—I could almost hear her pointing in my direction—"is going to be a ballerina. It's what she wants. No more of this shit. Steamed vegetables and fish. She's too young to know how bland it is anyway."

"Brandy—"

"I'm her mother!" She shouted this. The house seemed to ring with the sudden ferocity of her tone. "*I* am her mother. Not you. Thank god for that. Jocelyn!"

I waited the right amount of time and then made it sound like I was running down all the steps and hadn't been lurking like an unnoticed owl.

She stormed out with me in tow, leaving the freshly baked cookies and my beloved Mimi behind.

We got home, which was dark and uninviting with its busted porch light.

I felt sick and tried very hard not to admit that it was because I'd eaten a bunch of raw cookie dough. Eventually it got too bad, and my mom got immediately furious with me.

"Let's go," she said, trotting me to the bathroom. It was there that she told me to stick my fingers down my throat until I threw up.

She left me alone at first and I tried, but it made me feel like I was going to die. When she returned, this time with a glass of liquor, she leaned on the bathroom counter.

"It's for your own good, Jocelyn. You shouldn't have eaten all that crap. It's no wonder you feel like shit. Crap food will make you look like crap and feel like crap. Honey, you're not even trying."

I took a deep breath and then stuck my spit-covered fingers back down my throat, this time gagging.

"There you go," she said.

And then it happened. It was hot and made my stomach cramp and ache and made my ribs feel like they were splintering. The pizza, Sprite, and cookie dough all felt like what the ocean churns up in the middle of a deadly storm.

Afterward I felt raw and red and empty and filthy. My mom washed my hands and then took a warm washcloth and wiped my face, kneeling in front of me.

"There, that's better, isn't it? You didn't want all that nasty stuff in you, did you? All that icky grease and cheese and sugar?"

It made me feel nauseous all over again, but I thought if I threw up again I might flip inside out like a pair of peeled stockings.

I shook my head.

"If Mimi ever makes you eat that stuff again, I want you to go straight to the bathroom and get rid of it."

"Do you do that?"

She smiled and then laughed, and I could smell the liquor on her tongue. "Only if I make a mistake and eat something bad. But that's why we eat right, isn't it?"

I nodded.

She led me out to the kitchen, where she poured me a glass of water. My head was pounding.

"I have an idea," she said. "We'll do it together."

"Do what?"

"Fix our diets! We'll eat really well and we won't eat any more crap. We eat too much as it is. You're a ballerina." She shrugged. "The truth is, ballerinas don't eat much. Like princesses. How often do you see Ariel or Jasmine eating?"

I shrugged. "Not really ever."

"And they stay little. Like you're going to. You're going to stay delicate and little just like you are now. We'll count our calories. It'll be fun, like a little game."

Then the next day, for my birthday breakfast, I was given two egg whites and a sliver of salmon. For a drink, she gave me a glass of lukewarm water, also filled with lemon juice.

The salmon made me gag, but I ate it, as it seemed that she had gone through the pantry and thrown out everything. I mean everything. No boxes of pasta or bags of rice left. Just some boring things like lentils, salt, and pepper.

Then we went to the aquatic center for my party.

I was allowed to invite everyone from my ballet class, and no one from school. My mom said it was just better that way. It didn't really matter to me, but the only friend I really had was Sadie.

We played Marco Polo for a while, then went to the deep end to play Sharks and Minnows. And that's when it happened.

I got out of the water to dive back in, and then, as if the sharks were real, one of the other girls shrieked and pointed at me, saying, *"Blood!"*

I looked down at where she was pointing, my body dripping chlorinated water, me still catching my breath, and saw.

It was streaming down my legs in a diluted cascade.

All the other girls started shrieking and pointing at me, and I felt my eyes begin to well with tears, my throat to fill with a big lump, and my skin to grow fire-hot.

Sadie hoisted herself out of the pool and stood in front of me. She had a voice that could always rise above the rest, and she used it to say, "Hey! *Shut up!*"

The other girls started to quiet, all of them clinging to the side of the pool as far away from me as possible. "But it's gross!" said one of them.

"It's not blood, you idiots, it's dye from her new bathing suit." She rolled her eyes theatrically. "It's just a nice one, so it's made with red dye. Just because you guys can't afford it isn't Jocelyn's problem. Come on, Jocelyn."

I was shaking. It wasn't true, in my gut I knew that, but I almost believed her. The other girls looked shamed.

She wrenched my arm and pulled me with her as we went to the bathroom. Once there, she pulled me into a shower stall and wrenched the shower curtain shut.

"We have a problem," she said.

"The dye?" I asked, idiotically.

"What? No, I know that's not true. You just started your period. Is it the first time?"

I hesitated, finally understanding what was actually happening to me. "Yeah."

"Okay, it's not a big deal." She patted me on the shoulder with a wet hand. "I have two big sisters, so I know all about it. I'm going to go get your mom and we'll figure it out."

I nodded. The tears started to come and I willed them to wait until she left.

"Oh, it's okay, Jocelyn," she said. Her kindness had the adverse effect, and brought the tears tumbling over my lower lashes.

"It's so embarrassing," I said.

"It's not, it's just your body." She shrugged. "Those girls believed our little story, so it's okay. I'll go get your mom." She hesitated. "Or . . . do you want me to get my mom?"

I nodded before even deciding what I wanted.

Five minutes later, Sadie and her mom came to the shower stall where I was sitting on the slimy floor with my legs crossed, feeling like a disgusting, ugly child.

"Sweetie, are you okay?" her mom asked, with enough softness to make me almost start crying again.

Instead, I took a deep breath and nodded.

"Okay," she said, "do you want me to get your mom?"

I shook my head vehemently.

"Okay. I actually had some trouble finding her on my way in. I've got my purse here, we've got a few options. It's all going to be okay!"

She made it sound like no big deal.

Twenty minutes later, I was cleaned up and had a waterproof pad in. I felt like everyone could see it. Like a stupid baby in a dumb diaper.

I walked out of the locker room feeling self-conscious and silly. Sadie's mom told me I could keep playing and swimming, but I didn't believe her.

"I just don't feel like swimming anymore," I said. I looked around and couldn't find my mom.

I caught Sadie and her mom exchanging a look.

"How about we go get you a cheeseburger or an ice cream from the little restaurant, then?"

My stomach churned with hunger, but I shook my head. "I'm not—" I almost said honestly that I wasn't allowed, but at the last minute, I just said, "I'm not hungry. Thank you."

I sat on one of the chaises and acted like I was over the whole party. It was the first time I ever acted bored and bitchy to hide my embarrassment.

When my mom finally came back in, Sadie's mom intercepted her and—I could tell—told her everything that was going on.

My mom looked angry. Not concerned or worried about me, but pissed.

"Fuck's sake," I heard her saying as she came over to me. She adjusted her tone and facial expression before reaching me. Once she did, she said, "Party over?"

I shrugged. We didn't get to play any of the games I wanted to play or do cake or anything, but I was an inch from crying again, so I said nothing.

And then we left. All the other girls were still there when we did. I don't know what I expected, but of course they stayed. Just because I had to leave early didn't mean they shouldn't keep playing.

I felt like I was leaving behind a more innocent version of myself as we walked out of the locker room, passed through the lobby, and loaded into the car. I felt envious of the *me* I had been when we arrived, of all the other girls who could swim around and jump and dive without being concerned that a waterfall of blood might pour out of them. I used to be so carefree.

I was being very melodramatic. Sadie's mom had told me I was growing up. Maybe I was. And maybe growing up meant that everything got worse and worse. Maybe that's why my mom was the way she was.

The thought made me terribly melancholy, a feeling for which I didn't yet know the word, but that I could experience all the same.

When we got home, my mom asked if I wanted to open presents. This lifted my spirits a little, and she told me to go shower first and put on my pajamas, and then we could do presents.

I washed my hair with my mom's Herbal Essences shampoo and conditioner and L'Oréal Crème Ribbons body wash on my skin. It wasn't until I got out of the shower that I realized I needed another pad or something.

I traipsed into the living room and asked my mom for help. She helped me, seeming irritated the whole time, and then I went back to my room to get into my pajamas.

They suddenly seemed babyish and too young for me. A matching set of pink Little Mermaid pajamas I'd gotten years before, but could still fit into. As if fun, whimsical days and things were behind me.

I came out with brushed hair, the way my mom always wants it to be. She had Duran Duran playing, and she was drinking wine. It was always different with her, but usually this meant she was in a good mood.

"Would you like some water?" she asked.

"Okay," I said, thinking of the chocolate milk Mimi would be offering me right now, if I were at her house.

We went into the living room, where a small pile of presents sat on the coffee table.

The first one was a small notebook.

"A diary?" I said, happily. Most of my favorite movie and TV characters had diaries, so I was excited.

"Sort of!" she said. "It's for food journaling. You can keep track of the calories you're eating in there, and make sure it's not too many or too few. Open your next one."

She handed me another. I felt a little deflated, a feeling that worsened when I opened the next gift to find a beige-and-gray-covered book called *Food: Its Calories, Its Purpose*.

I flipped through. It was like a dictionary, only instead of definitions, there were measurements and numbers.

"You can look up anything you eat in there, and it'll tell you how many calories are in it. It's fun!"

I nodded. For my birthday I had been hoping for . . . other stuff. Sadie got hair chalk for her birthday and now she always had streaks of violet and pink and blue in her hair. I also wanted things like a TV in my room I'd never get. I wanted clothes, shoes, games. Other fun things. Not whatever this was.

"Thanks," I said anyway, feeling a little heartbroken.

I opened my next one. This one was better. A beauty kit.

"Oh," I said. "This is cool."

I looked closer at the set of pink tools. A label on the outside said:

INCLUDED: TWEEZERS, LASH COMB, LIP SCRUBBER, PORE EXTRACTOR, AND MORE!

My next present was a huge, heavy book. The cover had a black-and-white photo of someone beautiful. It was as big as my whole lap.

"It's Gelsey Kirkland," said my mom. "The most beautiful ballerina on the planet."

I flipped through the pages. She was very pretty, but also very, very thin.

"Okay, last present," she said. "This one is for both of us."

Fun.

I opened it, and it was a framed quote from Kate Moss: NOTH-ING TASTES AS GOOD AS SKINNY FEELS.

"It's a good reminder. She didn't actually come up with it, but it's one of her mantras."

"You got me a lot of stuff about eating," I said.

She sighed, then took a big swig of her white wine. "I know. It's because I feel like a shitty mom. I've been letting you eat whatever. A bunch of junk food. Your health is more important than that. When you're a ballerina, you just can't live like that. It's so American of me. I'm being such a normal American woman."

"You are a normal American woman," I said.

"Yes, but that's no reason to behave like one."

CHAPTER NINETEEN

Somehow, I manage to resist Alistair's offer to see the apartment. Everything in me is begging for him, begging to spend any time with him, in any proximity.

I know it's a bad idea. Already, every second I spend with Alistair draws me in more. Especially when I already know how good he is in bed.

When I met Jordan, I had an immediate attraction to him, too. An intense drawing-in. But it was like our souls were connected, and they always had been and always would be. This isn't that. I felt like I was supposed to be with Jordan forever. Partners. Parents together, maybe. Grow old together. But also have gorgeously hot sex with good communication.

I just want to *fuck* Alistair again. Very, very, very badly.

It's not just that. With Jordan, I never had to yearn. There was nothing to forbid our lust. We took a few months to get together because we weren't in the same country, but there was nothing truly stopping us. Just logistics.

The logistics are not the problem with Alistair. With Alistair, it's about pure desire and the taboo nature of it.

I don't get the feeling he's necessarily a good guy. I don't get the feeling we could stay up all night talking. But I do get the feeling that his teeth clamping down on my nipples would send me straight to climax.

I shake my head. No. He's right. I will be the one who loses their job if I'm caught in an inappropriate relationship with my donor. Nothing will happen to him.

I can't risk my job. It's a risk for only me.

My thoughts briefly go to one of the young dancers I forgot about at NAB who was fired on the spot when the wife of a donor went to the director and accused the dancer of seducing her husband. She accused her of being a sex worker, who set out to manipulate men like her husband.

The dancer was nineteen. And she was a total wreck. I knew the story behind it—she had been pushed by the *ballet* to be charming and to dance with the man at a gala. It was *he* who pursued *her*, sending flowers constantly, and when she tried to stop him, he even threatened to get her in trouble if she wasn't nice to him.

But none of the facts mattered when his wife found out. He threw the girl under the bus and she got fired.

I shake my head as I think about her. I can't even remember her name.

I used to feel so lucky, never having any of this donor drama, but now, I am more than making up for it.

We sit in the back of his car on the way back to Arabella's, and the chasm of space between our knees, though quite vast, feels charged with a hot, pulsing energy. Fuck, this is difficult.

Spanish guitar plays on the speakers, and I stare out the window, trying to distract myself from the heat between my legs.

I feel his eyes on me and turn to look at him, but when I do, he's looking straight ahead.

My heart squeezes and more heat fills my chest. The space between us tightens, and I find it hard to breathe.

No. No. No.

We get to the building, and the car slows to a stop.

"Thanks," I say as I rush out. "It was very nice of you to get champagne for us."

"I'll wait here, make sure you got in okay. Text me when you're inside with the door locked. I don't like this area for you."

I nod. "Okay, will do."

I need to get out of the car and away from him. He puts a complete spell on me.

I've never had someone worry about my safety like this. Jordan is so relaxed, so unruffleable, he never seems worried about something like an unsafe area. He just seems comfortable.

"Jesus," I say to myself, going up to the building door, collecting myself. Someone is walking out when I walk in, so I don't have to worry about trying to get Arabella to answer. Which is good, because I don't know what her mood is going to be like after earlier.

I walk up the steps, go to the door, lift the mat, and—

The key isn't there.

Oh, hell.

I try the knob, but it is, of course, locked.

I knock on the door. Once. Twice. Three times, and loudly.

No answer. But I can hear people on the other side. I press my ear to the door. It's laughing.

"Arabella, can you let me in, please?"

There's no answer, and I hear someone say *shhh.*

God. What are we, teenagers?

I'm not sure what to do.

My phone buzzes, and it's a text from Alistair.

All ok?

I knock on the door one more time. "Arabella, this isn't funny, can you just let me in? This is so fucking—ugh, Arabella!" I pound harder.

Nothing.

I step back and stare at the door. No wonder she didn't give me a key. This is her way of keeping control over her harem.

I look both ways down the corridor, not sure what to do. But then I see my canvas bag in the corner. I open it and see that almost all of my clothes have been smashed into the bag.

What a bitch.

I go back downstairs and to the car. Alistair rolls down the window. "Problem?"

"She locked the door and hid the key. She won't let me in. She's there, but she won't let me in."

"That girl. Get in." He opens the door and slides over.

I hesitate and look up at the window. I see a face vanish and a curtain close.

What the fuck is her problem?

I get in the car, really hoping she doesn't go spreading this around to everyone. She locks me out, forcing me to get back in the car with my donor, then tells everyone I'm fucking him or something. I can see it. It's not my first time dealing with a psycho ballet bitch.

He tells the driver where to go, and then, after a nod, the driver closes the partition between the front and back again.

"It's all right," says Alistair. "This is why you should stay at my spare flat. You need a place of your own. You can't be depending on someone you can't trust."

"Can I trust you?" I ask.

Our eyes lock, and I feel an electric current go between our gaze. Like if I don't break it, he might see into the deepest corners of my mind.

I avert my eyes, blushing.

"Of course you can," he says. "You can ask me for anything you need. You can tell me to stop. You can tell me you want more. Anything. I'm here to make your life easier. Not harder. Even if you are making things harder for me."

It's clear what he means. He means he wants me, too.

A deep relief washes through me.

I've never *been* taken care of. I've never been protected. No one has ever said they wanted to make my life easier. And to know that he's tempted by me, too—it makes me feel less crazy. I'm not making up this chemistry. It's there.

I take a deep breath.

"Jocelyn."

He says nothing more, so I nod quietly, my heart pounding. "Okay."

He looks out the window. We pull up to a building with a salmon awning that says, in an old deco font, IVORY TOWERS.

"We're here."

I feel overwhelmingly happy suddenly. I have a gorgeous place to live. I have a wonderful job dancing again. Even if Alistair changes his mind in a few months about the flat, this will give me more time to decide what to do about Mimi. I still need to figure that out, but at least I can start saving everything.

The driver opens the door for me and I get out, Alistair ready to lead me into the building.

"Mr. Cavendish," says the doorman, opening the glass door.

"Tobi, good to see you."

I wonder if Alistair has come through here with other women. It's probably the classic story of the wealthy guy with the secret apartment he uses for scandalous rendezvous.

"I'm surprised he remembers me," he says. "I'm never here."

It's like he read my mind.

We get in the gold-clad elevator, and he pushes the button for PH. Penthouse. I look up at the mirrored ceiling and then catch eyes with Alistair again.

We laugh and look away, like nervous teenagers.

There is a crystalline *ding* and the doors open.

"Oh my god, are you serious?" I say, immediately.

The place has soaring ceilings and massive windows, not unlike the studio at RNB. It smells like fresh linen and roses. There is a huge white sofa that looks like it's never been touched. There are shelves filled with Taschen books and expensive, delicate-looking ceramics.

"This place just sits here?" I ask.

Fuck the rich, I think. Then I remember that my mother used to say that all the time. She meant it as a double entendre. I suppose I do, too.

"You know, I grew up with nothing. My father and his father didn't get along. He wouldn't let him have any of the family money. My granddad thought my dad would gamble it all away. And he probably would have, to be honest, as that's how he tried to make up for it. At horse races, in casinos." He walks, hands in his pockets, to the center of the room, where he looks up at the soaring ceiling. "My mom made money working down at the local pub. I worked doing odd jobs wherever I could for people in the village. My dad drank himself to death after too many bad bets.

My grandfather gave the money to my mother. Said he thought she deserved it. He was right. She was a good woman."

"Is she still alive?" I ask, getting closer to him.

He shakes his head. "No. Neither's my granddad. It's just me and my younger sister. She's inherited my dad's bad decision making. God knows where she is. If I'm honest, when I bought this place, I bought it and designed it thinking she might come stay here. Might get herself together. But she'd rather wake up in the middle of the afternoon, party 'til daybreak, and find men to fuck and give her drugs. Once she got her inheritance, it ruined her life. She lost her ambition. I'm pretty sure she's partied it all away."

"I thought you got this place because you and Clementine were on the rocks," I say. I'm not trying to catch him in a lie, but I realize suddenly that it might sound that way.

"That was part of it. Especially once it became clear Marian was never going to set foot here. I have a lot of trouble pleasing the women in my life, for some reason," he says. "My mother was never happy. My wife and I are separating. She rarely wants anything to do with me. My sister would rather rely on strangers than on me."

"Maybe it's them, not you," I say. "I don't know, I haven't known you long. You might be a monster. But you don't seem like it."

His eyes find mine, and he smiles. "If it's me, I can control it. If it's not, then . . . well. I can't. I guess that's why I keep thinking if I do a bit more, work a bit harder, try to be better, then maybe I can change things."

For the first time since I met him, his guard seems down. He's vulnerable. My draw to him starts to deepen, to crack into something more as I watch him.

I tend to run from vulnerability. To hide from intimacy. I'm not the type to be drawn in by a sob story. I heard my mom spin a million lies to get what she needed. I know people just say what they need to in order to get by. I know people don't like to admit the power of pity. But I believe Alistair. I feel like there's nothing he could possibly want from me. And for some reason, he's dropped his cold exterior.

"You letting me stay here is such a huge gift," I say. "I really appreciate you for that."

"I just want to help," he says. "You stay here as long as you want. I hope you stay for as long as you're with the RNB, or until you meet some nice guy and you decide to move on. It's yours as long as you want it."

I don't know what to say, so I just nod and say, "Thank you."

He takes his hands out of his pockets, puts a hand on my shoulder. "I've got to go."

He doesn't explain any further and I can't help but wonder where he's going.

"Oh, of course," I say, feeling a little shy now. "Definitely."

"I hope you don't mind me not giving you the tour. I'm sure you'll figure it out. I'll have some groceries sent over in the morning while you're at rehearsal. Just leave a list in the kitchen. If you don't, I'll just send over some salmon."

I look at him, thinking he's serious, but I can see that he's kidding. Maybe he's not as dour as he seems. Maybe he's just very dry.

"Okay. Thank you."

He gets in the elevator, and as the doors close, he says, "Good night, Jocelyn."

"Good night."

And then I'm alone.

Holy shit.

I look around for a few minutes, then figure out the sound

system and put on a radio station made for Alistair. Hidden speakers throughout the flat start to play "Rock On" by David Essex.

There are two stunning bedrooms, but it's clear which is the primary. It has a creamy duvet on a plush, king-sized bed and fur rugs on either side. For some reason I feel strange about sleeping in that one, so I choose the ever so slightly smaller—yet equally gorgeous—one with the enticingly warm-looking velvet duvet in dusty rose. I drag my bag to it, then change into my pajamas.

As I head back to the kitchen I pass a darkly wooded office with books and encyclopedias and priceless-looking tchotchkes.

The whole place is worthy of *Architectural Digest*. Back in the kitchen, I open the glass-doored fridge and find bottles of San Pellegrino. I help myself to one, and then as I'm opening it I hear my phone buzz on the marble counter. I lean over to see a text.

I don't have the number saved, so I don't know who sent it, but when I see the text, I freeze.

Don't trust him.

CHAPTER TWENTY

I sleep better that night, in that massive bed under the velvet duvet, than I have in months. But when I wake up, the first thing I remember is the mystery text.

Don't trust him.

Who would send it? I can only assume it's in regard to Alistair. Who else?

My first thought is Arabella, but it can't be. If she didn't think I should trust him, she would have just let me into the flat last night. I could *hear* her inside, I know she heard me. It would have been one thing if she was just passed out. But she was in there. She was laughing. You don't do that and then turn around to send a text like that.

Cynthia?

No, that girl barely likes me.

And I honestly don't know any of the other girls at the company well enough for them to send it. First of all, no one knows me yet, especially not well enough to care *or* to have my number. Although I'm sure someone could find a way to get it. Second of all, ballerinas only rarely look out for each other—I should have known Arabella wasn't as nice as she seemed. Third, no one knows about Alistair being my donor yet. As far as I know. Though news travels fast in this world.

Does it travel fast enough to someone who might be trying to look out for me?

There's also always the chance that it was someone fucking with me to get me to mess this donor situation up or just literally getting the wrong number.

All I can do, besides text back **who is this**, which I already did, is wait and see what happens. I can see if anyone acts different in class and rehearsal. I can keep an eye on Alistair and see if he's sketchy.

It's raining out, but the flat is only a ten-minute walk from the theater, so I walk. When I arrive, my face is chapped from the cold, and as much as I want to spend fifteen minutes in my cozy dressing room, around the radiator, before changing into my warm-ups and going into the cold hallway, I have to hurry. I want a spot at the barre before Arabella arrives. I know if she's already there and I walk in, there will be that whole cafeteria feeling where you stand there with your tray and don't know where to sit.

I do beat her to the studio, thankfully. I feel relieved, thinking that maybe she'll go to the other class and I might get through the whole day without an awkward run-in.

No such luck. I forgot about the company meeting before class. Dammit.

I've just finished warming up my ankles with my TheraBand when I reach for my water bottle and look up to see Arabella walking over to me.

"Jocelyn," she says.

"Arabella." I let out an exhausted sigh, and then say, "Can we just sort out whatever is fucked up? I've done the whole mean-girl standoff thing before with my best friend and we should have just talked. Can you just tell me why you locked me out?"

This catches the attention of the girls around, but they all pretend they're not listening. I know they are.

"Okay," says Arabella. "I think it was fucked up for you to blow us off for some guy."

I give her a look and then gesture at the hall. She follows me.

I turn and round on her once we're alone.

"You left *me*!"

She looks irritated. "Only because you had clearly checked out of our time and into something with him."

I want to ask her if she set up the meeting with Clementine, but by the light of day, the suggestion sounds crazy.

"I didn't tell you to leave. He took me home after we talked about the ballet, and then you locked me out. And left my things outside. That was fucked up."

She runs her tongue over her teeth, as if she's just sharpened them, and says, "Okay. I'm sorry."

I'm taken aback by the abruptness of contrition. "You're . . . sorry?"

"Yeah." She shrugs. "Sorry."

I don't know what to say. I can't keep hammering her, trying to convince her she's wrong; she's already copping to that.

"Um. Okay," I say. "Thanks, then."

"Do you still need a place to live?" she asks.

"Actually, no. How did you know that?"

"Just had a feeling." She shrugs again. Then she completely changes. She smiles and puts her arms out. "Come here, *cariño*, I'm sorry for being so testy. It's my Spanish blood, you know, I just can't help it. I'll help you move the rest of your things over later."

"How did you—"

"Small town, love."

I let her embrace me, feeling completely thrown for a loop. I hug her back gingerly and then let go as fast as I can without offending her.

"So," she asks, "did you fuck him?"

"What? No!"

She asks it loudly, as more dancers go into the studio for the meeting.

She laughs. "I'm surprised. You two looked like you were on a hot first date."

"Okay, well, it wasn't. Be quiet," I say, with a hushing finger at my lips. "You got me into this company, and pushed me to get a donor quick, and now are you trying to get me kicked out?"

She laughs. "Of course not, love. Why would I do that?"

"I have no idea," I say.

We go back in, just as Sarika claps her hands and says, "Okay, okay, enough chatting, quickly before class, I want to introduce you to someone. As you know, *Manon* rehearsals are starting this week with casting to go up shortly. Of course, the basic has already been done, so please go to the rehearsals you're on the basic for, but as always, our minds can be changed." Between each of the last five words, she claps once. "For better or worse. And as we do have a week of *Swan Lake* left, please stay focused on that, too."

Arabella and I take our places.

"She means that," whispers Arabella conspiratorially. "Be careful."

My phone buzzes. I look and see that it's a text from Joel Carson, my mom's friend.

Hi Jocelyn, your mom's house sold.
Call me later. Joel.

I inhale sharply and shove my phone into my warm-up vest pocket. I was not expecting that. I look up and rejoin the meeting happening in front of me.

"I'm going to give the stage over to Isabella Von Fleet," says Sarika. "She is here from the MacAvoy Trust and will be staging the ballet."

A woman steps forward, does prayer hands at Sarika, then walks in front of us all.

"You can relax," she says, with a breezy American accent. "This is just a quick little introduction. We have lots of rehearsals ahead of us to get to know each other more."

She says *relax* in a soothing, long way, stretching out the *a*.

Some ballerinas sit. Arabella and I do not.

Sarika looks at us both, briefly squinting her eyes and then looking to Isabella.

"*L'histoire de Manon*. We call it *Manon*, don't we? I know you're all familiar with it. What ballerina hasn't yearned to play the lead role?" She gives an odd little giggle, then goes on. "When Kevin MacAvoy was choreographing the ballet, he was quite loose with his direction for our Manon. He left it open to the interpretation of the dancers, believing that authenticity was at the core of this character. But what made those in the role shine to MacAvoy was their ability to embody her poverty. He believed that what drove her was her desperation to change her station in life. And it will kill her."

I think of the text from Joel, and then of my mother. The irony is, the ballet ends in the swamps of Louisiana, which is actually where my story began. And where my mother's ended. I suck in my breath again sharply.

My ears begin to ring and I feel like I might pass out. I can't breathe. My knees buckle beneath me. I catch myself.

"Are you all right?" asks Isabella, looking over at me.

I nod. "Sorry," I say.

But I still feel woozy. I bend down and get my water bottle, drinking a few sips. My mouth has gone so dry that I cough.

"Excuse me," I say, because everyone is looking at me, and then walk quickly out of the studio.

I go straight down the hall to the bathroom, where I splash freezing-cold water on my face and breathe in deeply. I feel dizzy and sick. My mind keeps spinning around, then the sound of a car crash fills my heart and head. Memories of Louisiana float into my mind. My mom. My mom is dead. I feel a sob build in my throat and then explode out of me. And then the crash I've been waiting for.

A sob bursts out of me so deep I can't breathe.

She's gone.

The house is gone now. What is left for me? There's no *home* left. There never was much of a home, but now it's really gone.

I cry hard, one hand on the sink, one hand on my open mouth. I let myself descend to a crouch, my tears wetting my Adidas warm-up pants.

It's the kind of crying that just can't be stopped. The kind that's bigger than any self. Everything I've been suppressing the past few weeks is hitting me now like a fucking tsunami at fucking work. I feel like I can't breathe. My chest feels tight. I put my head between my knees and try to calm down.

A few minutes must go by as I sit there, falling hard into the feeling, tears still falling uncontrollably down my cheeks, and then the door opens.

My self-consciousness asserts the rest of me and I regret I didn't hide in a stall, but it's too late to run into one now. I try to breathe and pretend I wasn't being so small, so weak.

It's Isabella.

Now that I see her up close, I see that she is quite beautiful. Blond hair with some gray. Hazel and honey-colored eyes, dappled with kindness and a sharp, present attention.

"Jocelyn? Right?" she asks. "You all right, sweetie?"

I nod, but the tears are still spilling. "I'm fine," I say. "I'm sorry."

She comes over to me and crouches down in front of me. "What's going on?"

I bite my tongue and shake my head.

"It's okay," she says. "You can tell me or not. Would you like me to leave you?"

The answer is no, so I find the strength to say, "My mother died recently."

It's the first time I've said it out loud.

God.

"Oh, dear. Oh, I am so sorry. I'm just so sorry."

"I hated her. I don't know why I'm so upset," I say, trying to laugh, but the tears keep coming.

"We all hate our mothers," she says, smiling kindly, a hand on my arm. "But we all love them, too."

I nod and hide my face, sobbing silently into myself.

"Jocelyn, honey, can you do me a favor?"

I sit up. "Sorry, yes. Sorry."

"Don't apologize. It's something I want you to do for yourself. Stand up. It's okay, I've got you, stand up."

She takes my hands in hers and I stand up.

"Okay, now I want you to get really big for me. Your whole body is crouched into a tiny shell. I want you to open up that chest for me." She does what she's telling me to do. I mirror her, and she says, "That's right. Now put your arms out as wide as you can and take in the biggest breath you have all day. Maybe all week. Okay? Let's go."

We both breathe in together.

I let it out audibly, and I really do feel better.

I nod. "Thank you."

"It's nothing, don't worry about it," she says.

I breathe in deeply again. She does it with me a few times.

"I'm actually from Louisiana," I say, like that would explain my breakdown. "I think just hearing you bring up Louisiana triggered something." I go on, feeling stupid now. "It's where I'm from. And it's where my mother died. It wasn't that long ago."

"Wow. It's a bit like fate."

I suddenly can't stop. "Even the fact that she's broke—I grew up *completely* without money, just trying to find success in ballet. To be honest, I think . . . I think this ballet has always been a little too close to home. Hearing you talk about it in the company meeting really awakened something I've been suppressing. Because in a weird way, even though it freaks me out, this ballet has always been a dream of mine to perform. I was with NAB in New York for six years, but it was never in the repertoire to perform it. I remember the first time I saw it live here in London four years ago, it really spoke to me. I know I'm a mess right now. I shouldn't even be saying any of this and it's probably going to make my chances worse, but I know I'm made for this part. I am Manon." I finally take a breath. And then, "Oh god, I'm sorry for dumping on you."

She takes in what I'm saying, her eyes looking even more observant than before. Then she smiles and says, "You're a strong girl. I can tell."

This makes me ache. I want to hug her. I want to fall asleep beside her like a lapdog while she drinks tea and reads Proust or whatever it is she probably does.

God, I am *so* fucked up right now. I'm like the bird in that old book running around pecking everyone on the head and asking, *Are you my mother?*

Talk about Mommy issues.

"I'm going to give you some space. I'm running downstairs to meet Charles. I believe class just started, but maybe breathe a minute and then do your own warm-up class today?"

She pats me gently on the arm, and then drifts out of the bathroom.

I decide to not take her advice, and head back to the studio to join company class. I notice that no one will look at me. But it's fine, because I really don't want to look at them either.

CHAPTER TWENTY-ONE

NINE YEARS AGO

I crept through the house, careful to avoid all the creaking floorboards and squeaky hinges. It was a sweltering August night, which meant that the house was noisy with the sound of deafening box fans. The perfect cover-up for a sixteen-year-old girl determined to sneak out but who knew she'd be murdered if she got caught.

It was just after midnight, but my mom had worked the brunch shift at her bar that day and she had to work the same shift in the morning, so she was definitely asleep.

I stepped lightly past her door, my gait gentle and silent from the years of ballet. I basically had to jeté over the loudest of the wooden floorboards, but I landed as quietly as a cat.

I paused for a full minute to make sure the small sound didn't wake her, resolving to simply say I was getting a glass of water if she did come out.

My ears strained for the hint of every sound, my gaze locked on a spot in the dark living room as I waited.

When I heard nothing, I moved toward the door, which I opened as soundlessly as possible. I pushed open the squeaking screen door, then urged it closed, trying to prevent the rusty metallic hinge from doing the loud *boing-click* sound it sometimes made, since it barely worked anymore.

But this time, it obliged me. Even the house was on my side.

Nick had been my boyfriend for almost a year. My mom knew and she didn't approve. Not because she was trying to keep me pure or anything; she was not weird in that particular way. It was actually that she objected to the relationship side of things. She must have told me a hundred times to stay out of serious relationships while I was young. She preached endlessly about how long-term relationships were pointless in high school, how they were designed to be painful and were doomed to fail. She told me that men were bad enough, but to catch them while they were in puberty and try to wrangle any sort of commitment out of them or to have any expectations from their underdeveloped brains was just stupid.

But I knew that Nick was different.

He had floppy brown hair and a smattering of freckles across the bridge of his nose. He had brown eyes, but they were a pretty, chestnut brown. He played baseball, so he understood my commitment to ballet. He'd also been in piano lessons since he was a kid, so he had a sensitive side to him, too. One time I snuck over to his house in the middle of the night like this, but his parents were out of town. We lit candles like we'd seen in movies, and he played old music on the piano for me while I watched his hands.

He was one of the good ones. I knew he was.

I walked quickly down the street from my house. There was a soundtrack of cicadas in the trees and frogs in the swampy ponds nearby, and it met with the electric buzzing of the streetlights that cast pools of golden light onto the hot asphalt below.

Once I was far enough away, I broke into a run, the rubber of my Goodwill Nike sneakers padding on the pavement, the zipper pulls of my backpack rattling. My heart was pounding, not from the cardio, I was beyond used to that, but because I was going to see Nick.

Almost a year, and I still felt excited to see him. I knew enough to know that was unusual. Most of my friends who'd had boyfriends or girlfriends broke up after like three months, seven months max. But we were more in love than ever.

And tonight, I was going to do it. *Do* it, do it. For the first time.

I was waiting to lose my virginity for the right time, the perfect time. But it's never the perfect time. We didn't have access to hotel rooms or peaceful, private places where we could do it romantically like a movie. In theory, the night I went over to his house and he played piano would have been the perfect time. But we hadn't been together long enough then. I wasn't ready.

I turned the final corner toward the park where we'd decided to meet. It was romantic, with weeping willows and long grass, a few benches there along the brick pathway. There was a fountain of a little girl pouring out a bucket of water that was constantly running.

I found him just where he'd promised to be, and when he saw me, his face broke into a smile. He was the only person I knew who had perfect teeth without braces. He also didn't seem to get pimples and his face was always clear and perfect.

"Hi," I said, slowing my pace when I got close. Suddenly, I was bashful.

"Hi," he said, taking his hands out of his pockets. "Come here."

I beamed and then ran to him, jumping into his arms and throwing my own around his neck. We kissed once, twice, then again, then more urgently. There was a desperation in our touch, his hands on my back, my legs tightening around his hips.

"I want to," I whispered into his ear.

"You want to . . ."

I nodded. He knew what I meant. We'd been talking about it forever.

He looked up at me and then ran his fingers through my hair, tucking it behind my ear and then letting me back down to the ground. "Are you sure?" he asked.

"I'm sure."

I took off my backpack, set it on the bench, and then pulled out a blanket.

I held it up and laughed. "You're always teasing me for being unprepared, but I am this time."

"Do you have a condom?" he asked.

Disappointment welled in me as I said, "Oh, no."

He smiled. "It's okay, I have one."

"You do?"

"I always do. Just in case."

I rolled my eyes, but didn't have time to do much more, because his hands were on me again, his lips on mine. Barely disconnecting from one another, we laid out the blanket and spread it on the grass. The water from the fountain streamed and the sound of the bugs was even louder here, since there was so much greenery.

Despite the heat, I was shaking, especially my legs, which felt like Jell-O.

I lay on my back and he was above me, kissing me for a moment before saying, "You're sure you're sure, right?"

"I promise."

I don't know what I expected, I guess a little more ceremony or something, because the next thing I knew, he had taken off my shoes, socks, and jean shorts and was about to take off my underwear, and it all felt so fast.

"Just—" I said, stopping him before he took off my purple thong. "Can you kiss me for a minute?"

He was patient, just nodding and then obeying. And then after another moment of that, he took off my underwear, sliding it down my tan legs and putting them in a pile with the shorts and shoes.

I was completely exposed to the night air and I felt cold even though that was impossible in the ninety degrees.

He then unbuttoned and unzipped his pants and pulled out his . . . thing. He put on a condom that he retrieved from his wallet, and I smelled the latex and thought of the doctor's office.

I knew it was about to happen. But instead of feeling a sense of warm anticipation, my mind was distracted by how odd it was that he had to get so much less naked than I did. I was naked on the bottom half, and he had pushed my tank top up to expose my padded bra.

From behind, you wouldn't even know he was exposing himself at all.

Then it happened.

It was a strange, unfamiliar feeling, a shock of searing pain that I pretended didn't happen. My mind was racing, thinking again and again that I just couldn't believe it was happening, that I was really doing it.

The movements felt natural and yet completely foreign. I was aware of how to move with him, but the strange, primal nature of that compulsion made me feel disconnected from the experience itself.

There were moments where it started to feel good, but mostly I felt nervous and eager for it to end. I was suddenly anxious we would be caught. If we were, I'd be so . . . bare.

I could tell it was almost over when Nick's breathing changed and his posture shifted.

And then it was over.

My legs were shaking worse than ever as he climbed off of me, panting and saying, "I love you so much."

I said, "I love you, too," in a voice that felt far away and small.

"That was so good," he said. "You're so good."

I wasn't sure how this was possible as I had pretty much lain there. But I said, "You too."

I scrambled to put everything back on, surveying the area around to make sure no one was there, watching us.

Then a surge of panic, almost like buyer's remorse, hit me and I asked, "Was everything—like, normal with the condom?"

He laughed. "What do you mean?"

"Like—it didn't break or anything?"

"No, it was fine," he said. "Fuck. That was so good. You're so fucking hot."

I smiled, but felt a little cold toward him and I couldn't put my finger on why. He hadn't done anything wrong. It was my idea. I wanted it. So why did I feel so . . . off?

"I should get back," I said.

"Already?"

"My mom wakes up sometimes, it's just better if I'm there. I don't want to get caught."

"Okay. Do you want me to walk you home?"

I shook my head before thinking about it. "No, that's okay. If she woke up or something, it's better if I'm alone. I can just say I went for a walk or something."

He shrugged. "You're sure, then okay."

I gave him a kiss and then said, "Well . . . bye."

I couldn't figure out why the hell I was feeling so *awkward*.

I ran the whole way home, my body feeling weak and hollowed out.

I turned onto my street, feeling weird that it was so the *same* as it had been just a little while ago when I left. My whole world had changed. So how were the frogs here singing the same song as ever?

The house was obliging yet again as I snuck inside, and I was grateful. I stepped lightly past my mom's bedroom door, then into my own room. I shut the door.

I slept in my clothes that night, not really wanting to be naked again. When I woke up the next day, it took me a moment to remember why I felt so different inside.

I went about the day normally, acting like everything was fine, and even sometimes believing it was.

Just before dinner that night, as my mom made the usual healthy stir-fry, my phone rang.

"It's Nick," I said, answering the phone and covering the mouthpiece. "I'm gonna go out front for just a minute."

My mom said nothing, only exclaiming as she nicked herself with the knife as she cut the onions.

I shut the front door behind me and stepped out into the lavender dusk and sat on the front step.

"Hey," I said.

"Uh, hey."

"What's wrong?"

He let out a big exhale, and then said, "I didn't want to do this on the phone."

Every function in my body froze at the words, knowing exactly what they meant.

"Nick?" I asked, the syllable coming out as a sharp staccato.

"Last night was just kind of weird for me," he went on.

I was almost surprised he didn't hear my racing heart through the phone.

"It was weird for me, too," I said. My tongue wrapped clumsily around the words.

"Yeah, I could tell. I don't know, Jocelyn."

"Are you breaking up with me?"

There was a long pause of confirmation and I felt my soul pool at my feet.

"It just didn't feel right," he said. "I don't know what else to say."

It didn't feel right for me either, but somehow, even though we were saying the same thing, it didn't feel like we meant the same thing.

"I've got to go," he said. "I'm actually at practice right now."

"You're—you're at practice, but you, like, stepped away to call and break up with me?"

"Jocelyn, come on. Don't do this."

"Don't do what?"

I felt clammy all over. I was spinning my anklet around my ankle again and again, the small chain scratching deeper and deeper with each revolution.

"I'll see you around," he said.

I shook my head, though I knew he couldn't see it, and never got a chance to say anything else because he hung up without waiting for a response.

I hadn't even noticed that tears had begun falling down my face.

The phone dropped from my hand and then so did the heartbreak.

I curled over my bare knees and cried so hard I couldn't breathe. I was there for a few minutes when I heard the front door open behind me.

"Jocelyn?"

I braced for her to yell at me. For her to tell me to get inside, to tell me she'd been waiting for me. For her to realize what had happened and start lecturing me about how she'd known it would happen all along and how I should have listened to her.

I heard the screen door open, too, then my mom's footsteps behind me.

I cried harder, dreading whatever was coming.

She sat next to me, put an arm around my shoulder, and pulled me into her. "Come here," she said. "It's okay. I know. It's okay."

I cried even harder at the unexpected kindness, and for ten minutes, that was all I could do. She said nothing, just rubbing my arm and telling me it was okay.

When finally my breathing started to normalize, my mom said, "Did you have sex with him?"

The moment with my mom was so precarious. I didn't want to tip her in the wrong direction and receive her wrath. But I couldn't muster the energy to lie, so I just nodded.

"Ah," she said.

"It—it was only last night," I said.

She hesitated a moment, and said, "You had sex with him last night? For the first time?"

"Yeah," I said, choking on my breath.

"Your first time?"

"Yeah."

"His?"

"I don't think so."

She let her head fall, gave it a slow shake. "Fucking men," she said, then.

I couldn't have possibly been more surprised by this reaction.

"You want to know the best thing to do when you're upset?" she asked.

I sniffed. "What?"

"Go to the movies. Go see a sad movie and just cry it out in the dark theater. What do you think?"

"What do—"

"Let's go to the movies. We can get some popcorn. Come on." She patted my tear-covered thigh twice and then stood up. "I'll put dinner away and we'll have something out. Come on."

I stood weakly and followed her inside.

An hour later, we were at the local movie theater watching some sappy romantic drama. I didn't remember the name, and I barely knew what was going on, but it helped. I just cried and ate salty food and sugary candy.

My mom cried, too, and I wondered if it was about the movie or something else.

It wasn't until later that night as I crawled into bed that I realized and understood what I had learned about my mom that night. My mom understood heartbreak.

And she went to the movies an awful, awful lot.

CHAPTER TWENTY-TWO

A week has gone by, and I haven't yet been added to any of the *Manon* rehearsals.

I'm freaking the hell out.

It's Saturday afternoon, and the last show of *Swan Lake* is tonight. The week has been exhausting. One ballet is finishing and another is beginning, so rehearsals are going on for both ballets: *Swan Lake*, which I can basically do in my sleep at this point, as over the course of my career so far I have probably danced it two hundred times, and *Manon*, which is widely known in the ballet world to be emotionally draining for the leads and a blast for the corps and soloists. I envy the girls I see walking out of the rehearsals for the brothel scene. They're all giggling with big smiles on their faces, alight from doing such a naughty ballet.

Swan Lake, on the other hand, is quite serious.

To keep from panicking about *Manon*, I have thrown myself into the last *Swan Lake* performances and rehearsals, despite how dreary they feel in comparison to learning something new and different. The ballet *Manon* is not full of classical stature and tutus like *Swan Lake* but instead with tight-laced corsets, jewels, and freedom of movement. I've been sneaking in to watch some *Manon* rehearsals this past week when I have a moment.

And I've been devouring the book on my breaks, having come to realize that what I said to Isabella is truer than I realized; the story deeply mirrors my own life.

Every night, when I go home, I sleep like a rock. It's like I spent the day crying or fucking. I just fall into an exhausted rest. I've pushed myself to return to peak performance at a grueling pace. The last of the weight I needed to come off has fallen off this week.

It feels good.

I have always loved ballet. It has always felt cathartic. When I was a heartbroken teenager, I used to throw my fury and sadness from my soul to my fingertips and let it rush down my legs and out of my pointed toes. No wonder I was so mad at Jordan all the time.

I wasn't dancing.

Or maybe that's the definitely-very-expensive bed I'm sleeping in.

Maybe it's both.

Yet, despite the deep connection I feel to *Manon*, I still haven't been cast. I remind myself that the changeover from finishing up the run of one ballet and switching to another is *always* hectic. Plus, I'm new and so maybe they just forgot about me? It feels like the casting was done ages ago, and so far no changes were made. Not even adding me to the basic. The basic is the list that tells all dancers what parts they are learning. The closer to the top you are, the more likely you are to perform the role. I don't care where I'm put, I just need to be added.

I want to go ask, but I'm also terrified. Maybe I royally fucked up with Isabella. About halfway through the week, I started fearing that it's from my conflict with Arabella. For some reason, she seems to have a lot of power around her. The girls look to her for reactions. There's a lot of *whatever Arabella wants, Arabella gets*. She's the top ballerina at the company right now and it's extremely obvious that everyone looks to her as the Queen Bee.

I've tried to keep busy by performing my best at every rehearsal, and then at night after a performance, being well-behaved and going back to Alistair's flat instead of for drinks with some of the other dancers. At Alistair's I feel like I'm staying in a hotel, except that at a hotel, I move things around and make myself more at home. The other day I splashed a little Campari on the white countertop and was terrified it might stain.

Yesterday, I decided that I needed to stay on Arabella's good side. I made a few jokes and said something about how she should come over and see the flat sometime soon. She gave me a funny look, but then said she'd love to.

Rehearsals have finished early for the day, and I take a deep breath as I leave studio two and consider approaching Sarika or going to look for Isabella to ask about the casting.

I see Isabella across the hall through the glass door in studio three. She's talking to one of the other girls, smiling warmly and coaching her on her arm movements. Her por de bra in *Manon* needs to be opposite to the strict classroom technique of *Swan Lake*, and it can take time for some dancers to let go.

I almost get up the nerve to walk in, but then wuss out. I'll do it Monday. I'll definitely do it Monday.

I head instead to the canteen to grab a bag of almonds and a banana before getting ready for the last show of *Swan Lake* tonight. I'm stopped by the rehearsal coordinator, Kiki, just as I arrive at the elevator.

"Jocelyn, there you are! I'm glad I caught you."

"Hey!" My chest surges with cold anticipation. Is she going to tell me I've been put on the cast list? "The Princess rehearsal finished early," I say, referring to Waltz of the Princesses, which we spent the last hour doing over and over. "I think we have it down by now." I laugh, nervous.

She doesn't laugh. Poor Kiki. She's always flustered with the thankless job of organizing the lives of over sixty dancers.

"Okay, great." She sounds stiff. "I came to tell you that you've been added to *Manon*. You can start attending rehearsals Monday."

"Wait, are you serious?" I let out a howl of relieved breath. "That's great!" I'm sure it's just a soloist role or something, but I'm just ecstatic to be included. It was a big scare thinking that maybe I'd get left out. "Okay, so what rehearsal shall I go to, for which role?" I ask.

She looks at me like I'm stupid. "I just told you."

It takes me a few seconds while she looks at me like a disobedient child. She's clearly unwilling to clarify.

"I'm sorry, I don't follow. Which role is it?"

"*Manon*?" She squints at me with an impatient shake of the head. The embodiment of *ugh!*

"O-oh! For the actual—for the part of Manon? *Manon* Manon?" My mouth drops open as it dawns on me. "You're not fucking with me, are you?"

She rolls her eyes and walks off. She can't be fucking with me. Kiki is too busy and, ironically, *bored* to fuck with me.

Fuck the almonds. I need to go home—or "home"—and study up on this role.

"Aah!" I hear a screech down the long hallway, then turn to see Arabella running toward me with her arms out. "You got added to *Manon*!"

"I did!" I say. "God, how did you hear that already?"

"Honey, when are you gonna learn? I know everything that goes on around here. I've got ears everywhere." She says this last part in a sensuous, threatening way, like a Bond villain. Then she cracks up.

"I'm just kidding, it's on the basic in the lounge. You might be the last to find out. Anyway, I'm so happy you've been added to learn Manon, behind me, of course!"

She reaches over for me, then hugs me hard and tightly, kissing me all over my cheeks, then giving me one kiss on the lips, sweeping her tongue briefly over my lips as she does.

"Thank you," I say. "It's very exciting. And I couldn't have done any of it without you."

It's true, but I am not sure if giving her the credit was the smartest move.

"I know, right? I'm like a little angel, helping all my little kittens get what they deserve. Ugh, I've got to go, but I'm so happy for you, baby."

"Thanks," I say again.

She gives me another hug, this time leaning in and whispering in my ear, "It's really hard to believe you're not fucking Alistair."

She then bites my earlobe way too hard.

"Ow, Jesus Christ, Arabella!" I instinctively push her off me like a bad cat that just took a swipe at me.

She widens her eyes and turns scarlet. "What the fuck is your problem?"

I glance around us, clutching my ear. I pull away my hand. There's no blood, but it sure as fuck felt like there would be.

"Arabella, that fucking hurt."

"What the fuck ever," she says.

She's clearly one of those people who can't take being embarrassed without getting aggressive. She reminds me of the kids on the playground who played too rough, then cried when they got told off for it.

"Thanks for the congratulations," I say. "I have to go."

My ear is throbbing.

"Whatever," she says. "I'm just saying. It's a little suspicious to show up here and get such a big role."

"Maybe I'm just right for it," I say.

"Or maybe you're fucking him," she whips back.

Smarting from the searing pain, and angry from it as I always am when I get hurt, I snap back. "I don't need to fuck anyone to get a role. Maybe that's just you."

CHAPTER TWENTY-THREE

It might just be my elation, but the theater feels alive tonight. The show is amazing. The last night of a run can always be hit-or-miss. The exhaustion of being overworked sometimes kicks in; the tiredness catches up. But it's best when the adrenaline hits. The feeling of *This is it, this is the last chance until next time.* And for some, the hopefulness that next time they will be in a better role. For the corps de ballet, they are praying this is their farewell to being one in a flock on the side of the stage. The soloists hope they have a shot at the Swan Queen next time. In a way, everyone dances as if it's their last dance.

Tonight there is a magic onstage that simply cannot be pinpointed. The audience is there with us. A show depends not only on the dancers but on the audience as well. Sometimes I get onstage and feel like I'm performing in a darkened auditorium of bored teenagers. Other times it feels as though everyone in the theater was meant to be there on that very night. Like serendipity that leads to some unknowable resolution of fate.

I danced Big Swans and Princesses. I always laugh at the term *big swans*, as if being five foot six and a hundred and eight pounds is considered big.

I sent my friend Sylvie a text tonight before I went on, with a silly picture captioned, **how the mighty have fallen!** Last time I danced *Swan Lake*, Sylvie, who is a petite waif, was a little swan and I was Swan Queen. Sylvie quickly responded.

Ha! Big Swan, never! Odette better watch out you might eat her! . . . But for real Jocelyn I'm so proud of you! I love you and hope to see you soon!

The difference between a big swan and a little swan is literally two pounds and two inches. Finally, though, my muscles are starting to remember, and I'm starting to feel as limber, lean, and agile as I was before. I feel good tonight. As if a soft warmth radiates throughout my body and seems to get hotter and hotter until I nearly feel as though sparks are flying from my fingertips and toes.

I'm ready for *Manon*. I have found my way back to my career, to myself before it escaped.

The shadow has lifted tonight, and it is the first time in months there hasn't been a dark, murmuring cloud over my head. Whenever I've not been focused in a rehearsal, my mind has wandered to my mother, to Mimi, and to Jordan and, unfortunately, Alistair. Try as hard as I might, I can't stop thinking about him.

But not tonight. Tonight, I am Jocelyn. Sylvie is right to be proud. I'm the strong rebel she met all those years ago.

After the curtain call, we head up to our dressing rooms to take our makeup off, releasing our bones from the beautiful costumes, all the while knowing that outside, the audience is pouring onto the chilly street, chatting about the show or about where they're going for drinks. Most people don't know Balthazar across from the theater says they close at eleven p.m. but that's just a lie they tell tourists.

A week ago, I sat there until two in the morning with one of the guys in the company. We shared green beans and wine as we bonded over ballet faux pas. His was accidently asking a principal to move barre spots. He thought it was a new corps member, not the new guest artist.

Now, as we all remove our costumes and makeup, I feel warm at the memory. Like maybe some things are falling into place.

Natasha, another soloist, announces to the dressing room that it's snowing outside.

There's an excited din at the news and everyone starts to get ready to leave a little more quickly. There's a day off tomorrow, so people are talking about their plans. As I head to the showers the soloists share with the corps girls, I overhear that Arabella invited a group to her flat. I feel a little embarrassed. The age-old feeling of being left out. I quickly replace the feeling with a peaceful gratitude, knowing that Arabella is just jealous and bitchy. Plus, I am going home to a gorgeous flat, and soon I'll be in *Manon* rehearsals.

Plus, I think, as my ear burns with the memory of her bite, who the hell wants to go hang out with Arabella when she's clearly been possessed by the still-living soul of Mike Tyson?

If I wanted a booming social life, I could have flitted around with Jordan or sucked up to Arabella, but that's not my focus right now. I'm a ballerina. That means *work* is my life. I have plenty of time to hang with filler friends the rest of my life.

I bundle up for the cold and prepare to walk home. It seems

like my Louisiana blood might never get used to cold temperatures despite my living in New York City for six years.

I leave the dressing room and start walking down the hall, when I hear my name.

I turn to see Luca. He quickens his pace, smiling that absurdly gorgeous grin. He reaches me and says, "Congratulations."

I'm a little stunned by his beauty. I don't even know if I'm attracted to him. He's just one of those people who is so undeniably gorgeous that he is everyone's type.

"On—oh, on *Manon*?" I stutter.

"Yes, I'm dancing as Des Grieux. Your penniless lover."

He has a strong Spanish accent, and I crumble a little under how beautiful the words sound.

It's just laughable how hot he is.

"Yeah! I can't wait. It's really exciting."

As I step out of the stage door, I think back to a few years ago when I met Sylvie for brunch on the Upper West Side. It was snowing then, too, and I was even less prepared for the cold than I am today. That day, I remember distinctly that I was idiotically dressed in a short skirt and sheer tights.

"Okay, I'll see you soon for rehearsals," he says, giving me a friendly wave, and then heads off in the other direction.

I blink after him for a moment, watching him go, seeing that he's meeting up with a group of people. Not dancers, just friends waiting for him.

I breathe in the air, which has that distinct snow smell, and take off down the road. I already know tomorrow, Sunday, the streets will be peaceful and quiet, everyone tucked into their little flats.

Yet there it is again. That sad little ping in my chest.

There's a chance I'm kind of lonely.

I hate that word. *Lonely*. It's so pitiful.

I think about my mom, then wonder why. If she was alive right now, I'd be staying as far from her as possible, not hunkering down to endure the storm with her. I guess it's just that there's something lonely about losing family, no matter how estranged. Besides Mimi, and whatever random rich dude my mom was fucking, she was my only known relative. So now Mimi is all I have, and she doesn't seem to recognize me most of the time.

Yeah, that's probably a pretty good reason to feel lonely.

It doesn't hurt that I can't stop thinking about Jordan and also Alistair. I can't stop thinking about what either one is doing.

I sigh. There's no use thinking about Jordan. He has a new girlfriend. That fucking blonde. I need to remember that. And I really shouldn't be thinking of Alistair.

I need to stay in good spirits. It was such a good night. I don't want to sit here, dragging myself down, remembering all the things that should be depressing the living shit out of me. I'll call Sylvie later. We always have something to laugh about.

I get back to the building, Ivory Towers, and am allowed in by the doorman, who then calls me the elevator. I thank him, and he tells me to have a good night.

Once in the flat, I take my coat off and hang it in the coat closet by the front door, kicking off my shoes and letting my aching feet relax on the plush rug that sits in the entryway.

Usually, when I arrive home, there is fresh produce, and often there is dinner waiting for me.

There's never anyone else in the place, but there's evidence they've been there.

Someone has cooked and prepared dinner; someone has cleaned the bathroom and made the bed.

Someone has handwashed my ballet clothes and done laundry.

Someone has brought in an extravagant bouquet of fresh flowers.

It really is like living in a hotel and, from what people say, like visiting a nice parents' house where they just want to take care of you. Except that I'm hyperaware of every little spill, slosh, and stub.

Tonight, however, there is no dinner. I feel like a psychology test subject: how long does it take her to *expect* a warm dinner prepared every night?

It's not that I feel entitled to it, only that it's what usually happens and I haven't really prepared for what to do if it's not provided.

I open the fridge, and see that there's not really anything but eggs and random ingredients like a bed of wheatgrass and microgreens.

I'll have to order something. I've done the eating-nothing-but-eggs-and-spinach starving-ballerina routine for the past few weeks and now I'm working hard enough that I feel like I don't need to do that. Not tonight at least. Not when it's snowing and I've got good news to celebrate.

First, I decide, I need to get out of these clothes. There are lots of places open late on a Saturday night, and it's not that late yet, so I don't think I have to worry about places closing, even in the snow.

I put on an old Beyoncé album and get into my loosest sweatpants and an old, oversized Nike T-shirt from the nineties that I found at a thrift store once and have worn to sleep in since high school. I put my hair in a loose bun and paint dark green mud onto my face. I grab my phone and the book *Manon Lescaut* to read again and curl up on the sofa.

I sing along with the music and scroll through Deliveroo, trying to drown out the urge that is once again creeping into my mind. Jordan versus Alistair.

I really want to text Jordan. I want to tell him I got the role. In some weird, perverse way, I want to show him this crazy penthouse and have him enjoy it with me. Yet, there's another part of me fantasizing about being here with Alistair.

Ugh. I need to stop obsessing.

I want him to like me. Like I like him. I want to know if he thinks of me.

I shake off the forbidden thoughts of Alistair. I'm only thinking about him because I'm living in his space.

As much as I miss Jordan, I can't call him. Or text him. Out of sheer pride, I have to resist. I mean, he hasn't *once* tried to contact me. Not once. Probably because he's got that other blond girl in his life now who says *I love you* and picks things up from his place. And who has a *key*, for fuck's sake.

If I texted him, he'd probably say something awful like, **I'm so happy for you. It's good to hear you're doing well.** Something distant and uninvolved, something that makes me seem like a distant friend who just got out of rehab and is really getting her life back in shape.

Or he could ignore me. Or he could tell me to leave him alone.

Then there's the *small* chance he'll say something like, **I'm so glad you texted. I can't stop thinking about you.**

How likely is that, though? Not likely, since he hasn't even tried to call. Not even after too many glasses of wine or late on a lonely night. Even if he *did* say that, would I even be ready for that? Or would I just push him away again?

There's no reason to text him. There's no good outcome.

Instead, I just sit with my feet on the chair beneath me, the novel of *Manon* in my lap, my fingernails between my teeth, and I stare at my phone still resting on the coffee table.

I'm startled out of my skin when I hear the bell of the elevator ring, the sound almost lost in the loud music, but startling nonetheless.

Is it someone dropping off food? They usually do it when I'm not here, but maybe?

The doors open, and to my horror, it's Alistair. I honestly think it would have been more desirable to see a cat burglar.

"Ah!" I say, seeing him. I open the book and put it in front of my face.

"Don't you look pretty?" he asks, with that wry tone of his.

"Alistair, why—I didn't know you were coming. I—"

"I texted you," he says.

"Did you?"

I look at my phone. He did indeed text me. My phone was still on Do Not Disturb from the show tonight. He only texted a few minutes ago, but that might have at least given me a chance to get myself slightly more presentable. I would have seen it if I hadn't been paralyzed with indecision about Jordan.

"Um—one second, I'll be right back," I say, walking quickly sideways so he doesn't see my face.

"I can come back," he says. "Perhaps I shouldn't have come, I—"

"No, no! Just wait one second."

I run into the bedroom where I've been staying.

I feel suddenly very exposed. Not just because of the mud mask and my ugly pajamas. But because the place isn't tidy. It's Saturday night, so I was taking it easy.

This is all made worse by the fact that shutting the bedroom door on him feels wrong considering that it's actually *his* house. I look too comfortable.

I wash off my face. It's the kind of mask that dries to a hard, cracking shell, so my face is all red and splotchy beneath it.

I redo my hair to look a little more collected, and then stand in front of my closet. Do I change? If I put on something else, won't I look like I'm trying too hard?

"I can really go," he says from the other room.

Fuck it, I decide, no time to change.

I leave the bedroom and see that there's a big brown bag on the counter and that he's standing awkwardly in the middle of the room with his hands in his pockets, as if he's never been here before.

"I'm sorry about that," I say. "I didn't know you were coming or I would have—"

"No, no, I'm sorry. I'll call next time, make sure I get you before I just waltz in. I feel like a prick. I thought the doorman told you I'd be stopping by. Did he not?"

"He did not. But seriously, you're fine!" I say. The truth is, I'm happy for the company, even though I wish I looked better. "Come over whenever. Obviously."

He smiles awkwardly and I don't know what to say, so I just smile back.

At the same time as he says, "I brought dinner," I say, "Is that food?"

"I was at the show tonight," he says. "I took a colleague. He's considering becoming a donor himself. I caught up with Charlie afterward, and he told me the good news."

"Good news?" I'm so flustered by all this that I momentarily forget. "Oh, the role?"

"Yes. It's good. I'm glad to see you're rising through the ranks as promised already."

I blush a little. "I'm trying."

"It wasn't until I was out of the show that I received a text from one of my employees telling me that they had been detained by the bad weather and hadn't been able to drop off your dinner. So I stopped off and picked something up."

"Really?" I say, genuinely surprised. "That's so nice of you. You don't need to be providing me with dinner at all. I was just going to order something."

"If you don't like the food, then—"

"No, it's great!" I say, scrambling. "It's delicious, it's not that. It's just that you're being—well, you're really going above and beyond, that's all."

"You're a priority and I'm not going to lie, it's refreshing to be around you."

I can't hold his gaze, so I look down at the floor, noticing that my pedicure has rubbed off of two of my toes. It's almost impossible to keep the polish on when dancing.

"It's ramen," he says, walking over to the bag. "I was in meetings all day, so I picked up something for myself as well. I hope that's all right."

"Of course," I say. "More than all right."

He glances at me, and then takes off his coat.

"Here," I say, taking it.

"Thanks."

I run it over to the coat closet and hang it beside mine, a strange thrill running through me at seeing them hanging side by side, both damp from the snow.

"I wasn't sure what you would like, so I got two different kinds. You can have whatever you prefer."

I go back over to the kitchen and see that he's rolled his sleeves up to his elbows. My eyes linger on the ropy muscles of his forearms.

"Let me do it," I say. "I can heat it up and everything, just—"

"Sit," he says with a gently commanding tone.

"Are you—"

"Sit," he says again, this time gesturing at the stool across the counter with the chopsticks in his hand.

I look at the expression on his face, searching for anger but instead finding an unexpected shadow of amusement there.

I look on the counter and see that there's a bottle of champagne.

"Where did that come from?" I ask.

"The wine refrigerator," he says. "In the study."

"Huh. I haven't gone in."

"Not very curious, are you?"

"I am, actually," I say, suddenly defending the fact that I'm more likely to snoop than evidence would suggest.

"I suppose I won't have to check to make sure you haven't stolen any Caymus out from under me."

"I don't even know what that is. I thought this was a booze-free household."

He makes a face. "That would be uncivilized."

"I just thought it was because you were trying to keep me in prime shape."

He pops the bottle and then says, "A fair assumption. You would like some, yes?"

I nod eagerly. I'm glad to have stopped partying like I was after finding out my mom died, and then after Jordan and I broke up, but there's nothing like a good glass of champagne. Especially after a good show.

He pours me a glass, and pours one for himself. He then holds his aloft and I follow suit.

"To *Manon*," he says.

"*Manon*," I repeat, the glasses clinking, our eye contact lingering.

My heart skips a beat and I take my sip. It's delightfully bright with lots of tiny, sharp bubbles. I feel my body relax immediately.

"It's quite impressive," he says, pouring the ramen into a saucier on the gas stove, then lighting it with the *tick-tick-tick* sound before the flames light. "I might not know much about ballet, but I have a feeling it's hardly the usual to slip into the leading role this early on at a company."

I flush with color and heat and say, "Yeah, kind of, but I'm not cast yet, just added to the casting list; and, not to brag about myself, but I was a principal at my other company. I'm good."

"Do all the other girls hate you for it?"

I shrug and take another sip. "It's ballet. No one's ever happy for each other. Ever."

I think about Arabella earlier. My hand gravitates to my ear.

Just then, the song changes to "6 Inch," Beyoncé's old song with The Weeknd. It's just a little too sexy.

"I'll change the music," I say. We're trying to be good.

"I got it," he says, then pulls an iPad from god knows where, and changes the music to something else without lyrics. But it is, I consider, also very hot music.

"I thought Arabella and you were close," he says. "Wasn't it Arabella who connected you with the company?"

"Yes," I say. "Which is why it's strange that she's treating me so weirdly now."

"Hm."

The soup is already warm, so he dumps it into a large bowl that looks expensively designed. He heats up the second one.

"I think you're exceptional," he says. "I've never watched someone with such interest before. Not even Victoria."

"But everyone loves Victoria Haley," I say, in a slightly mocking tone.

"My wife loved her. Not me, so much. I thought she was a brat."

I laugh in surprise. "Wow, I didn't expect you to say that."

He puts the second soup in the second bowl, and then says, "Let's go to the table."

He leads me to the dining room table, and we take two seats where we can look out the windows at the snow.

"It's so pretty out," I say.

It occurs to me then that the weather might not make it easy for him to get home. I haven't been in London long, but I do know even a little bit of snow here stops everything. I wonder then where he lives.

"Gorgeous," he says.

And then, before I can stop myself, it falls out of my mouth. "My grandmother, Mimi, would love it here."

I try some of my soup as he tries a bite of his. It's one of those subtle, delicate kinds. I usually go for the spicy kind that knocks your socks off.

"Here, try this one, see if you like it more," he says, reading my mind and sliding the other bowl over to me.

Sharing food is actually very intimate, in my opinion. It's something done by close friends, family, lovers. Not donors and their dancers.

But I accept anyway.

I like his way more.

"Take it," he says, reading my mind again. "I prefer the shoyu."

He takes my bowl and pushes his toward me.

"Thank you," I say.

"So where is your grandmother?" he asks, taking another bite.

"Louisiana. That's where I'm from."

"I've been to New Orleans a few times. Does she like it?"

"She used to. She's in a memory care center now. She has dementia and rarely remembers me anymore, but I really miss her. Or . . . I miss who she was."

My throat tightens with emotion and stress as I think about the house. When I called Joel back to talk about the house sale, it turned out that it didn't sell for as much as they had hoped.

Even more pressure on me to figure out how to pay for her bills in addition to all of my own.

He looks at me and says, kindly, "That must be very hard."

"It's all right." I shrug. Then, unable to help it, I spill. "Actually, I'm not all right. I'm responsible for her bills and I'm scared shitless. I can't afford it. I—"

Tears threaten, and I breathe in deeply, trying to steady myself.

"It's okay. I told you my life story the night I brought you here."

I relax a little and then he gives me a small smile.

We sit in peaceful silence for a few minutes, both of us eating, the music adding a deep, thrumming intensity to the quiet.

"I know this is something of an inelegant transition," he says, "but I cannot stop thinking about the night we met."

This surprises me, and I choke on my wine. "You can't?"

"No. And I shouldn't say it out loud. But I . . . find myself breaking a lot of rules when it comes to you."

My eyes catch his, and there is something strange and intense there between us.

I cannot think of a word to say.

I grow hot, speechless, and full of pulsing desire.

This is so unlike me. I'm strong. Not the girl who goes weak in the knees over a handsome man with an accent.

His eyes search mine and I get the psychic feeling he's asking me for some kind of permission.

If this was not my donor, if this was not a married man, then I would find it very hard to resist him.

I don't know when exactly or how this intense attraction came to be. How, mixed in with all of my rehearsing, all of the strangeness with Arabella, and all of the darkness—how I managed, through all of that, to wind up where I am now.

Staring into the eyes of the one man on the planet that I cannot have and should not want, trying to stop my body from acting on its own volition.

I slide back in my chair, unsure what I'm going to do. Get up? Excuse myself and go to the bathroom? Run away?

His eyes have followed me.

"Jocelyn." That husky voice.

He pushes his soup away.

I'm delirious with desire. The part of my brain that makes decisions has been cut off from the rest of me. I am simply human for him.

He moves his chair away from the table, so that he's facing me. "God, you are really doing something to me," he moans, and runs his hands through his hair.

Instead of running, like I should, I drop slowly to my knees and put my hand on the armrest of his chair.

I spread his legs apart and put my hand on his stomach. It's hard with muscle and warm to the touch.

I allow my hand to move to his chest.

He lifts his own hand and wraps it around my wrist, and for a moment, I don't know what he's going to do.

He takes my hand and places my palm on his jawline.

Air escapes my throat at the strangeness, the *badness* of this. So much different from our night in the hotel room as strangers.

I put the slightest bit of pressure on him and he leans down toward me.

I'm so close I can count the specks of hazel in his tourmaline eyes.

Then his lips are on mine.

The familiarity sends an electric shock through me so intense I don't know if I can stand it. It feels exactly like the night we met. When I knew him as Max. Like a month hasn't gone by.

I press my tongue against his lips, and then I taste his tongue on mine. And then we are kissing with an intensity and hunger I've never quite known before.

His hand is on my waist, his other now on my neck, my fingers are in his hair, his five-o'clock shadow is scraping against the softness of my raw, clean face. His lips are on my neck, my nails are in his flesh.

He shies away from my fingernails and I know instantly that it's because he doesn't want to be caught with marks on him.

He did the same thing the first time.

This lights me further for some reason, and I pull back, biting his chest just hard enough for him to feel that I'm not leaving marks on him.

Alistair then pushes me gently off of him, still keeping his hands on me, still looking at me like he wants to devour me in one bite.

"I should go," he says.

I nod urgently. "Yes, of course," I say. "I don't know what—"

"Don't," he says.

I'm not sure what he means. Does he mean *Don't apologize, it was me, too*, or does he mean *Don't say another word, I need to start pretending this never happened*?

I stand up, my legs as stable as bamboo in a heavy breeze.

He looks unbalanced, too, running a hand through his hair as he turns in a circle and then says, "My coat?"

"Oh, sorry." I go to the closet and pull it out for him. "Here."

"Thank you."

"Thank you for dinner—thank you for everything, really."

"Yes, of course, and congratulations again."

God, this is so awkward. I am not looking forward to the night of embarrassment ahead of me. And tomorrow—what if it's worse than embarrassment? What if I get fired?

Oh my god, I've ruined everything.

I keep it together. I just need to wait until he's out of the apartment.

He gets in the elevator and presses the button for the lobby.

"Have a good night," I say.

He nods.

The doors begin to slowly close, and I feel that I am only a few seconds from breaking down completely.

But just as the doors are about to shut, he sticks his hand between them.

They relent and open back up for him. He keeps a hand on one and looks me in the eye.

I'm braced for anything. I'm ready to be reprimanded.

"Jocelyn," he says.

"Yes?"

"I just want you to know that it is taking everything from me to step into this elevator right now." His eyes drop briefly to my completely hidden body. "It's taking everything. I'm trying to be a good man."

He then gives a half shake of the head and grits his teeth.

I wait for him to say something else, but instead he releases the door and steps backward, his eyes dropping down one more time to my body before landing on my eager, heavy gaze.

"*Fuck,*" he whispers.

The doors shut.

CHAPTER TWENTY-FOUR

I've been replaying the kiss in my head all day. How did that *happen*? What were we thinking? What was *I* thinking?

Every time I picture it, I'm struck with the feeling of shame and embarrassment at my boldness, but then, dichotomously, with the excited thrill of how good it felt. I want more. I want more *badly*.

Every time my mind wanders to desire, it comes crashing back down with the guilt again.

How had I been willing to risk everything? What was wrong with me? I must control myself. I must. My phone dings with a text alert. It's from him.

I'd like to pay for your grandmother's care. Please send me the name of the facility. Xx

Oh my god. My thoughts are racing. I can't believe he's doing that. I think I just fell for him more and also he didn't mention the kiss. Ugh, I can't help but think he must regret it.

I distract myself with other things, first thing being that I call Mimi. It's been too long since I've talked to her.

I set up an appointment to talk to her, so an aide is going to set up FaceTime for her on an iPad. I sit, anxiously waiting for the call to go through.

I breathe in deeply. It always makes me nervous.

Mimi is sitting in a large, plush armchair in a warmly decorated room. She's reading a magazine and listening to Louis Prima.

"Mimi," I say, smiling as I see her.

She looks up, her face lighting up when she sees mine, but then her eyes dim a little as I see that she does not recognize me. I feel even worse for the few and far between calls I've done with her and the fact that I moved so far from her. I know her memory loss is degenerative and not necessarily attached to how much or little I interact with her, but I have to believe that if I saw her more, she'd know me more.

The truth is, it scares me and upsets me to see her without the strong sense of self she had for my entire life. It feels unkind of me to protect myself in this way, feeling like after a lifetime of her being so devoted to me, it was only fair that I give her the kindness of engaging with her now even if it's uncomfortable. But it's easy for me to rationalize it away since she doesn't know if I do or not. If she was merely ill, then I would have kept in closer contact.

"It's me, Jocelyn," I say, struck as always with the incorrect feeling that I am condescending to a grown woman. "Your granddaughter."

She nods. "Of course, of course."

I know she doesn't quite remember, but it's clear she knows she should know me.

"Your room is looking nice today," I say.

"Oh, I'm only staying here for a little while, I'll go back home soon."

"Right," I say.

"I talked to a friend of yours today," says Mimi.

"You did?"

"Yes, I did. Handsome boy. I can't remember his name—Morgan or . . . or something like that."

"Alistair?" I ask, thinking this makes some sense. But not a lot.

"No, no, no," she says.

I tilt my head, not believing my next guess. "Jordan?"

"That's right. Oh, he's such a nice boy, darling, you two would make such a nice couple."

"He's—I think you might be confused, Mimi. Jordan and I broke up. I don't think—"

"No, no, I'm sure of it," she says.

"Okay," I say, going with it even though I don't believe it. "What did you two talk about?"

"Who?"

"You and Jordan?"

"Who, dear? I'm sorry, my memory is just—" She makes a squiggly hand gesture and then looks at me to fill her in.

"It's not important," I say. "What are you reading?"

For the next hour, we have some version of the same conversation over and over. Her memory comes and goes, fleeting and thin. I don't mind, I can be patient with this cyclical nature.

My mom had been impatient with her, but in a warm, familiar way. She would say, *Ma, I just told you!*

At some point, I ask Mimi to show me the pictures on the wall behind her. Even through the shitty quality of the international call, I can see that they're mostly of me and my mom. More of me.

I lean closer to puzzle out one of them, one I've never seen before.

"What's that picture behind you, Mimi?"

She turns and looks and I instruct her to which one I mean. She takes it off the wall and holds it in front of the camera.

Her hands shake a little, but I can tell that it's my mom in a classic ballerina outfit. The pink leotard and tutu, pale stockings, pink satin shoes, her hair in a bun tied with a pink ribbon. She's in Mimi's backyard.

I know it's my mom, but it's hard to believe. I never knew my mom to have had any interest in ballet besides through me.

"Is that my mom?" I ask.

"No, no, that's Brandy," she says, confirming that it is, indeed, my mom.

"Did she want to be a ballerina?" I ask.

She furrows her brow in thought. "I think that was Halloween."

"Oh, I see."

"But she always wanted to be a ballerina. She went as one for Halloween almost every year. She was always too tall for it, and we didn't know how much she wanted it until she was too old to get started."

She looks lucid enough as she says it, but I have to believe she's got something wrong. Maybe conflating her memories of me with the scattered remains of movies or something.

I realize with a sad drop in my stomach that I'll never know for sure. The three of us were all we had. And now . . . well, now it's really just me.

"Listen, Mimi, I've got to go, but I'm going to call you in a few days, okay?"

She smiles. "Okay, honey."

Sensing the end of the call, the aide comes into frame, saying, "Thanks for calling!"

"Yeah, thanks—hey, I have a question. Did someone named—" I feel ridiculous even saying it. "Did someone named Jordan speak with my grandmother today?"

She looks quizzical and then says, "Let me check the call log. We always keep track in an app, here, it's somewhere . . ."

She puts the camera at an unflattering angle as she goes through the iPad.

Finally, she says, "Looks like someone named Jordan Morales called around nine. Now that I see his name, I remember he calls fairly often. Checking in."

"Huh."

"Is that all right, miss?"

"I'm sorry, it's fine," I say.

"Do you want me to remove him from the list of callers?"

"No, it's okay. I was just surprised he called," I say. "It's good."

She nods. "If you change your mind, you just let me know. You're the secondary contact on the account and have been given full privileges, so anything you need."

"Secondary? So the primary would be . . ."

She checks her computer. "Alistair Cavendish."

I let out a humorless "Ha."

After Alistair's offer, I sent the information to him, but part of me didn't actually believe he would do it.

When she sees the expression on my face, she says, "Is everything all right, Ms. Banks?"

No. And yes. I don't know.

"Of course," I say, pleasantly. "Thank you so much, I'll see you next time."

I hang up.

I need a drink.

I put on my shoes and leave the apartment feeling more unsettled than anything else. It's like finding out there's a camera in your home, that someone could be or has been watching you for longer than you knew.

I talk myself into feeling better as I walk against the cold wind, pulling my knitted hat down over my ears.

Alistair just did what he thought I wanted. And it *is* what I wanted. As for Jordan, well, he loved Mimi. He hadn't known her long, but the two of them really connected. The first time he met her, I saw tears in his eyes when we left her, and when I asked him why, he just said that he wished he'd known her when there was more of her to know.

My heart threatens to break, and I remind myself of *Manon*, and how the bills are paid, and how nothing is actually wrong.

Everything is just fine. Totally, completely, absolutely . . . fine.

Definitely.

I have gravitated toward the theater, which is the area I know the best, and decide to dip into Gravitas, the little wine bar where the dancers often go after rehearsal if they're being bad and not just going home to have water and herbal tea.

I just need a drink and maybe a carb. I can tell that the reality of all the things I have to deal with is simmering under the surface, threatening to reach a boil and to spill over. I know that if I go home, I'll just feel worse.

I wish Sylvie was here. Or any friend.

And that's when I walk in and see the perfect, most ideal distraction in the world.

CHAPTER TWENTY-FIVE

Luca is sitting in the corner of the dark bar at a table with a tea-light lamp, a half-full rocks glass in front of him.

I know that one of my options is to turn around and leave. Do I really need to risk complicating everything further?

According to Cynthia, one of the appeals of Luca is that he doesn't make *anything* complicated. All the gossip I've heard about him has only confirmed it. The dancers act like he's a rite of passage. A favorite toy to be shared around, everyone understanding that it's a matter of turns, not possession.

"Hey," I say, walking up.

"Jocelyn!" He looks delighted to see me and puts down his book—*The Last Nude* by Ellis Avery—and stands. "Come, sit, please."

I take off my scarf and coat, which he takes and hangs up for me.

"What would you like to drink?" he asks.

"Um—what are you drinking?"

"A Negroni made with Montenegro instead of Campari."

"That sounds perfect," I say.

"You got it," he says. His accent lilts over the very American expression, and I sigh at how adorable and appealing it is.

A moment later, he returns with two more cocktails and sits down at the table with me. He, of course, smells incredible.

"So, what brings you to the bar on our day off? And by yourself? Surely a beautiful girl like you has many men, no?"

"Uh, no," I say, with a laugh. "And, I don't know, I just got off the phone with my grandmother and then . . . fancied a drink."

For the next two hours, we chat about everything and nothing. We talk about the book he's reading, which he's reading because a girl he knows recommended it to him, we talk about movies, great restaurants, and then, eventually we come to where we grew up.

He grew up in Northern Italy, in an absurdly idyllic-sounding setting. His father was a poet and his mother an opera singer. They had him when they were both on the older side, his father fifteen years older than his mother. His mother would travel around singing in various operas, but his father was always home. They were both dead now, his mother having had a condition that meant she would always live a relatively short life—he didn't know the English word for it—and his father having died in his eighties.

Naturally, this led to him asking about my upbringing. And for some reason, it felt very safe to tell him.

I told him about Louisiana, and my contentious relationship with my mother. My wonderful relationship with Mimi. Where Mimi was now.

Eventually he asked, "And your mother? Do you no longer talk?"

"She actually died. This past winter."

His face falls and he shakes his head. "No. Life . . . life can be so painful, can it not?"

"Yeah." I play with the condensation on the side of my glass. "It's actually the first time I've really said it out loud like this, except, unfortunately, to Isabella on her first day," I say with a cringing laugh.

He laughs. "Well, Isabella is the perfect person to spill to. She has a good heart. I've worked with her a few times now. I'm sorry to hear about your mother."

"Thanks. Yeah. It was really shocking," I say. "How she died. I mean, it wasn't until Isabella started talking about Manon dying in poverty in Louisiana that it hit me. Even though I wasn't particularly close with her. I wasn't . . . I mean, I wasn't close with her at all. She was kind of a stage mom—do you know that expression?"

"Yes, I've learned it," he says.

He's listening intently, but without putting pressure on me. He's leaning on his fist, elbow on the table, eyes scanning mine as he listens.

"Well, anyway. Yeah, and she was kind of a shitty mom in that way. But I also really wanted to be a ballerina. I didn't have that much discipline, or at least I wouldn't have. I never would have given up ballet, but I might have been too flaky to really succeed. She didn't let that happen. I'm . . . I mean, I'm grateful for that."

He nods, and when I take a sip of my drink, he follows suit.

"So we didn't talk much in the last several years. She's always trying to sleep with wealthy men to get the life she wants. Or— was always. And wanted. So she was driving on a road near our house, her house, on a road she's driven a million times. And I have no idea what happened. She wasn't drinking or anything. It seems like she just lost control of the car. It was late. They think it was maybe an animal she was avoiding or something. She drove off the road and hit a tree."

"Terrible."

"It is," I say. Another sip of my drink. "She was hospitalized. I didn't—"

Here's the part I've really never said out loud. Jordan was with me, so I didn't have to admit to it. He'd seen it. But I've never said it out loud. Especially to someone who might judge me. I don't think Luca will, but it still feels scary to say.

"I didn't go visit her," I say. "I knew she was in critical condition. I could have gone. I wasn't dancing at the time or anything, I can't even pretend I had a conflict or something. I just didn't want to go."

"Why do you think that was?"

I think. "I . . ." I pause again, unable to say what I'm really thinking. How I thought she would recover, and we would have more time.

We're silent for a moment, my gaze locked on a knot in the wooden table. When I look to Luca, I'm afraid I'll see a cringe, a separation between me and this guy I barely know, wedged there between us by my selfishness. My inhumanity.

"How was your Christmas?" he asks.

Tears brim in my eyes as I laugh and say, "Actually, really"—I gasp as the tears start to fall—"really beautiful."

He gives me a compassionate smile and then says, "Do you mind if I touch you?"

I sniff and shake my head, and he moves his hand to my shoulder. He rubs it and says, affectionately, "You got what you needed from her. She couldn't give it to you without you taking it. I'm glad you stayed here. Took care of yourself."

"You don't think I sound like a monster for letting my mom fucking, like"—my breath catches—"die alone?"

He shakes his head. "It's complicated. Life is complicated. You did the best you could. You listened to yourself. It's the best you can do."

I bite the tip of my tongue and nod. "I couldn't imagine going. God, sorry, I'm such a mess!"

He laughs. "What ballerina isn't?"

I laugh, relaxing a little. "You're really amazing."

"No." He waves a hand.

"No, you know it. I mean seriously, how are you so perfect? It's kind of unfair to the rest of the men on the planet."

"I'm not perfect," he says. "I spend all my money and I have a very small penis."

The last comment is so unexpected that I burst out laughing in his face, falling forward into his chest. I can't breathe for laughing, and I can feel him laughing, too.

A while later, he's walking me home. It's already dark out.

"Thanks for walking me home," I say when we arrive at Ivory Towers.

"Of course," he says. "I don't live too far from here, but not in a place as nice as this."

"It's my donor's extra flat," I say. "I can't afford something like this. I can't afford anything."

He laughs, and that makes me laugh.

"I'm glad you have a nice place to stay."

"Do you wanna . . . see it?" I ask.

He looks down at me. He's six foot two, so he stands a lot higher than me. I look up at him.

"You want to show me the flat, or something else?" he asks.

I shrug. "Whatever."

"You don't have to," he says. "You know that. I find that women often feel guilty for crying and things like this. If I come up, I expect nothing from you. Not in the least."

I know he's saying something nice about consent and respect, but I'm distracted by his incredibly sexy accent.

"Oh, it's fine," I say, blowing him off and pulling him in by the hand.

We go inside and up the elevator. For the first few minutes, he just walks around saying, "This is amazing. Just amazing."

I go to the study and I grab something at random off one of the racks of wine, making sure it's not too old or special looking. I end up with something white and French.

For the next hour, we just talk more. I find that it's too painful to say Jordan's name, and too hard to really bring him up at all, especially to another guy. So I basically tell Luca, honestly, that I'm still in love with my ex, so I don't want to talk about him.

Of course, he understands.

It's not until nearly nine thirty that something in the tone shifts enough that I think we might actually hook up after all.

It starts because we start talking about sex.

"So what's the worst sex you've ever had?" I ask, sipping my wine, feeling tipsy and happy. I know Luca well enough to know I can ask him anything at this point.

"I don't like to answer that!" he says. "I've never had bad sex. And it was definitely never the women."

I roll my eyes performatively. "I mean, that's a very nice answer, but come on. There must have been something."

He thinks for a moment, and then says, "Okay, I've got one. It was a three-way. Two girls from Sicily. Gorgeous, both of them."

"I did say *worst* you ever had."

"I know! I know, okay, so these two girls. I meet them at this hotel in Positano. I was there visiting family, staying alone; they saw me at the bar, and they walk right up and ask me if I want to fuck them."

"Damn," I say. "Bold."

"*Damn* is right. So, I was twenty years old at this time, I couldn't see why to say no. So I take them back to my room, and—"

"You're really bad at this."

"It's true, it's the worst! We were all there, you know, in the bed"—he blushes—"and I don't know, there was something about it that just felt bad. It didn't feel like sex, it felt like something else. Sex is about connection. This felt like it was something else, something more about the feeling itself. Or about saying *Look how crazy we can be*, but I couldn't see to what audience we were performing. Each other, I guess?"

"Okay. Okay, I can give you that. I had a weird threesome thing once, too."

"Really?"

"Yeah, it was with my best friend, Sylvie, and this, like . . . absolute asshole named Sebastian. He was the ballet master at the time, and in retrospect it was a total abuse of power. But basically we all kind of fooled around and then later on when I was asleep, the two of them started hooking up without me. I didn't want to be part of it, but I still felt weirdly, like . . . excluded? If that makes sense?"

"Definitely."

"Then they also went on to have this crazy affair. So it felt even weirder, like I felt like I had actually been in the way that time we all hooked up. Like an obstacle."

"Did it feel good?"

I sigh. "Well, kinda, but same as you said, I was too preoccupied with the performance of the whole thing. I was on Molly at the time, though, so that helped."

"Ah, I see."

"I've had a lot of bad sex," I say.

"Really?" he asks with genuine surprise.

"Yes. I mean, I've had great sex, too. My ex was amazing, but that really had more to do with my connection to him, I think. I still was all in my head about it. I don't know, I just have trouble letting go."

His eyes stay on mine for an extra moment, and I feel my skin grow warmer under his gaze.

"That's a shame."

There's a silence then, neither of us seeming sure what to say next. The music we have playing on the speakers fills the void, but something is unquestionably building between us.

It's crazy, because as physically perfect as he is, I'm not all that attracted to him. Do I want to fuck him? Yes. But not in the way I felt compelled to Jordan. Or even to Alistair. With Jordan, it was love. With Alistair, it's lust.

With Luca, it just seems like fun.

"Should we . . ." I bite my lip and wedge my foot a little deeper under his thigh.

He touches my bare leg and says, "On one condition."

"'Kay, what?"

"It's all for you. Nothing for me."

I squint at him in confusion. "You mean, you don't want to fuck me?"

"That's not what I said. I said, nothing for me. Not tonight."

I consider, and then say, "Okay, your loss."

I then set down my glass of wine, get up, and run across the apartment.

"Oh, wow," I hear him say.

Then he comes after me, and I fall, laughing, onto the bed with the velvet duvet.

I was already stripped down to a pair of sweat shorts and a T-shirt. I had washed all my makeup off when we got back, since I ruined it by crying anyway, and didn't really feel the need to impress Luca.

He has a gentle, firm touch that I feel comforted by as he takes my clothes off. He takes off his shirt, exposing an excessively attractive, lean body. He's got an intense eight-pack and that sexy V between his hip bones. Male dancers always have good bodies, but for one thing, they're not always straight, and for another thing, they are *rarely* this good.

"Jesus Christ, you're not human," I say.

"Coming from a goddess like you," he says, lifting me and scooting me back further onto the pillows.

He doesn't remove my bra or thong right away. First he comes over me, and kisses me. He has just the right amount of softness in his lips, not so much as to be feminine, but not too little either.

He kisses like he was sent from God, his tongue so correctly gentle, his lips against mine in such a satisfying way. He groans a little at how good it feels, and I can feel his hardness on my leg. I know now, for sure, that his *small penis* joke at Gravitas was indeed a joke. He's huge. Of course he is, because he's a perfect specimen.

Luca kisses my cheek, my forehead, my jaw, my neck, and then in my ear he whispers, "You have to do me a favor."

"Going back on your one condition already?" I writhe a little under him, overcome with comfortable desire.

"No," he says. "You must tell me what you like. Don't be afraid."

He touches my waist gently and I suck in a breath. "Fuck," I say.

"You like that?" he asks.

I nod against him.

"Mm," he says, and then he spreads his palm flat on my waist, then tightens his grip.

"Ah, my god," I say, jerking in pleasure at the touch.

He moves down, kissing my chest, touching my breast through my bra, then kissing that same spot on my waist. He drags his mouth across my flat stomach, flicking his tongue a little. He puts a hand flat against my back and brings me even closer to his kiss.

I feel so completely comfortable. Drained, in a nice way, after crying so much, at ease in the arms of this nice, beautiful man, who only wants to make me feel good.

"Do you want me to touch you here?" he asks, gently touching me through my underwear.

I nod. "Yes, please."

Still through the fabric, he begins to touch me, using his thumb against my clit, planting his ring and middle fingers firmly against my vulva.

I bite my lip and gather the blanket in both of my hands.

He does this until I can't stand it anymore, and without me needing to tell him, he puts his fingers inside me.

"Fuck," I scream. "That's—so—"

He finds my G-spot and I flatten my hands against the mattress, then cover my face with my arms as he finally puts his mouth against my clit, moving the thong to the side.

"That's good, right there," I confirm, though it's clear he knows it's the right spot.

"You taste so fucking good," he says. The words themselves

would be hot enough, but combined with his accent, I actually feel a wave of orgasm come close. "You're getting so tight. Fuck."

I gasp as his mouth envelops me, his tongue moving rhythmically. It's as gentle and satisfying and plush as his kiss.

"Where's your vibrator?" he asks.

"I don't think I need it," I say.

"Do you want it?"

I think, and then laugh, nod, and point to where it is.

Luca releases me, and the absence of him makes me even hotter for him.

He retrieves it and comes back over, this time with slightly more intensity. He plunges his fingers into me, just the right amount, and then kisses my inner thighs while he turns on the vibrator.

It has a low, quiet hum. I didn't want something loud. I could be in the same room as someone else and they wouldn't even know it was on.

He puts it on my clit and I let out an *"oh,"* while he groans against my thighs.

"You're so good," he says.

The silicone head of the vibrator buzzes against me, his fingers move inside me, and he uses his mouth wherever he can.

It's not long until I feel it coming.

"I'm close," I say.

"Take your time, baby," he says. "I could do this all night."

He really says all the right things. So often, sex feels performative or rushed. Like I have to *get there* faster than I can or want to.

But I believe Luca when he says to take my time.

I don't need to. Only a minute after he starts using my vibrator, I feel the warm tsunami start to churn within me, then it all hits the right rhythm at the right time, and I say, "I'm close, I'm close, I'm—"

And then I let out a scream of pleasure. Then another, and another. Then I feel the tsunami again, and I can tell I'm going to climax again.

He takes away the vibrator and uses just his tongue and fingers, and I feel it build and then finally crash over me. I scream loud and long, and he says, "Yes, baby, yes."

When I finally finish, I feel completely empty. Spent. The most relaxed I can remember feeling in a very, very long time.

He comes up to me, shutting off the vibrator and then putting it away from us; he pulls me into his chest and we lie there for a while.

I must fall asleep, because the next thing I know, I'm tucked under the comforter and he's sitting on the edge of the bed.

"I didn't want to wake you," he says.

"It's okay, I didn't realize I fell asleep."

"Do you want me to stay?" he says, moving the hair off my face.

I consider.

He says, "It's okay either way, truly."

His voice is so gentle.

And I realize I don't want him to stay. Not because it wouldn't be nice. But because I kind of want tonight to be its own thing.

"You don't have to stay," I say.

He smiles and says, "Okay. I'm just going to clean up and then I'll go, okay?"

I nod.

He shuts the lights off, leaving on only a dim one in the corner I hadn't even known was there. I hear him bustle around in the kitchen washing out the wineglasses. I hear him wash my vibrator in the sink. I hear him putting away our takeaway.

And then, he goes.

I don't love Luca. I don't even feel particularly compelled by him, despite his beauty.

But he might just be the most perfect man I've ever met. Why, I wonder, as I drift off into a soothed sleep, is it that I cannot just want a man like that?

CHAPTER TWENTY-SIX

I'm so excited that I have to practically tie my ankles together to keep from showing up to rehearsal an hour early. It's how most people describe Christmas as a kid. Joyful, almost frantic anticipation. And the little rendezvous with Luca didn't hurt giving me a great sleep.

I still get back to the theater early. I have to stop myself from walking at top speed from the flat to the studio.

After getting changed and doing a short Pilates practice and some other warm-up exercises, I wait in front of the elevator, shivering a little from excitement.

When the doors open, I feel my gut sink.

"Jocelyn!" Arabella gushes, stepping out and toward me.

My ear throbs as a reminder that she can't be trusted.

"Arabella."

"*Cariño*, I thought about you all day yesterday. We're like Spanish lovers, aren't we? So much passion between us. We're here, we're there."

She laughs, flippant and confident. I recall the first days I knew her, when I thought she was so glamorous and interesting. Sort of like a more sexual Holly Golightly. Now her erratic mood swings feel more like those of a kid who's been prematurely prescribed psychiatric medication.

Girls push by us and get in the open elevator.

"Are you coming in?" asks one of them, the girl Anastasia, who I met on that first night at Arabella's.

"No, we need a minute," says Arabella.

They let the doors shut, and I see them look at each other just before they close all the way.

Fuck. I do not want to do this with her before rehearsal. She's first on the basic for *Manon*, so I was hoping to just stare at the back of her head the whole time and learn the steps from her, never having to actually interact.

"I'm sorry, Arabella," I say, reluctant to give her anything, but knowing things work best when Arabella is happy. She leans on the wall, arms crossed, waiting for me to go on. "I shouldn't have implied that you"—I look around, making sure no one is listening—"fucked for your roles. I know you're good. I know you didn't do that, and I shouldn't have said that."

I hit the button again for the elevator.

"Of course, darling! I forgive you. I said we're like lovers, aren't we? So we get heated. I like this fiery side of you that's coming out. It's sexy."

It's not a completely accurate reporting of what happened. It's not as if we were arguing and things escalated. She *bit* me, for fuck's sake. After having more than one tantrum at me. And I snapped and said her rude words back to her. That's what happened.

I think of her and Cynthia, who scream at each other more than speak. I wonder why Cynthia puts up with it.

The elevator dings and then opens again.

"Well, see you." I give a little wave and step into the elevator.

She gives me an amused, puzzled look as the doors shut again.

"God," I whisper to myself.

Thanks to the little run-in, I don't get to rehearsal early at all, arriving right at three. I open the door to studio five, seeing that the earlier rehearsal has dispersed and the dancers are grabbing their things and dance bags and starting to rush off to their next rehearsal, break, or costume fitting. There is always something next.

I set my bag down and quickly get ready. Pointe shoes on, warm-ups off. Today, I'm in a drapey lavender chiffon practice skirt that hits right below my knees. I take a few stretches, breathing deeply, trying to release the stress of the conversation with Arabella.

After a few minutes, I glance at the clock on the wall. It's three oh five. Where is everyone else? There are only stragglers putting their warm-ups back on or stretching while scrolling their phones before heading off. None of the dancers who should be here, are here.

There are three other women learning the role of Manon. They should be here with their partners. The room should be abuzz with all of us. Am I in the wrong studio? I must be, right?

I go over to the pianist. "Excuse me."

She looks up from the notes she's writing on the sheet music. "Yes?"

"Am I in the right place for Manon and Des Grieux rehearsals? It was supposed to be three to five, but I don't see anyone here who should be. Except you, obviously." I laugh awkwardly.

She smiles politely. "You're in the right place. It actually begins at three fifteen. Union rules, there has to be some space between rehearsals. I don't know what good that does, I'd rather get home fifteen minutes early if we're taking time somewhere."

"Right. Okay. Well, thank you."

Just then, the doors swing open.

Isabella, who is setting the ballet, and with her is Luca.

I knew he'd be here, of course, but I didn't expect the little lift of glee I feel when I see him. Not romantic feelings, more like the feeling of having a secret with your very best friend.

"Hello, Jocelyn. Please forgive us for running a little late. Or at least, it's late to me, I usually prefer to be early. I'm glad to see you do, too."

"Of course," I reply. "I was a little confused at first," I confess. "I thought the other dancers would be here by now."

She looks confused, and then, understanding, she says, "Oh, no, dear. It's just you and Luca. I need to catch you up."

Luca smiles at me, and I smile back.

I breathe out a sigh of relief, glad I'll have a chance to be caught up, and gladder that he is my partner. I know he's an incredible dancer, and I know for certain now that he has a very gentle touch.

"I've danced the ballet before, so I've got you, Jocelyn," Luca says softly.

"Thank you," I say.

"All right." Isabella claps. "Let's go ahead and start with the act one pas de deux between you two."

My heart skips a beat. I can't believe I'm Manon. It keeps hitting me.

"So," she goes on, "Jocelyn, you'll start sitting in the chair. You've been watching him dance. Luca, let's go to where you end your solo on your knee in front of her."

We take our places. I vaguely know the steps, from having

studied a million videos online and having been given a brief run-down, but it's pretty difficult to know it with one hundred percent certainty without having a partner to learn it with.

"So, Luca, remember when you offer your hand to Manon to come dance with you, you're both shy at first. You have this immediate, intense attraction to each other, but it's so strong and overwhelming that it scares you. You're young and you're nervous. It's the transcendent, deeply affecting feeling of . . . how can this stranger see my soul already? Hear my heartbeat already?"

Her words echo through the studio as she circles us.

"You feel like you finally found each other. By this point, here, go to this arabesque position, Jocelyn. Luca, hold her waist *just so* . . . yes, just like that, and pivot her slowly to face you."

I think of his hand on my waist last night. *You like that?*

We do as she says, Luca's eye contact deeply penetrating. He's got these sharply blue eyes that see right through me. It's like he's cast a spell, and now my mind is swirling with complicated emotions around Alistair and Jordan.

Isabella goes on.

"This moment, *this* position, is when your souls connect. It's that blissful, whirlwind feeling that you get when you meet someone and you just *know*. It is love at first sight, it is the anticipation that pain might lie in your shared future, but that it's one that you, neither of you, can avoid."

I take a deep breath. She seems to be describing exactly how I felt when I met Jordan. I felt completely drawn in. I was so sure I had finally found my person.

Why did he never call?

I refocus on Isabella's voice.

"These moments are *very* important to your characters. First your hands touch, there is electricity there, then this arabesque moment when you come so *close* to kissing—"

Luca and I bring our faces together. He smells like peppermint and sweat. In a good way.

Now Alistair, that kiss, is in my mind.

Luca, his tongue inside me.

Christ, I need to focus.

"And with that, you both let your walls drop. Now, again!"

We go back to the beginning and start from the top of the pas de deux. Luca moves me and holds me with expert strength and grace.

My mind will not *shut up*. It's whirling and swirling.

"Yes, Jocelyn, that's it!" she says, her voice rising and filling the room. "Feel like you're flying. Keep that torso strong but let your arms be free. Okay, Luca, you can run a bit faster with her up in the press lift."

We try it again and again and again. And I don't mind at all. I'm so glad to be back in the studio, back in the arms of a strong, sexy man that I know I can trust.

After an hour, we're both damp with sweat. My muscles are burning. It feels incredible.

"Okay, I think that's looking good," says Isabella. "Go ahead and take your five-minute break. Jocelyn, do let me talk to you for a quick moment first."

I catch my breath and go over to her. "Thank you so much for this," I say. "No role has ever meant more to me."

"Of course. You're a gifted dancer. I was watching you last week in class in *Swan Lake* and your movement intrigued me. I felt like I could see your thoughts with every gesture. And"—she shrugs—"that's Manon."

I give an uncomfortable laugh. "Yeah. That's what this music and everything makes me feel, too. I feel like I really connect with it."

She gives me a kind look. "Of course, it's perfect for the performance and I'm delighted to have found someone who can play Manon with all the inner turmoil and who seems to understand the inner conflicts so deeply. It's great for the role, but how is it for you? How are you, Jocelyn?"

She puts a hand briefly on my arm and then lets it drop, waiting for me to respond.

There is so much compassion and care in her tone and in her expression. I feel completely naked in front of her, almost a little embarrassed to be so completely empathized with. The only person who has ever really treated me like this is Mimi. She did everything a mother was supposed to do. And now that she's gone, I realize it's been quite a long time since anyone has treated me with this brand of support.

"I'm okay," I say. Unexpected tears threaten to appear and then overflow, so I blink a few times and clear my throat. "I'm a little rocky sometimes, but I'm mostly okay. My donor actually . . ."

I start to tell her that he's moved me into his apartment, but I get a strong feeling that's crossing the boundaries a bit and Isabella might be concerned.

"What about your donor?" she asks, noticing my pause. "Is everything all right?"

She's on alert. A woman wanting to make sure everything is on the up-and-up for another woman. I appreciate it, but of course since I desperately *want* Alistair, it's conflicting.

"He's been really supportive," I say. "That's all, he's just been really great, is all."

"He? I thought Clementine Cavendish was your sponsor."

"Oh, right, well, it's the two of them. She and her husband. But I haven't met her yet, so. It's just been A—Mr. Cavendish."

Mister? Is that actually *weirder* than calling him Alistair?

"I see," she says, seeming to be picking up on the fact that something is a little off.

I'm in a dizzying mental spiral, so I just put my fingers to my temple and say, "I'm sorry, I'm going to run to the bathroom quickly."

What I'm not saying is that I want to fuck my donor, I miss my ex, and my dance partner spent an hour eating me out last night.

She is silent for a few seconds, and then she says, "Okay, why don't you take an extra five minutes, go freshen up? We'll resume at four twenty."

"Okay," I nod. "Thanks. Sorry."

Oh my god, I'm being so *weird*. It's just my guilt. Guilt has always made me a mess. When I did anything wrong as a kid, any little lie or extra piece of candy snuck, I was a complete wreck while I waited for my mom to figure it out. I always knew she would, and I dreaded it.

I go to the bathroom, and look in the mirror. My cheeks are pink, my skin dewy.

Everything is fine. I don't know why I'm freaking out. I need to just calm down and enjoy the fact that I'm Manon. It's all okay.

I was born for this part. I need to be calm and collected and not spiral out about everything else in the world that I can't control.

On my way back up to the studio, I see Mary Simon with a woman I vaguely recognize. She has dark blond hair, she's very thin, and—oh, fuck.

Clementine Cavendish. She isn't as blond as the pictures I've seen, and she's even thinner and prettier in person.

Oh, fuck, fuck, *fuck*.

The flashing memories from the other night are pulsing in my mind. I try to push them out of my head, but now that I shouldn't, all I can think of is his lips on my neck. His hands cupping my breasts. The way he tasted. Me living in his bachelor pad.

I wonder if she knows.

The two women walk toward me.

"Jocelyn," says Mary. "How lovely to see you again. I heard about the role. Congratulations. I knew I had a good feeling about you."

"Thank you so much," I say. "I'm very excited."

"I'm sure you are. Please, let me introduce you to Clementine. I understand you've only met Alistair thus far, yes?"

His name being said aloud, in front of Clementine, puts a grip around my heart. Like an alarm sounding at the door of a store when you know you have a stolen lipstick in your pocket.

"That's correct," I practically whisper. Then, "Hi." I hold out my hand. "It's so lovely to meet you."

I force myself to let my eyes meet Clementine's. God, she is so strikingly beautiful.

"Wonderful to finally meet you, Jocelyn. I've come to see your rehearsal. I hope that's okay." She smiles. "From what my husband tells me, you are very talented."

My husband. My husband. The words feel like a slap. I practically want to snap back with, *I know he's your husband, why do you keep reminding me?*

Oh my god, does she know? Did he go home and say I made a move on him? Oh my god. Oh my god.

"That's so great," I say, overcompensating. "I'm so thankful to you—and um, and to your husband both for supporting me. I only just started learning the role." I'm getting even more nervous. "So, I hope the rehearsal isn't going to be too boring for you."

"Oh, no, I love it."

Clementine has an effortless cool to her. A strong, clear voice with a slightly Americanized English accent. A relaxed posture. A comfort in her own skin that I only have when I'm dancing.

"Well, lead the way," says Mary, when I stand there a few seconds too long in stunned silence.

"Right, of course, yes, follow me," I say.

I have no idea how I do it, but once we start rehearsing again, I manage to block out Clementine, and all thoughts of her husband.

I focus only on Luca and Isabella. We move on to the bedroom pas de deux.

I do a pretty good job of ignoring them until the door opens and Alistair comes in. Mary waves him over.

I stumble at the sight of him.

"Fuck, sorry," I say.

Luca has caught me, and now he says, "My fault. Let's go again."

I regain my composure. I could dance in my sleep. It shouldn't bother me that he's here. It's fine. It's fine. But right now, I feel like the world's worst person having slept with a married man. I hate myself.

But I'm a little off my game. No matter how hard I try to concentrate, I can't do it. I keep slipping. I'm not hitting my marks.

Luca makes it look good, making up for my lack, just like he'd do onstage if something happened. Of course, Isabella's job is to be hyperobservant, and she notices.

She keeps stopping us and saying, *Focus, you two, let's try that bit again*. Which is generous, because I think we all know it's me, not Luca.

At the end of rehearsal, Isabella dismisses Luca, who gives me a commiserative look before leaving.

Isabella lowers her voice so the Cavendishes and Mary Simon can't hear.

"Is everything okay?"

"Yes," I say. "I'm sorry. It's just that I hadn't danced in a while, and it's just . . . personal stuff."

She scans my eyes. "You're extremely talented, Jocelyn. But you have to get it together. Whatever's going on, you have to find a way to leave it outside the studio. I have empathy for your situation, I understand you just lost your mother and things are tough. Unfortunately—"

"I know," I say. "I know, it won't happen again. I know."

"That was so fun," says Clementine, standing from her seat, Mary and Alistair following suit.

My heart in my throat, I smile as she approaches.

"No wonder my husband can't stop talking about you. You're fantastic."

My eyes flit to him and I smile politely as he avoids my gaze. "Thank you."

"I can't believe that was only the first rehearsal. Wow." Clementine looks me up and down, like someone might if they had just bought a fancy new car and she's kicking the tires. "He was right. You are special."

I shift my dance bag to my other shoulder for something to do. It's weird and hard for me to imagine what it's like when Clementine and Alistair talk about me. As I live in his clandestine bachelor pad and allow him to give me the most intensely sexual kiss of my life.

"Thank you so much," I say. "That's very nice to hear. I'm glad you're both happy."

"Definitely," says Clementine. "Definitely. All right, well, we have a party we need to get to. Congratulations on your role, and I can't wait to watch it all come together."

She shakes my hand, and I say, "Thank you, me too."

"Good to see you again," says Alistair, reaching out his own hand. I take it, shocked to find that there's a piece of paper hiding in it.

I try not to let my surprise show, and say, "You as well."

We break our grasp and he turns to follow Clementine. I look at Isabella, whose eyes are on my hand. She raises her gaze to mine. It's questioning, not accusatory. She's not sure what she saw.

"Good to see you," says Mary.

I'm desperate to look in my palm, read the note, but I wait, of course, until I have disentangled from the situation in the studio, going all the way to one of the bathrooms instead of the dressing room where someone might see me.

I unfold it.

Meet me in Mary Simon's office in 10 minutes xx

CHAPTER TWENTY-SEVEN

I take a deep breath and knock on Mary's door.

"Come in," Alistair calls.

It surprises me to hear his voice beckoning me in, though I don't put it past him to have the most power in any room he's in.

I step in and shut the door quietly behind me. Something tells me to keep this very private.

Alistair is alone at the desk. I don't know what I was expecting.

"Where's Mary?" I ask, and then, "Wait, aren't you supposed to be on your way to a party with your wife?"

I don't mean to say *wife* with a bite, but I do, and I hate myself for it.

"I told them I needed to make a private call. I'll catch up with Clementine. Mary generously offered her office."

"Have you already made your call?" I ask, playing dumb.

He gives me that heavy-lidded look that makes me feel weak and he says, "Come here."

My heart lifts a little and I walk over to him. "I'm sweaty from rehearsal."

He nods, running his hand down the back of my arm, lifting it toward him, and kissing the back of my hand and then my arm. He licks my skin and the weirdness of it makes my legs feel like jelly. In a good way.

"I know I said the other night I was trying to be a good man, but it's just too hard to watch you move your body like that. Especially with another man."

He pulls me closer and kisses me. I lean into him, parting my lips, responding. He smells like expensive things and he tastes like them, too.

When we pull apart, I say, "It's just dancing."

He cocks an eyebrow. "I wasn't talking about the rehearsal."

I narrow my eyes at him. "What do you . . ."

"No more guests at the apartment."

"Wh-what?"

He smiles at me and then says, "I have cameras at the place. Outside. Not inside. Don't worry. I didn't and wouldn't watch. I couldn't bear it."

I feel a plunge of embarrassment. "Oh, shit."

"I know I have no right to ask for this, but I couldn't stand thinking about you there with Luca. It didn't help seeing him handling you just now. I'm not usually a jealous man."

I know I'm beet red. "It's your place, I understand. I probably shouldn't admit it, but you have nothing to be jealous of."

He lifts my chin up to him. "Look at me."

I obey, looking up into his steely eyes. "Really nothing. You're all I can think about."

He kisses me again, more eager this time. His hands playing

with the strap of my leotard. It would be so easy for him to just pull it down. I moan, wanting that so desperately. He pulls back, smirking, and says, "Good. I know I have no right, but I like the idea that I consume you and no one else does."

He steps back. He knows he's completely being a tease.

"Now listen, I need to run," he says. "But tomorrow. Berretti's at six p.m."

Part of me thinks that I should cancel the meeting at Berretti's. The reality of meeting Clementine yesterday in rehearsal makes my forbidden thoughts about Alistair seem suddenly more inappropriate than ever before. I'm confused and I'm angry. What the fuck is going on? He told me he was separated. They didn't seem close, but they also didn't seem on the brink of divorce. And then what happened in Mary's office. Who am I becoming?

I could tell him I have an added rehearsal. Or I could say I need to call Mimi because I had a voicemail from her care home and something happened—no, first of all he'd probably know if I was lying, and second of all I don't want to jinx her. I believe in that kind of thing.

I try to remind myself that this is all part of the job. It's part of having a donor. It's part of keeping everyone happy. And maybe I should try to enjoy it. My mom certainly would. Berretti's is a beautiful luxury department store. If he's taking me shopping there, which is what I assume is happening, it should just be exciting.

Shouldn't it?

I arrive about ten minutes before six p.m., going through the old, ornate revolving doors, the warm gust of air a welcome relief from the cold, damp weather outside. It's dark out today, the moody, heavy clouds gathering low and opaque in the sky, seem-ingly just a little higher than all the buildings.

I decide to take the escalator up to the fifth floor to meet Alistair, wanting to take the time to admire each floor and its el-egance. Plus, I'm here early. This is why I showed up early.

I'm dressed simply, in a black fitted turtleneck and tight black jeans, my hair in loose curls, diamond earrings in my ears. I bought them for myself after my promotion to principal with NAB, deciding that I deserved them after a lifetime of cubic zir-conia from Claire's. It was an irresponsible thing to do with my money, but I have never regretted it. Every time I need to elevate myself for my surroundings, they're the first thing I grab.

Despite them, though, I still feel like a fish out of water. There's a sophistication to this place that makes me feel like I'm about three generations of wealth behind on knowing how to shop here.

The first floor is jewelry, makeup, and handbags. The glass counters glow as spotlights land on sparkling diamonds, gold, platinum, and silver earrings, rings, bracelets, necklaces, and even—I spot—a tiara. The makeup looks more glamorous here than it ever does in a makeup bag, every little compact and brush looking like something to be treasured. The bags are all perched on their own little pedestals. The place smells like roses and leather.

The next two floors I pass are women's designer labels. I see Prada, Dior, Celine, Yves Saint Laurent.

The fourth floor—my heart nearly stops as my eyes land on all of them at once—is shoes. Fucking amazing shoes. Patent leather loafers gleam beneath the lights, sparkly pumps glisten, and deli-cate stilettos that hardly look as though they could support the weight of any woman. Even a carb-starved ballerina.

Finally, I get to the fifth floor. Menswear. I feel a flush of embarrassed disappointment. Maybe I wasn't brought here to be treated, but instead to help him. Help him with what, though?

Surely he has people for that. And plus, all of his suits look custom-made.

When I don't immediately see him, I find a clerk. There's a woman adjusting the belt on a mannequin, a little obsessively, if I'm honest, as the adjustments she's making are almost imperceptible.

"Excuse me," I say.

She turns. She's an older woman, one of those women who looks like she never goes anywhere without her "face on."

"Yes, miss?"

"I'm looking for Special Services."

She gives me the tiniest, microscopic flick of judgment, then says, "Right this way."

It was like the famous *Pretty Woman* moment, only a micro-aggression.

She leads me to double doors with frosted glass. She gestures at them with a small bow, and then walks away.

Okay then, I guess I'm on my own.

I knock.

No one answers. I knock again.

Nothing.

I can hear distant voices on the other side of the door. I glance at my phone. It's six now, and I don't want to be thought of as late.

I push the doors open.

There's a small, elegant waiting area. Cream chairs and a glass coffee table. Silk wallpaper. Wooden molding on a low ceiling. An intricate chandelier.

"Um . . . hello?" I call out, once in.

I hear a woman laugh, and then, in a strong French accent, "This way, this way!"

I round a corner, then walk down a short hallway and through an open set of glass doors.

I can hear the woman's voice speaking in French, but I can't see where she is. It's a round room with mirrors and racks of clothing. Beautiful dresses with long hemlines or tight waists and puffy skirts. There are thick coats with beautiful stitching. Silky blouses and camisoles as light as air.

I let my hand run gently over the materials.

This is the kind of thing that literally filled my dreams when I was a kid. I would fall asleep on a creaking mattress with four fans blowing on me, hot without air-conditioning. I would escape on fictional journeys, imagining myself in dreamlands of shopping, vacationing, being in beautiful places. I dreamed of tulle tutu-like dresses—and sky-high heels. I wanted to be a beautiful ballerina with a gorgeous life.

Right now, that's what it feels like I am.

There is a velvet couch in the center of the room, and on the table in front of it, an ice bucket chilling a bottle of a champagne called Agrapart & Fils. I've never had it, but as my heart floats to the top of my chest, I realize I'll probably be given a glass any moment.

The woman comes out from behind a rack, scaring the shit out of me.

"Jesus!" I say by accident, eliminating any sophistication that I might have briefly appeared to have.

"Jocelyn! I am Laura, your personal shopper."

She's a petite brunette with a messy bob and the sort of messed-up teeth that somehow look glamorous on the right kind of chic European.

"My . . . ? I'm sorry, I don't understand."

I think I might. I think I might understand that this shopping extravaganza *is* about me, but I want to be sure.

"I wasn't sure of your taste, but Alistair said ballerina chic and that you are *tiny* tiny. And you are! Look at you, I definitely guessed right for the size on most of the items."

"Wait, are you saying . . . is this for me?" Then, dumbly, "Doesn't the store close soon?"

"Oh my gosh, yes! Of course it is for you. Ah, did I ruin the surprise? I'm sorry about this, dear. For the Cavendishes, we keep the store open late."

Of course they do. I kind of can't believe I asked. I'm really making myself sound like a rube. Next, I'm going to ask if there's a charge for bags.

I look around, trying to take it all in.

My eyes stop on one of the racks I didn't notice before. Lingerie.

My heart is beating so fast, the poor, broke child inside me absolutely alight with excitement. I can't help but smile.

"Why don't I pour you some champagne and you start looking about. Alistair's instructions were to let you have anything you want, but you need a dress for an event tonight. You really only need the one dress, he said, but asked that I pull extra, thinking that you might need to fill out your wardrobe. So I obliged, as you can see." She smiles.

"Is Alistair coming here?"

"No, no," she says. "Don't worry, it's just us girls."

I feel a little disappointed, but I pretend not to. It's easy to pretend, considering I'm looking at an entire room of expensive clothes, knowing I can have anything I want.

For the next half hour, I look through everything, feeling my greedy little heart explode as I see the labels and mentally guess how expensive they are. The clothes in this room could buy a house. A nice house.

Laura has stripped me down and helped me into a stunning dress when I hear my phone buzz.

"Oh, could you—" I gesture. "I'm sorry, I don't want to mess up the—"

"Of course, darling." She steps off her pedestal and retrieves my phone.

I look and see that it's Alistair.

I hide the screen from the woman, and read the text.

**Send me a picture of what you're
thinking of wearing.**

I take a picture of myself in the three-way mirror I'm standing before and send it to him, along with a text.

**So ... what event is this? Sorry about
the guest by the way.**

He texts back quickly.

**The event is at nine. I'll pick you up at
Ivory at quarter-til.**

He says nothing about the guest.

Do you like the dress? I ask.

It's an Alexander McQueen, a strapless, draped chiffon dress in hot pink.

I think it would look ridiculous without diamonds. Have Laura pull some for you.

"Um," I say.

"Is everything okay? Am I pinching?"

"No, it's just . . . Alistair asked that you pull some diamonds."

"Of course, dear," she says. "You see how this feels as you move around, and I'll go get some. I had some set aside just in case."

And then I'm alone in all this opulence.

I take another picture, a more relaxed one, and send it to Sylvie.

My donor is buying this McQueen dress for me. Fucking crazy

She responds after a few minutes, saying: **no strings attached??**

I write back, **idk, I don't think so . . . ?**

She sends back a cringing emoji, and then adds, **it looks fucking amazing though.**

I respond, **the shopper woman is literally grabbing some kind of diamonds to go with it.**

She answers, **omg that'll look so good with that pink. How are you tan, you're in LONDON.**

I answer, **that Louisiana poor kid tan just never left me.**

She says, **lol**, just as Laura bustles back in.

"Okay, darling, I've got a few options."

She drapes diamond necklaces over my collarbone as I look on in the mirror, again feeling like I'm in *Pretty Woman*.

"I like this, but it won't work without the matching earrings.

But this looks nice with the studs you're wearing. These are real, correct?" She flicks my earlobe.

Proudly, I respond, "Yes." I stop just short of adding that I bought them myself.

"We'll need bigger ones to make the look work. Take them out."

She doesn't mean any harm, but I feel a little slapped by this. I put them safely into my purse and then allow her to put much bigger ones into my ears.

The effect is stunning. I feel like Audrey Hepburn in *Breakfast at Tiffany's*, only instead of a tiara, I'm in a long delicate diamond chain and matching earrings.

She picks out a few pairs of shoes and I go with a strappy pair in the same shade of pink by a designer I don't recognize.

I pick a few other items, feeling shy and that maybe I look like I'm taking advantage, and then she packages them up for me. Someone brings them downstairs for me, and just as I'm becoming aware that I'll have to walk out onto the city streets with thirty thousand dollars' worth of merchandise, I'm informed that there is a car waiting for me outside.

I get into the back of it and the driver takes me to Ivory Towers, where the doorman retrieves my packages, and I walk upstairs empty-handed.

Rich people really just don't have to do anything, do they?

Upstairs, I get ready using my own makeup. I do a simple look with clean skin, light mascara, and a pale pink lip. I don't have the skill or will to do anything much with my hair, so I put it back in a slick ponytail and call it a day.

I consider the fact that there's no glam squad waiting a confirmation that Clementine is not involved in any of this. A woman would have known that with a five-thousand-dollar dress and many more thousands' worth of jewelry, you should not leave someone like me to my own devices with the rest.

At eight forty-five sharp I'm waiting in the lobby and I see headlights pull up out front, checking to make sure there's no one around, conscious of not wanting to be seen with him in case it's another shit show.

My phone buzzes. A text from Alistair.

Here. Come.

CHAPTER TWENTY-EIGHT

The car has completely opaque blackout windows, and the driver opens the door covertly and I see Alistair subtly shielding his face, I assume in case anyone happens by as I climb in.

I slide into the back seat with Alistair and see that I was correct to assume he would be alone.

"Will Clementine be at this event?" I ask anyway.

"No."

"Did you . . . tell her about—"

"Of course not."

I nod, feeling embarrassed. "Right."

The car takes off.

"Champagne?" he asks, pulling two glasses from a built-in bar.

"Sure."

He pops a bottle of Krug and pours me a glass. I take it and say, "Thank you."

He pours his own, and then holds it out. "To art."

"To . . . art." I clink my glass against his.

We both take a sip. It's so good.

It's amazing how lately I have been unable to think of Alistair without feeling uncontrollable desire. Sometimes I want him so bad just from the memory that I gasp at the thought.

My night with Luca was beautiful, but it definitely did not have the same effect. That felt more like a nice night with a boyfriend of many years or something. It didn't have the electricity of the kiss with Alistair.

Well, of course it didn't. He's completely off-limits. Married. My donor. I'm an idiot.

"So where are we going?" I ask.

"An art show. I need to buy a piece, and I know you have a good eye. I need someone young to tell me what's working."

"You're not that old," I say.

He gives the smallest hint of a smile, and says, "No, but I also didn't spend a year with one of the most popular emerging artists. I can only imagine that some of Morales's taste rubbed off on you."

I feel shocked by the sudden appearance of Jordan in this conversation. I take a bigger sip of my champagne.

"Am I wrong?" he asks.

"No, I heard him talk about all kinds of artists that are selling right now. I don't know how much I remember."

"It's better than I could do without you. This is an important purchase."

"Why?" I ask.

"It just is."

It's clear I'm not meant to ask for further clarification, so I just nod and look out the window. I swallow the questions I want to ask about his and Clementine's relationship.

"You look beautiful, by the way," he says.

"Oh, thank you—thank you, by the way, sorry, I can't believe I didn't lead with that."

"It's all right." He smiles.

"Yeah. It's not hard to look good in a dress and jewelry like this."

He hesitates, then says, "Just take the compliment. You don't need to give the dress credit."

"Women are always doing that. Having trouble taking compliments. I blame men."

This elicits the first real laugh I've gotten out of him.

The gallery isn't far, and when we get out, there are paparazzi. Holy shit.

I smile and try to look pretty and less normal than I feel.

My mom would love all this. God. I can't believe she won't see the pictures. Little as we talked, I would have shared them with her.

Alistair doesn't touch me as we walk in, and he answers one of the paparazzi asking *who is that* by telling them that I'm Jocelyn Banks, a ballerina with the RNB.

We walk up the red carpet and into the gallery.

I felt a little ridiculous just being myself in this dress and everything, but here, in this context, I can see that wearing anything else would have been a huge mistake. Everyone here *drips* of money.

I nibble on pieces of cheese and drink champagne as Alistair mingles. It's not until an hour in that I see the only other person there who is not dripping of money. But just like me, he's dressed the part.

Jordan.

And he looks stunning.

He's in a tailored suit that looks exactly on trend. Someone else must have dressed him. He's not one of those guys who wears button-downs and khakis, not at all. But he's not *this* trendy.

I find myself drifting toward him like a ghost, my heeled feet moving of their own accord.

He sees me and does a double take.

"Just one moment," I hear him say to the man he's talking to.

He comes toward me.

"Jocelyn."

"Jordan. What are you doing here?"

He gives a sheepish look. "I have a few pieces in the show."

"Oh—duh, of course. Yeah. Of course you do."

He smiles. He looks more handsome than last time I saw him. How? Did life without me suit him that much?

Or do I just not remember him accurately?

I am about to ask why he never texted me when someone walks up to us.

"Everything else here is shit," she says. "Oh, hi!"

Up close, she looks familiar. I can't place her, except that I'm certain she's the same woman from Jordan's apartment.

"Jocelyn Banks," I say, holding out my hand.

"I know—we've met." She glances at Jordan.

"Jocelyn, you remember my sister, Adrienne."

"S-sister?"

They both look at me with confusion and then everything clicks back into place.

"Holy shit," I say. "You look—you look a lot different. Or am I wrong? Sorry, I feel so rude for not recognizing you, Adrienne, yes, of course I remember you."

I don't feel that bad actually, because she looks almost unrecognizable. Last time I met her was on a FaceTime call when Jordan and I first started dating. She had long dark hair and she weighed about forty pounds more. The worst part is that we've texted a *lot*. Like, a lot. Not since Jordan and I broke up, obviously. But before that, a lot.

"It's fine," she says. "My own mom didn't recognize me. Long story short, I divorced my boring husband and moved my kids to L.A. Now one goes to school with J. Lo's kids and I do yoga every day—oh, I'll take one of those."

She intercepts a glass of champagne off a passing tray.

"Wow," I say. "That's amazing."

"I didn't tell anyone right away, not even Jordan. I don't know why, I guess I was embarrassed to be trying to *make it* in L.A. or whatever. But yeah, actually everything's been great. I chopped all my hair off and work out every time I feel depressed, and now I'm super skinny!"

She laughs, and that gives me permission to laugh.

Last I knew her, she was living in Orange County, working a job she hated, with a husband who never wanted to do anything more with his life than he was already doing. Most of what she and I talked about was Bravo TV, so I'm not surprised I was not someone she confided in.

"You look incredible," I say. "I can't believe it's you."

I feel so relieved that this isn't some gorgeous woman Jordan is dating that I can hardly breathe.

She glances between us. "Great to see you, Jocelyn, but obviously this is awkward, so I'll let you guys catch up. I'm going to go look at some pretentious art and find the caviar."

Once she's gone, I look back at Jordan's face and I feel compelled to touch it.

I don't, of course.

"Jocelyn, I—"

"Jordan Morales," says Alistair, appearing at my side. "I hoped we'd get a chance to meet. Alistair Cavendish."

Jordan's eyebrow flicks at the sound of the name. "Nice to meet you," he says.

"I hoped Jocelyn could introduce us," he says. "I'm interested in buying one of your pieces. In fact, I have a proposition for you."

CHAPTER TWENTY-NINE

Jordan and Alistair then step away from the crowd. Away from me. Away from my control and my listening ears. Jordan gives me a last, conspiratorial look before he goes, something that acknowledges that, yes, this is very weird.

My heart lifts, unexpectedly, at the little moment of *us*-ness, and I steady myself by taking a glass of champagne off a passing tray and saying, out loud to myself, "Okay, okay, all good, everything's fine."

I busy myself by staring into the abyss of dark ruby crimson in the piece closest to me. I look at it without really seeing it, my mind whirling as I try simultaneously to guess what Alistair could be proposing and also try to take my mind off of it.

I drift around the gallery looking for Jordan's pieces, my mind a million miles away, but find myself coming back to the present as I realize I don't recognize some of his work.

It hasn't been that long since we broke up. Only a few months. Last I was around Jordan, he was in kind of a slump. Painter's block. Nothing was coming to him. Every time he went to his studio, he came home frustrated because ever since moving to London, he'd been completely dry.

But judging by the unfamiliarity of some of these pieces—and the fact that the information tiles beside them say they were painted this year—he's been extremely prolific since we broke up.

What is he, Adele? He can only create his art after a breakup?

His pieces are all gloomier than they had been previously. Lots of cadmium red and Prussian blue. Payne's gray and onyx black. Instead of the soft varnish he usually does, these are all finished in thick, high gloss.

So he's not with anyone—or at least, the blonde was his sister, not a girlfriend—and he's been making moody art ever since we broke up. So then how is it possible that he hasn't tried, not even once, to get in touch with me?

I take a sip of champagne and look across the gallery at Jordan and Alistair, who have been joined by a man in thick-rimmed glasses and a narrowly tailored suit. If I had to guess, I'd say that Alistair is making a purchase and that man is the gallery owner.

Why does Alistair want to buy a piece of Jordan's? Not that I don't think they're good, have value, or have an appeal to a rich man who likes to acquire things, but why has he brought us here?

Is he fucking with me?

My defenses rise, and I remember that he's given me no reason not to trust him. Except for the whole *he's married* thing—but that has nuance.

Or at least that's what I keep telling myself.

The three men do a round of handshakes. Alistair looks pleased, and so does the gallery owner, but I'm fluent enough in Jordan's body language to see that he seems uncomfortable. Something is off.

He looks around the room for a moment, searching, and when his eyes land on me, I see a look I can't translate.

I start to walk toward him, but am stopped by Alistair approaching me. He gives me a wink and then stands by my side, where he whispers, "Nice guy," before asking a server if they have any scotch hidden somewhere in the back. The server nods and goes off to find it for him.

The gallery owner puts a little scarlet dot on the info panel by Jordan's painting nearest to us. It's a mix of grays and blues and something about it gives me chills.

I know that the little dot means it sold.

"Did you just buy that painting?" I ask.

"I did. For quite a bit above its value, in fact."

"Why—why did you do that?"

"He's a great artist. He's up-and-coming. And by buying it at this price, I'm raising the value of his other work, which I've started buying up recently."

"You didn't tell me that. Why didn't you tell me that?"

"I own a lot of art, Jocelyn; would you like me to tell you every piece I own?"

I start at this, but look up at him to see a wash of amusement in his features. He's kidding. It just didn't sound like he was kidding.

The server returns with his scotch, and he accepts it, slyly handing over a twenty-pound note as he does.

"One more thing," he says. "I put it under your name."

"Put—the sale of the painting?"

"Yes. Hope that's all right."

"Why did you do that?"

"Let's just call it diversifying my assets. I paid for it, of course.

And the sale should register as anonymous, should anyone look into it, but if they look too deeply, they'll find your name instead of mine. I can hardly escalate the artist's value if I'm buying them all for myself, can I? Plus, if I gift it to you, it's a tax write-off, isn't it?"

I feel a little lost. This is not a side of art or wealth I've ever been exposed to, and I'm not sure what to say in response.

"Okay," I say. I try not to expose how shocked I am.

"I thought you'd be pleased," he says. "You're now the proud owner of a painting worth hundreds of thousands of pounds."

I cough on my sip of champagne. "Hundreds of—"

"That's right," he says.

I look around to find Jordan, and I see him in conversation with another rich-looking man and the gallery owner. Jordan looks a little ruffled.

Last I knew, his pieces were selling for a lot, but not for *that* much.

Christ, if the gallery owner ratchets up the prices on all the others to match Alistair's purchase, and everyone knows it just sold tonight—well, Jordan could leave tonight a millionaire.

I start to understand what Alistair's intentions are.

"But why do you care about making the pieces worth more?" I ask. "Don't you already have more money than God?"

He laughs. "You haven't spent enough time in the upper echelon, have you?"

"I'm a ballerina, I've spent plenty of time with men like you," I snap back. "Your obscene wealth doesn't impress me. And isn't it your wife's, anyway?"

It's a daring thing to say, and for a moment I'm sure I've said just the wrong thing.

He arches an eyebrow and gives the hint of a smile.

Just when I'm finding myself annoyed with him, my unrelenting desire for him kicks back in.

It's those steely blue eyes. They get me every time.

I try to hide my smile and when I don't, I feel him laugh beside me. "What do you say we get out of here?"

Jordan's eyes land on mine once more, and I feel a deep, confusing pang of love for him.

Two girls, both gorgeous, tall, and thin, walk up to him.

"Yeah, let's get the hell out of here," I say.

We walk for fifteen minutes, mostly in silence. I try not to fill it like I always do.

My thoughts are in a tangle anyway. My feelings on him purchasing the painting, my feelings about the painting itself, the relief that Jordan isn't dating some gorgeous blonde, the devastation that this means his lack of contact with me makes even *less* sense.

"You seem tense," says Alistair finally.

"Do I?"

"You do."

I honestly don't know, for a moment, if he's right. I don't have time to examine it, as his pace slows and we stop in front of an unassuming building.

"We're here," he says.

"We're . . . where?"

A security man with an earpiece walks out the front door of the building. He's dressed in all black and he looks like he could kill anyone in a matter of seconds.

"Mr. Cavendish, welcome."

The man's voice is as deep and resonant as Idris Elba's.

"Thank you, Michael," says Alistair, gesturing for me to step through the opened door.

I do, and then Alistair leads me confidently down a dark, industrial hallway. He opens another door.

It's like when Dorothy walks out of the sepia and into the world of color.

It's staggering.

It reminds me of old pictures of the Cocoanut Grove in Los Angeles back in the thirties. Hedonistic chaos, a loud brass band, and people everywhere dressed in gorgeous clothes.

Alistair guides me through the pulsating throngs of people, weaving our way through the maze of tables and chairs. The band is playing a song that sounds like something you'd hear at a Jay Gatsby party.

The dance floor is full of elegantly dressed couples swaying to the music, and I'm kind of in awe of the opulence and extravagance of the club.

The walls are adorned with gold and silver, and crystal chandeliers hang from the ceiling, casting a soft glow over the room. The air is thick with the scent of expensive perfume and the sounds of clinking glasses and laughter.

Alistair leads me to a table in the center of the room, and we sit down at a reserved table lit by a tea light. A server immediately approaches us.

"Mr. Cavendish, welcome. What would you like this evening?"

"A bottle of champagne. Your best, whatever you have tonight, thank you, Sal."

The server goes off.

"Where the fuck are we?" I ask.

"It's called the Seven. An exclusive club you can only visit with obscene wealth. Even your wife's."

I feel a little embarrassed for having said that to him earlier. "Sorry," I say.

"It's fine," he says. "It's why I like you. You're sparky."

"Sparky?" I ask with a laugh.

The server returns quickly with our champagne. He opens it and pours for us both.

"Cheers," he says.

"Cheers."

We clink glasses and the crystal makes a distinctive *ding* sound.

"So why is it you hate money so much?" he asks. "You don't like fancy clothes, beautiful flats, and exclusive clubs like this?"

I look around us. Everyone is laughing and having fun. It's a gorgeous, colorful atmosphere. Exciting. Charged. Relaxed.

I grew up poor and can confirm that even at the nicest of barbecues and block parties, there's never quite the same sense of relaxation there. Unlike the people I grew up with, these people just simply don't have to worry. Conversations at block parties are usually about the rising cost of something or the cost of repairing one's roof. Here, they just find new ways to talk about success while making everything sound like stoicism.

Why *does* it make me so mad?

"I don't know," I say. "It's not like I don't like this. I love the champagne. I love the dress."

We have to raise our voices to be heard by each other over the festive din, and I find myself doing that thing where I gesture in half-made-up sign language to make it clear what I'm saying in case he doesn't catch every word.

"So what's the problem?" he asks.

Then he surprises me and moves me closer to him by my

waist. "That's better, now we can hear each other properly." He's so close it tickles my neck and sends chills up my arm. I barely suppress an involuntary moan.

He really is gorgeous. The dark hair, the dark lashes, the pale eyes. The lips I know can make me go crazy.

"Like I said, I don't know." I think for a second, and then say, "It's probably to do with my mom. She spent her whole life chasing wealth. It made her miserable. It made *me* miserable."

He nods. "Makes sense. Did she ever get it?"

I think of the dilapidated house in wild Louisiana. The medical bills.

I shake my head. "Not really. The last time we talked, she was just breaking up with this rich guy, George. I don't know. She just spent her whole life trying to marry rich."

"Why do you think she did that?"

I hold up the champagne and gesture at *all this around us.* "She wanted this," I say. "She said it was because she was making it possible for me to do ballet, but"—I shrug—"I don't know."

A memory starts to form in my mind of an evening before I moved to New York and I shake my head to make it go away.

No. I can't think about that right now.

"Well, you made it, baby." He smiles slightly. "You'll always be okay now."

Something in me relaxes a little when I look in his eyes. "I don't know," I whisper.

"Maybe your problem isn't that you're going to turn into your mom," he says, interpreting everything I've said and synthetizing it into something like a diagnosis, "maybe the problem is you can't accept peace when it's on offer. Maybe your life is actually falling into place, not falling apart."

He holds my gaze for a second and I feel my breath catch.

Oh my god. What if he's right?

"So what do you think I should do?" I say. He looks at me so intently and I think he hasn't heard me, so I repeat, *"What do you think I should do?"*

He leans even closer, whispering right into my ear. "I think you should let go."

He shrugs.

"Let go?"

"Just for a while. See what happens."

I smile and then shrug, gesturing that I'm not sure.

"Maybe," he goes on, "maybe I'm not going to betray you in the end. Maybe you're actually hanging around with a good guy who's really just trying to look out for you."

He moves one hand to my thigh and I lean on the table with my elbow, taking a sip of my champagne, and study his face. The heat of his hand on my leg stirs me intensely.

Is there any chance that this guy is for real? And if he is . . . what does that mean?

I play with the idea in my mind. What would it be like to be with someone like Alistair for real?

To be in a place like the apartment where he's letting me live now, but to know that it's my own. To know that it can't be stolen away or taken away.

You can make good money as a dancer. Especially as a principal, like I used to be. But with Mimi's bills, it's plunged me right back into the past. Right back to the beginning of my career. All the uncertainty. All the worry. All the fear that I'd become like my mom, scraping by.

I remember Arabella, right in the beginning, telling me that I had trouble accepting help. Is that true?

What if Alistair isn't a threat? What if he's just someone who likes me, has a complicated relationship, and also happens to have a lot of money?

I smile at him, trying to breathe away the worry. He gently squeezes my leg and moves his hand up a bit further.

"You're right," I say. "I should just enjoy it." I move my hand to his, putting it under the hem of my dress and guiding him higher.

He gives me a crooked smile and then I watch his gaze drop to my lips and then back again. "God, I want to kiss you." His hand is reaching closer to my black lace thong, his pinky finger starting to tease the fabric.

I gasp, my body responding aggressively. "But we can't. Because we're in public?" I then move his hand away, teasing him.

He groans. "You're intoxicating." He puts a hand back under the table, and as I move my knees apart, desperate for him, he hikes my dress up, going straight to my thong and slipping his fingers in. "If you let me in, you won't be able to get me off of you."

"Fuck," I say, my breath catching. *"Fuck."*

He moves his fingers expertly in and out of me. I'm so fucking wet he can barely stay inside.

I try to keep my breathing even as my pussy tightens around his fingers. I feel like I could faint, but right before I finish, he quickly removes his fingers. I pant and stare at him wide-eyed. It's like jumping into a cool pool on a hot day and not feeling the splash.

He smiles. "Do you want more?"

"Yes," I whisper, not correcting his understatement.

"Good girl, I know you do. I like to tease you. I bet no one ever makes you wait."

"Ha," I laugh, but I don't correct him. Instead, I boldly put my hand onto the outside of his pants and feel that his cock is so hard it seems as if it's going to burst the zipper.

"I want more, too," he says, confirming what I already know.

He moves my hand away playfully and we sit up like normal people out for a drink.

I'm breathless as we both take a sip of our champagne. We catch eyes and then, smiling, we look away from each other again.

We watch the singer, a gorgeous woman with a dress dripping in emeralds, a massive headpiece on her head. If it weren't for her 1970s-style curtain bangs, her ensemble would look exactly like a costume straight out of *Gentlemen Prefer Blondes*.

She sings in Spanish, saying something about love and loss, and I try to soak it all in as if it's mine. As if I belong here.

And yet I'm aware we're playing with fire. The two of us, out, like this. Like an exposed nerve. And yet I feel safe. Unafraid. Protected, with him. Insulated from the real world. As if we have time-traveled together, to a time where no one knows us and no one can catch us.

I want to. I want to own it. But something inside me tells me not to trust it.

I think of the text I received when I first spent time with Alistair. The one I never got a response on.

Don't trust him.

Alistair refills our glasses, then gives my hand a squeeze. "Come with me."

I follow him, splashing a little bit of drink as I go.

He pulls me through a door and into an old phone booth. The window has been covered with opaque film. He urges me in, and then looks around before getting in with me, shutting the door behind him.

It's cramped, but bigger than the phone booths usually look in movies. The proximity doesn't feel smothering; instead it just feels hot.

He puts his hand on my jaw and kisses me. He runs his fingers along my lips, and then when I open my mouth, he puts them inside. "Do you like the way your pussy tastes?" he groans in my ear. "Lick them, Jocelyn. Show me how much you love yourself."

I do as he says, feeling hungry for him. At the same time, he puts his other hand up my dress, planting his fingers flat against me.

I let out a gasp of pleasure and surprise, releasing his fingers from my mouth. He drops to his knees, putting his tongue against the mesh of my thong.

"Fuck!" I say, planting my hands against the walls, bracing myself as my knees weaken. "Fuck, Alistair."

He moans against me and it drives me even crazier. Then he moves my thong aside and flicks his tongue against my clit.

I finish almost immediately, the surprise an aid in my deep carnal satisfaction. As soon as I do, he unzips his pants and unbelts, asking me, "May I please fuck you, Jocelyn Banks?"

I nod and say, "Please, please fuck me." Feeling almost dizzy.

He lifts me up, flips me around, and plunges into me and I yell out. Loud. He covers my mouth with one hand while the other holds tightly to my waist. He laughs against me.

"Sorry," I say, muffled against his hand, laughing for a moment myself before it feels too good to do anything but revel in the feeling.

He fucks me hard, one hand on my waist, the other pulling my tit hard.

Fuck, he's so hot. I turn my head back to look at him. He's *so* fucking good-looking.

No wonder I can't pull myself away from him. He's everything I want. Good-looking. Likes me. Protects me. Is *incredible* in bed. And with him, I don't have to worry about things like awful medical bills.

I reel my mind backward, taking it away from the stressful thoughts, and wrap my arms and legs around him as he gets somehow even deeper inside me.

"I'm close," he whispers. "I'm so fucking close."

"Yeah?" I push my hips into him hard. Both his hands on my waist driving me hard. I begin to move with him. Every time he slams into me, I lift my hips up again for more.

We both breathe fast and hard, the din of the party outside feeling a million miles away. He finishes inside me and I cum just after.

When I've caught my breath, he pulls me up, kissing the back of my neck, then says, "You do something to me, Jocelyn."

"Yeah, you too," I say.

We compose ourselves, then he walks out first. I wait a moment, then go out, too.

We hold hands for a second, both of us laughing at how outrageous we are.

That's when the flashes begin. One after the other after the other.

A swarm of paparazzi.

CHAPTER THIRTY

SEVEN YEARS AGO

I was just another teenage girl listening to Lana Del Rey, wishing life was different than it was.

I lay in the backyard on an old Barbie beach towel draped over a rubber-strapped pool chair. The sun was blazing and the bugs in the trees would have been deafening if I didn't have in my AirPod knockoffs, blasting "Brooklyn Baby." My skin pulsed with the heat, and whenever it got too hot and I needed to cool down, I took the hose from beside me and pulled the trigger on the nozzle, letting a fine mist of water fall over me.

Poor-girl pool party.

I'd been out there every day since school ended. I usually did this during the summer, but that summer was different. It was different because usually I knew what was going to happen to me. I knew that I was whiling away the days until the end of August, when school started back up. But I'd graduated in May, and now I had no idea about my life.

In my mind, I was a ballerina. In practice, I was a ballerina. I had been dancing since I was a kid. I had taken every opportunity I had ever been given. I had succeeded as much as a girl can when she comes from Tristesse, Louisiana. And everything hinged on the audition I'd had for the North American Ballet in April. I had thought I'd have heard by mid-July, but I still hadn't, and it was driving me crazy.

The platonic ideal of an American summer after graduating from high school was usually that the seventeen- or eighteen-year-old had the summer of their life with their friends. They all wore sweatshirts with their future college scrawled across the chest. They made promises about forever that they could never keep. They put their arms around each other's shoulders and swayed back and forth to songs that felt like *their* story and they drank cheap beer at a bonfire or keg party or something cliché like that.

They had a summer of freedom between high school and college, before real life started to slowly let them in.

I knew that that was the graduation story sold to me by American movies, especially the teen movies of the nineties that I had watched on loop ever since I discovered them. I knew it wasn't *real* real. But also, I knew that for some people out there, it was.

Just not around there. Not in Tristesse.

The people I graduated with, it didn't look like that.

My closest friend, Sadie, had a week after graduation where she got to relax and have a vacation with her family where they went to a beachside town in Texas. But when she got home, she had to start working full-time at her dad's restaurant, which he opened after he left his Hollywood career—after all, one day it'd be hers. She'd heard it her whole life.

Everyone else I knew had a similar story. Sure, a few people went off to school, the majority of them going to Louisiana State University, a few others going somewhere further. But most people I knew started life in Tristesse the way they always knew they would. They picked up a job at the grocery store or started bookkeeping at the local HVAC place. Like, four girls in my graduating class were getting their cosmetology licenses to work at the local hair salons.

No one around me had dreams. No one really talked about getting out of there. They talked about getting married, having babies, starting the whole ugly cycle all over again so that in eighteen years, their *own* kid graduated from high school only to keep propagating the species.

It freaked me out. I couldn't even *think* like that. I never had. I always knew I was destined for more.

Destined for greatness.

Not that I wasn't willing to work for it. For fuck's sake, I'd spent my entire life so far training for life onstage. Counting the days, even though I didn't know the end date. My entire life hinged on a success that came to so, so few people in a generation.

With every passing day of hearing nothing from the company I'd auditioned for, my fear grew. I distracted myself by spending hours and hours a day at the ballet studio. Trying not to regret turning down the offer at the regional ballet company. But I was too driven to settle there. I'd had a part-time job all year to save up for my hopeful move to New York. It was the next thing to happen to me, I just knew it.

At first, I was just dreaming. Happily anticipating the *yes* I knew I *had* to receive. It was how I had always looked at my future. Even when I was thirteen years old, I used to fall asleep thinking of it. Thinking of how it would *feel* to be a famous ballerina. To have my whole job be *dance*.

If I was accepted by the North American Ballet, then I'd get to move to New York City. I'd get to be around other dancers full-time. My life would be hard, but in the way I was willing to bear. In the way I was *eager* to be strong and resilient.

But after the first week, then the second, then the third week of hearing absolutely nothing, my anticipation turned to dread. I could not hear *no*. I couldn't. I couldn't stay in Tristesse, give up my dream, work at the restaurant with Sadie, and tell my sticky kids one day that I used to be a ballerina and hear them say they couldn't believe it as they begged for another Lego set from the Costco we'd driven an hour to get to.

Kill me. For real. I could never.

If they weren't going to accept me, I really had no idea what the hell I would do. I couldn't stop dancing. I couldn't stay there. But I also had no money. And how many people like me had gotten a job—just for a while—to save up to get out of their hometown and then, somehow, just gotten stuck?

Despite the heat, chills ran through me.

I thought I heard the phone ring inside and took out one of my not-AirPods to sit up and see if I was imagining it.

No, it was definitely ringing.

I jumped up to run inside to go answer it, but then saw through the window that my mom had already picked up.

It didn't look like an unusual call, i.e., the company calling to save me from a terrible life, so I sat back down and put the music back on.

Two or three minutes later, I felt the air on my body cool and blinked, shielding my eyes to see that my mom was standing in front of the sun, casting a shadow onto me.

Immediately, I was annoyed, sure that she was going to give me shit for using the hose and wasting water, when the drip by the end of the coil was only a little *tiny* bit of—

That was when I noticed she was crying. Hand at her mouth.

Oh my god.

I tore out my earbuds and then demanded, "What's wrong? It's not Mimi. Right? Is—"

My mom shook her head, catching her breath. "That was the North American Ballet."

My heart stopped. This was it. I knew it already. I knew I didn't get chosen. I just knew, deep down in my soul, that the moment of devastation was directly before me. I almost wanted a time machine. To delay the inevitable.

But another part of me wanted her to rip off the Band-Aid. Just to tell me they'd rejected me so that I could get on with figuring out what the fuck to do with the rest of my life. And how.

"And?" I asked, my fear making my voice sound irritated and disinterested.

She nodded and said, "They want you."

My heart started back up, now working overtime.

"Shut up."

"I'm not kidding," she said.

"Are you fucking serious?" I stood, both hands at my mouth. "Are you serious right now?"

She nodded again, still crying. "You're going to New York, baby."

I let out a breath I could swear I'd been holding my whole life, and then screamed and ran to her. We hugged hard and long, both of us crying, neither of us caring that I was covered in hose water and sweat.

"We have to celebrate!" said my mom. "What do you want for dinner? Do you want to go out to a restaurant? Make something here? What do you want? Anything."

"Anything?"

"Anything. Let's not worry about the diet or anything like that tonight. Just having fun. You earned this. We earned this."

I bristled a little at the use of *we*, but then answered her question. "I want to go have tacos at Mimi's house. The kind she makes."

I saw a small flit of something in her eyes, but then she smiled and said, "I'll call her right now."

"No, let me, I want to tell her."

I ran inside and called Mimi, hardly able to say the words, afraid that when I said them, my mom would burst into laughter and say *gotcha!*

I knew my mom wouldn't do that. She'd never fuck with me like that. It was an irrational fear.

Mimi was overjoyed and told us to come over at seven, she'd get a bottle of champagne.

I felt completely out of my skin when I hung up with her, finally calming down just enough to get the details from my mom. I asked a million questions.

When do I leave?

Do I have a roommate?

What do I bring?

When do I actually start?

How much did they say I'd be making?

How am I getting there?

Did they say anything else?

Are you sure, a hundred percent sure, this is for real?

It was happening. She had all the information, and most of it had been emailed to me.

Once she'd told me everything she knew, I took her laptop to my room, shutting the door on the rest of the house, and my mom, and squealed in the privacy of my room.

My hideous, awful room. I hated it. Hated the floor, hated the walls, hated the ceiling. I was going to have a new life. One that took me far, far away from there. I'd be traveling the world. Paris! London! Barcelona! Sydney! Montreal! Mexico City! Vienna!

The world was about to be my stage.

Being in my room, it already felt like I'd moved on. Like I was future me, looking back on that very moment. How long ago my present already felt.

That night, we went over to Mimi's, where the house smelled like garlic, onion, and cumin. The tacos I wanted were the Old El Paso kind that came in the yellow box at the grocery store, ground beef sold separately, a big tub of sour cream ready to be scooped, powdery shredded Mexican cheese on top. It was my favorite trashy meal, and I was rarely allowed it. Or, actually, the truth is that I was never allowed it, but Mimi made it for me anyway sometimes.

I was buzzing. I felt like I'd been asleep my whole life, and I was only just waking up.

Mimi gave me a huge hug when she saw me, and I said, "I couldn't have done it without you!"

She smiled and squeezed me again.

"I got a bottle of bubbly, if you want to open it, Brandy," she said, gesturing at the fridge. "I think we can let Jocelyn drink a glass or two, just tonight, don't you?"

I waited, ready for my mom to be a big drag like always, putting the kibosh on all the fun. But instead, she said, "I think that'd be more than okay tonight."

I beamed.

We drank Cupcake prosecco out of Mimi's fancy champagne

flutes, which had been covered in dust and needed to be thoroughly cleaned before use.

It had been a while since there'd been anything to really celebrate.

After we'd all had a few tacos and were on to our second glass each of champagne, I was giddy with the little alcohol I'd had and the news of the day, and honestly could not stop smiling.

"So when do you go?" asked Mimi.

"In two weeks," my mom answered. "I think we'll fly. I was considering driving, but I don't think that's a good idea with the state of the car. It needs so much work done."

I wasn't sure what I was hearing. "What do you mean, *we*?" I asked.

The phrasing was a little cold, but I meant the question. What *did* she mean?

"I mean . . . you and me," she said, smiling a little.

I felt suddenly out of control. "You're not coming with me," I said.

Mimi put down her glass and looked between us, an expression of worry on her face.

"Of course I'm coming with you," said my mom. "We've been in this together the whole time."

"No—what are you talking about?"

My fantasy was crumbling before my eyes. I envisioned being on my own. Free. Walking around the streets of Manhattan as late as I wanted. Never having to check in with anyone. I felt panicked, like she was suddenly telling me the NAB that had accepted me was actually just a small company in Tristesse that I'd suddenly never heard of.

Nothing about my life would change. Nothing good was coming. My misery would follow me.

"Jocelyn, stop this," said my mom. "I thought I'd sell the house, that—"

I gave a loud laugh. "Sell the *house*? Are you crazy? No, this is my thing, Mom, I'm going by myself. This isn't, like, our thing, this is my job, this is my future!"

I had salt on my fingers from the hard-shell tortillas, and I rubbed it between my fingers anxiously in my lap.

Mimi cleared her throat. "Jocelyn, you need to adjust your tone. Your mother has sacrificed everything for your ballet—"

Oh my god. Not Mimi, too. No, no, no.

"I'm the one who woke up early and worked out and ran and did yoga and Pilates and went to dance class every day for the last decade. Mom doesn't do anything but—but"—I was seething—"fuck random dudes and try to get a free ride off someone. Well, guess what, it's not going to be me."

I threw my napkin down and burst outside, letting the screen door slam behind me.

CHAPTER THIRTY-ONE

Alistair put me in a different cab than him. We couldn't be seen getting in the same car. I am in the back of an Uber without him, my hands shaking, the phantom camera flashes still hovering around in my pupils.

My phone buzzes. A text from Alistair.

They should never have been allowed in. I have no idea how they got in there. Someone must have let them in a side door or something. I'm so sorry.

At first I don't understand why he's apologizing to me. He's the one with the wife and the reputation. It wasn't *me* they were there to photograph. It was the super-handsome, ultrarich socialite out with the girl who was not, most certainly not, his wife.

But then I realize why he's saying that he's sorry. It's just like he told me all those weeks ago.

He isn't the one with anything to lose.

I am the one who might lose my career.

Oh my god, oh my god, oh my god.

I put a hand on my chest and grip, my fingernails digging into my flesh.

What the fuck have I done?

I worked so hard for this career. So did my mom. She made ballet her full-time job, almost as much as I did when I was a kid. Despite what I screamed at her the night we found out I'd be going to New York.

I hate that memory. It's been threatening to resurface ever since she died. But I haven't let it in. For some reason, as I stood there being blinded by the cameras, it spilled over in my mind. Like instead of my life flashing before my eyes, it was my regrets.

When I was accepted to the NAB, I was so happy. Scared, too, but in a way I knew I needed. I needed to break away from my old life, and my mom was part of that. But whenever I remember how I screamed at her, what I said to her, I feel sick with guilt. Nauseated with hideous shame. Embarrassed for my lack of gratitude. Compassionate for my younger self and wishing I'd had anywhere close to the ability to communicate my feelings in a way that hadn't come with so much rejection and ingratitude.

I think everyone has memories like these. Where they were horrible. Where they were wrong. Where they were the asshole.

The difference is, I never got to say that I was sorry. I will never get to tell her that I'm sorry. I'll never get to clarify what I meant, all those years ago.

I'll never get to thank her for how hard she worked to make ballet happen for me. I'll never get to thank her for how she managed to send me off to New York without punishing me for how awful I'd been, and how she never brought it up again.

I'll never get to tell her what I've started to realize lately. Which is that there is no such thing as a free ride. My mom wasn't sleeping with men to make her life easier. She was just trying to change her life, and she didn't have a lot of tools. She was trying to change *my* life, and she didn't have a lot of tools.

The life I was afraid of living, the dark fantasy I had where I worked at a restaurant in Tristesse, raising ungrateful children who didn't see me as a human being with a past—that was my mom's life. I was the one who couldn't see my mother for the person she was, and only saw her as a receptacle for my blame.

I can see it all so clearly now. The good and the bad. She had made her share of mistakes. She had been mean. She had helped me develop what is obviously, now, an eating disorder. She had been inflexible about my diet and my health.

She had also been firm, and did not back down from me. She gave me discipline. A work ethic. She provided me the opportunities I could never have had without her. She had kept me on track to have the success I said that *I* wanted.

I'm not turning her into some kind of saint now that she's dead. I'm not acting like she was a perfect role model, just because I suddenly understand a little more of what it feels like to be with a rich man and dance around all the eggshells in his life and to feel beholden the way I do. But I can finally see what I owed her. And I owed her more love.

I was right that she shouldn't come with me to New York. But I was wrong that we hadn't gotten me there together.

I burst into tears. Hard. They're angry tears. They're the kind that are pinpointed like darts at a bull's-eye. Not the confusing kind of grief where you don't know where the tears are coming from. I know. And it is okay to cry. I should cry. Losing my mom sucks. Losing her when I finally have begun to understand her? That sucks, too.

Being caught fucking a married man by a swarm of paparazzi who are about to splash it all over the *London Post* and ruin my career?

That sucks pretty fucking hard.

With trembling hands, I type out my response to Alistair.

What do we do?

The little gray dots appear to indicate that he's typing. But then they vanish. And no text ever comes.

CHAPTER THIRTY-TWO

It's been almost a month, and I'm living on borrowed time. I just know it.

When the pictures came out, they were blasted all around the Internet. The good news was that some gossip sites were applauding my whole look, calling it *iconic* and *mistress-chic*.

The bad news is fucking everything else.

Somehow, no one at the company has mentioned it. Not that they don't know. All the girls are looking at me like I've got *slut* written across my forehead. Even Sarika is being chilly to me. I swear I caught her shaking her head at me when I walked in the first day.

But I haven't gotten a text or an email or been summoned to Charlie's office. And I haven't heard a word from Alistair.

Something is way, way off.

Arabella is the only one to acknowledge it, coming up to me halfway through the second week of rehearsals, and saying, "My condolences for your career, *cariño*."

I shrug these thoughts off and focus my attention on the rehearsal in front of me. It's a painfully slow rehearsal, putting the ballet together with the full cast. The room is packed and smells like sweat, and it's basically a walk-through, piecing it all together before they start to run the ballet from beginning to end.

It's Saturday, the last day of rehearsals before opening night. Arabella is cast to dance as Manon Monday night, and I'm scheduled to make my debut Wednesday night. Today was supposed to be Arabella's stage run, but she's called out sick and they have given it to me. We're about to begin rehearsals when Kiki, the rehearsal coordinator, finds me warming up.

"Jocelyn, may I speak to you for a moment?"

Her voice is small and wary.

Here it is. I knew it was coming. I'm going to be fired.

"What's up?" I ask, launching off the barre and walking toward her. I can feel the eyes of the girls around us.

"Charlie wants to see you in his office."

"Right now?"

"Tonight, after rehearsal. He won't be in the building until then."

"Okay . . . um. Do we know what it's regarding?"

She gives me a look that says *yes*, but her voice says, "No. Sorry."

"Okay. Thanks, Kiki."

She gives a tight-lipped smile and then heads off. I see her take in a deep, relieved breath.

Well, that's it. I'm definitely going to be fired. Today is the last full run-through, and then . . . I'm out. I'm sure of it.

So, this is it. I have nothing to lose. This rehearsal could be my only chance to dance *Manon*.

We're called to the stage. I'm determined to give it my all.

I start the first act slow and steady. I'm young and naïve like

Manon, excited for the future and falling in love with Des Grieux, played by Luca. Our first pas de deux is amazing. It's miles away from the first rehearsal almost four weeks ago. We're connected deeply. I have a personal fondness for him, just like everyone does; it's not a physical attraction, but it works to serve as chemistry for our characters.

Luca can see in my eyes this is going to be different, and I can see in his that he's ready for it. We move as one.

Manon and Des Grieux are in love, and yet she is swayed by the allure of money. When her brother gets her alone, he presents a wealthy gentleman who gifts her ridiculous jewels. I almost laugh out loud at the mirroring of my life in this moment, and it comes across in my performance of Manon's pure giddiness at being swept off her feet and taken away.

The first act ends with Manon becoming the mistress of the wealthy gentleman, leaving behind her love, Des Grieux.

We take a ten-minute break here and everyone is very happy with Luca and me so far. It can be hard to tell with ten staff members watching and writing notes and an even more critical audience of about forty dancers watching from the wings. A few dancers from the first act receive notes in the break, but not me. I catch Isabella's eye as I grab my water. She gives me an encouraging smile. I realize with a start that Charlie is there. Despite what Kiki said. He's very much in the building, and he's watching.

His expression is unreadable.

I turn away. Now is not the time to focus on them. It's my time.

Act two begins and we fly through it. This act is, by far, the most fun.

It's set in a brothel and the dancers go wild. Honestly, it's because they finally get to act *onstage* how they act *offstage*.

Manon arrives at the brothel with her patron, and they capture everyone's attention. He has transformed her into an elegant woman. She is no longer the naïve young girl from the first act. She is mature, sophisticated, worldly.

Until she sees Des Grieux.

Luca has this character down perfectly. Playful, authentic, genuine.

Des Grieux ruffles her hair and in doing so, he reminds Manon of her young, innocent self. He actually cares for her.

The act ends with them trying to run away together and instead, Manon is arrested and accused of being a prostitute by the wealthy gentleman she dumped. She and Des Grieux are sent on a boat to what was, at this time in history, the French territory of Louisiana.

When this act ends I am confident. I don't even look to the front of the room. I know I'm killing it.

This final act, though. This is the one to make or break the ballet. This is Manon's death scene. Done poorly, it makes the entire show feel like a melodrama. Done well, it's a devastating tragedy.

Luca comes over to me in the wings. "God, you are incredible tonight."

I smile, feeling my own sense of loss as I prepare to say goodbye to the role. "You too."

He smiles back, then squeezes my hand. "You ready?"

I look up at him. We hold eye contact for an extra beat, then I say, "Yes."

He comes close to me and whispers, "I'm here so that you can fly. You've got this."

Tears brim in my eyes and I give him a quick kiss on the cheek before we go out.

Here we go.

The final pas de deux is here. The ending of the ballet.

Des Grieux has just rescued Manon from the jailer who was raping her. He kills him to protect Manon. And now they are lost in the swamps. Luca gently pulls me up from the ground. I face him and slowly rise en pointe. He holds my waist firmly with one hand and my chin with the other.

The music slowly builds with a cello's slow, low note held for several measures. It releases into two quick pizzicato notes. My head falls back as the music crashes into the banging of the timpani and the clanging of the cymbals.

Manon has a disease from the journey. If Des Grieux can just get her out of the swamps, he feels he can save her.

I feel dizzy myself.

Memories of my own mother swirl in my mind, mixing sickly with the realization that I have already lost Mimi, even though she's still, physically, here.

Jordan. I lost him, too. I pushed him away.

I break away from Luca as Manon is supposed to, my entire body nearly convulsing with the sadness.

Manon runs a big circle around the stage, lost, trying to find her way.

Des Grieux calls to Manon and she runs to him and he catches her in the air. It happens again and again. Manon is losing her mind to fever.

The music undulates with melancholic chords; piercing notes on the top feel like cries for help.

My mother did not have the tools she needed to have a different life. She used sex. She used her body. She looked for comfort.

Security. All she wanted was to be happy. All she wanted was for me to be happy. She was flawed. But I never got to tell her I knew she was more than that.

I move across the room en pointe, Luca helping me to float like a feather and guiding me to safety. We pause; then, as the music builds, he spins me and my leg opens just enough for his hand to slide under my right thigh and dip my whole body like a bow. Feet in the air as the point curves down to my head, close to the floor.

My mom was trapped. An endless cycle of bills swallowing her whole. Just when she might have been able to break free, she had me. Then I became her focus. Once I was taken care of, Mimi became her ward.

She never stood a chance.

When I'm lifted up, I pull away from Luca for the last time and bourrée fiercely to the far corner before the final throw in the air.

I finally see it. I finally understand why my mom wanted to come to New York with me. It was a way to change her life.

I run to Luca and feel as if I'm riding a wind at my back, and as I jump, I press my hands into his shoulders and propel myself up in two revolutions and he catches me around the thighs.

I'm pencil straight and dead still as I raise one arm up in the air above me, my body elongating into a long, stretching line.

The music is now crashing like an angry ocean, despite my stillness.

This moment is not about Manon and Des Grieux. It has transformed, and I feel that it is deeply about myself and my life.

I tilt my head to the sky following my arm and release my curled-up fist.

I know, deep down, my meaning. My future.

My head falls back and with that, my body collapses and Luca catches me and lowers me to the ground.

And then he does something that's not in the choreography. He lies down beside me and squeezes my hand and lets me and Manon have the moment instead of trying to wake Manon, as he is supposed to. Luca seems to know.

The music finishes and the room is deadly silent.

I lie with my eyes closed, at peace. A low rumble starts, almost like a downpour has begun outside, but it's not coming from above.

I open my eyes and sit up. The dancers around the room are stomping their feet and starting to stand. The staff are standing and clapping. They whistle and cheer for us.

No one saw that coming. Not even me.

A fter rehearsal I take a deep breath in my dressing room and gather my thoughts. I know I just did the best performance of my life. And my colleagues and boss saw it. When I get fired in about ten seconds, they can all remember me that way.

I walk through the hallways and past the lounge to the stair-well to go up to Charlie's office. I'm trying to ignore the looks I get even though they are in appreciation. It's a strange feeling to finally be accepted on my way to being fired.

I arrive at Charlie's office and knock on the door. There's no answer, so I knock harder.

"Come in."

Even through the door, I can hear how serious his voice is.

When I go in, he gestures at the chair on the other side of his desk.

I sit.

"I assume you know why you're here."

I nod. "Yes."

He sighs. "Jocelyn, I'm in a tough position. Today's run-through was exceptional. There's no doubt about it. Truly transcendent. And yet I have to ask you this. Have you been sleeping with your donor?"

I expected him to chastise me, not simply to ask me if it happened. Time to lie.

"God no," I say, looking as flabbergasted as I would be if he'd asked me if I liked licorice.

"You're not lying to me, are you?"

Go big or go home. Literally. Except I have no home.

"Of course not." I shrug, trying to look natural. "Mr. Cavendish asked me to accompany him to an art show. We went there, and then he took me to the Seven. He didn't tell me where we were going, and we had only just gotten there when the paparazzi showed up."

He looks at me like he finds all this very hard to believe, but I look impassive.

"You do understand how completely inappropriate and unacceptable it is to have an affair with your donor, do you not?"

"Of course I do. I would never do that. I worked my whole life for this career. I wouldn't give it up to sleep with some old married guy."

My stomach twists a little at my own words.

He stares at me, and then gives a slightly humorless laugh before saying, "Right. Well, Mr. Cavendish reached out and told me that the photos were unfortunate, but not representative of any foul play."

My heart lifts. Oh my god, am I really going to get away with this?

Why hadn't he answered me? We could have gotten on the same page with our alibi. Instead I spent a month in a state of horrible suspense.

I shrug, as if none of this is a big deal, and say, "Well, there you go."

He narrows his eyes. "You're awfully flippant. Your career is on the line, Ms. Banks."

He's right. I'm shrugging too much. If this really was a complete misunderstanding, I'd be panicked. Nervous. Everything I'm trying to pretend I'm not.

"I know it seems that way," I say. "It's just that I've seen this before. My friend at my old company got skewered by the press once for some terrible false story that went around. I can't control it. I'm here to dance, not to fight the free press."

Damn. That was pretty good.

He flicks his eyebrows. "We have been deciding what to do with you this week. I wanted to meet with you first thing Monday morning, but no one could agree what to do with you. We were ready to fire you . . . but that performance today. You blew me and everyone away. This meeting was supposed to go a lot differently."

"I understand," I say, trying not to overplay my hand.

"Jocelyn, you'll be performing opening night on Monday night instead of Arabella."

My heart lifts, but my stomach turns sour. What the fuck. I'm shocked. My mouth nearly falls open. I was not expecting him to say that.

"That's a dream come true," I manage to say, the first honest thing I've said since I arrived in his office.

"Right. Well." He shakes his head. "The thing is, and judging from today, especially, you're the best dancer for the role. And if you're telling me the truth"—his eyes land on mine and I try to look comfortable—"then it would be wrong to take this role away from you."

My jaw wants to stay clamped shut, but I give a breezy smile and say, "I agree."

I'm trying to use charm to fool this man, who is clearly too smart to trick. At least completely.

"And if you're lying to me," he goes on, "then this is completely unethical."

I nod and say, "I understand."

"I'll leave you and your conscience with that," he says. "But congratulations. Now go."

Holy shit. Holy shit.

"Thank you for having faith in me," I say.

I leave the office and run quickly to the bathroom, where I catch my breath and rub my face hard. *Fuck.*

I don't like lying. But I can't lose this job. I can't. It's what everything has been for.

I hate how I feel right now. Guilty for lying. Embarrassed for being caught. Ashamed for doing something so wrong. Confused. A little betrayed by the entire experience of being in London. And very scared of how Arabella is going to react when she hears the news.

I put in my headphones as armor and put my songs on shuffle. The song that comes on is "The Other Woman" by Lana Del Rey. The irony is not lost on me.

I let it play and walk through the hallways toward the stage door exit, through the girls, ignoring the many sets of eyes looking at me.

I push open the door to the outside, and I feel a tap on my shoulder and turn to see Arabella.

"Congratulations," she says.

"On . . . oh, on *Manon*."

"Yes, of course, what else would I mean?"

She has a hand on her hip and she's arching an eyebrow at me.

"I'm just out of it. Long week. Thanks for the congratulations."

"It's sort of funny, isn't it?"

"What?"

"You replacing me for opening night, when *my* helping you is how you even got here." She laughs. "I mean, if it weren't for me, you might be working at a burlesque show by now. I saw you dance that night with our friend David. I think you'd be good at it."

I can't tell if she's kidding or being mean or both.

"You're right, I owe you," I say.

"You're right, you do," she says, smiling. "So come out with us tonight. Yeah? We're going to this very cool new spot. I won't take no for an answer. You can buy me a drink for getting your career back."

"Oh, I don't know," I say.

"Oh, please." She pouts her lip. "That's so mean after all I have done for you, no?"

"Ha. Right, um . . ." I feel my ear throb from the memory of her biting me. A reminder that she cannot be trusted.

"Come on, just for a bit," she says. "And fine, *I'll* buy the drinks. You know, as evil as you may think I am, I can recognize when someone is the better dancer for the role. Have I ever done anything but help you?"

Somehow, for the most part, she's right.

"Come on, it's Saturday night. Live a little since you have all day tomorrow off."

"Fine, okay, sure, yes. Just for a bit."

She smiles devilishly and says, "Great. I'll meet you at nine. I'll text you the address."

Her smile turns to a grin and I nod.

Fuck.

CHAPTER THIRTY-THREE

I thought you would have been fired," says Arabella, as she hands me a glass of champagne.

We're in the back of a black car, and she's dressed like a witch with a heroin addiction. A tiny little black dress and fishnet stockings, pointy, sky-high boots.

I take the flute from her and she clinks her glass with mine. "To your success."

"That's . . . I mean. Okay. To yours, too."

I take a big swig of the champagne and she smiles after drinking her own.

"But anyway, I thought you would have been fired. How exactly did you get away with that?"

I suddenly become paranoid. Like, is she wearing a wire? Of course I know she isn't, but she's really zoning in on me.

"It was just a misunderstanding. The paparazzi got into that club somehow and just—"

"Please, honey, don't try to lie to me," she says. "I know what you look like when you just got fucked. Remember?"

She pinches my nipple and I shy away from her. I finish my champagne in one gulp and then say, "You're the worst."

"You love me," she says, putting her head on my shoulder and laughing.

Why the fuck am I here? I shouldn't have come. I'm only here because I don't like to make Arabella mad.

Why is my whole life about keeping everyone happy all of a sudden? Why is it so tense? So stressful?

It's not what it's supposed to feel like.

The champagne went right to my head, so I put down my glass and say, "How close are we?"

"Almost there," she says, looking at her phone.

Five minutes later, we pull up outside a club. It's exactly the kind of place I like when I'm with people I trust. When I feel like really losing myself. It's loud, it's dark, it's moody, there's loud, sexy music playing.

But I don't want to be here with Arabella.

One drink and then I'm going. That's it.

Then I realize there's a line around the block.

"Oh my god, no," I say, "I hate a line. I'm not doing that."

"Don't be ridiculous, lover, you're with me."

She loops an arm through mine and leads me to the bouncer. He smiles at her and lets us right in, which pisses off the entire line.

"Sorry, everyone!" she calls out as we walk inside, which really just adds insult to injury, I'm sure.

We squeeze through the many, many people and order a drink.

She walks up to the side of the bar and does a double kiss with the bartender. She orders something, nods, and then comes back to me.

"It's good to know people," she says over the crowd.

"Clearly," I say back.

The bartender comes back with two shots and two cocktails.

I said one drink. Now I've got a shot and a drink to take. Ugh. God. Fine.

"To an unforgettable night!" she says, then throws her head back in laughter.

I clink glasses with her, and then shoot it.

It burns all the way down and tastes stronger than usual liquor.

"What the fuck was that?" I say, when I can breathe again.

"Navy strength gin!" she laughs. "And caipirinhas!"

I want to drink my cocktail fast, so I get to leave sooner, but now that I just had a navy strength gin, I know the last thing I need to do is pound a third drink in a span of fifteen minutes. I'm sort of a lightweight these days, since I haven't been drinking as much and I've lost a lot of weight and have been working out so much.

Fifteen minutes later, I feel fucking wasted.

I'm slurring and my head is spinning. Sometimes booze hits harder than other times, but this is worse than usual.

"I'll be right back," I say, patting Arabella on the shoulder and starting to make my way to the bathroom.

"I'll go with you," she says. "We can't be splitting up!"

Something feels really off.

My eyes feel like they're crossing.

I hear my name faintly, mixed in with all the other loud voices. Then it comes in clearer.

"Jocelyn? Jocelyn!"

I turn and see Jane. Right beside her is Artie.

Oh god, please let that mean Jordan is here.

I suddenly feel like I need help.

I wave at them, trying to breathe normally. I stumble and they both reach out.

"Babe—oh my god, are you okay?" asks Jane.

Artie holds me up by the arm. "What's wrong with her?" he asks Arabella.

"Nothing, we just took a shot," she says, laughing. "Just a ballerina who can't hold her liquor. Nice seeing you again!"

She guides me away from them and I can't find my tongue enough to say that I don't want her to.

There's a long line for the bathroom and she says, "How bad do you have to pee?"

I shake my head.

"Do you have to puke?"

I shake my head again. I guess I just wanted to go to the bathroom to regroup. To figure out what's wrong. Why I'm so trashed.

"Do you want to go home?" she asks.

My body relaxes a little. Okay. She's not a terrible friend.

I nod. "Please."

"Okay, let's go home," she says.

Somehow, she gets me outside. I keep my whirling eyes out for Jane and Artie but don't see them again.

We get in the car and I say, "I'm so sorry, I'm so sorry," over and over again.

"It's okay, baby! What are friends for?" Then to the driver, "Take us to Ivory Towers, please."

She gives the cross streets and as she does, I feel my eyebrows furrow in confusion. How did she know that's where the apartment was?

I start to ask but can't muster the energy.

I feel my eyes shut. I struggle to keep them open and feel them cross.

This feels fucking awful. So, so, so fucking awful.

It may be an hour later, it may be five minutes, but the car comes to a halt and I feel myself jerk forward and my eyes shoot open like a baby doll's.

We get out of the car and the cold air hits me and makes me feel briefly better.

"Wait, my phone, my—I don't know where my phone is," I say, looking around me.

"I have it, come on, it's okay, come on."

She pulls me in toward the front door, and I say again, "I'm sorry."

"It's okay," she says, but I sense a hint of irritation that only makes me feel guiltier.

When the door opens, the gust of hot air that usually makes me feel welcome and soothed from the cold makes me suddenly sweaty and nauseous.

"Penthouse?" she asks.

I nod, and then wonder again how she knew where the apartment was. "How did you know—" I start.

"I just assumed; it's the Cavendishes, after all," she says.

"No, no. I mean how did you know where the apartment was?"

"I didn't, you told the driver where to go."

"No, I didn't," I say, confused.

"Yes, you did, come on, you're sick, let's just get you upstairs."

We get in the elevator, and the movement makes me feel even sicker.

"I'm gonna throw up," I say.

"Just try to wait until we're up there, we're so close."

I breathe through it, eyes shut.

The elevator shudders to a halt and a wave of sick comes over me. The doors, blessedly, open at that moment, and I burst through them as soon as I can fit through. I then run straight to one of the bathrooms and puke.

I throw up for five straight minutes, my body undulating and aching already as I throw everything up.

I *never* get sick like this from drinking. Everyone's made a mistake here and there, but this is *not* like me. Not like my body.

Is there a chance I was drugged?

No, there can't be. I only had the champagne with Arabella in the car, then the drinks from the bartender. I watched her get them from him.

Unless . . .

Another wave of vomit.

I flush the toilet after that, and then fall to the freezing-cold tile, my hair swept over my face. I feel like I'm dying.

I become vaguely aware of a figure above me and blink a few times to see that it's Arabella. She's holding a phone above me. At first it doesn't make sense, and then I try to ask, "Are you taking a picture of me?"

But it comes out as a terrible garble, one long syllable.

My eyes shut, and darkness falls over me again.

The next time I hear movement, I blink again to see another figure.

Then I feel myself being lifted up.

"Jocelyn. Jocelyn, can you hear me?"

I groan. I don't know who it is. I can only tell that it's a man.

"Jocelyn. Arabella, what the fuck did you do to her?"

Through the fog of my mind, I hear his question and register that he thinks she did this to me.

"No, no," I start to say. But then I start to wonder if maybe . . . maybe she did.

My thoughts aren't coming in clearly enough to firmly doubt or accuse. I feel my head flop backward again, and then I feel a hand on it, holding me like a baby.

"What the fuck did you give her?"

"I didn't give her anything!" she says. "She just can't take her liquor, that's it!"

"Bullshit. She doesn't drink like this."

"What . . . what is this?"

A woman's voice.

I blink slowly, over and over again, trying to get my eyes to roll back to where they're supposed to be. I can't see anything. I can only feel the solidity of the man who holds me and the icy, freezing floor beneath my bare skin. Am I naked?

Oh god. Please don't let me be naked.

"Fuck," says the man's voice.

"What the hell is this place?" the woman asks.

My head lolls and I see sparkling high heels on the bathroom floor a few feet away, then the slender legs of the woman wearing them.

"Can we not do this right now? We need to get her to a hospital."

"A hospital? What's wrong with her?"

"She's what's wrong with her."

"It's not my fault," says Arabella. "She was like this when I found her."

"I don't understand, I thought this girl didn't have any money. Explain what the fuck is going on!"

"Not *now*, we don't have time for this. Go call nine-nine-nine, *now*!"

I try to sit up, but my body feels like it's been hit by a train.

"Deal with your whore yourself," says the woman.

I see her shoes turn and go the other way.

"Dammit."

The man lets go of me, and I feel my body fall onto the ground as he leaves the room.

Then I hear laughter.

CHAPTER THIRTY-FOUR

I wake up the next morning with a pounding headache. It's dark in the room I'm in, and for a long, hazy moment, I can't tell where I am.

My environment materializes as if out of dust.

I'm in a bed. I'm under the covers. I'm in the bedroom of the apartment with the curtains drawn. I have no recollection of getting here.

I put my hands over my eyes, my muscles feeling shaky and uncertain. The last thing I remember was being on the bathroom floor and all those people—who were they?

Arabella, I know she was there. And she was being a bitch, I think. But then again, she did get me home when I needed to get home.

The man—it was Alistair, I feel almost certain it was him. He had me in his lap. But then there was a woman there. Who had that been?

My mind's eye squints through the blackened memory. The shoes. The legs. The voice.

Oh my god, was it Clementine?

Holy shit.

Well, that's it. I'm going to be fired. They came over and found me crouched over a toilet, blacked out.

What *happened*? I never get that wasted. I know I had that glass of champagne, then that strong gin, then some of that cocktail, but I only had a few sips of that. That's enough to get a little too drunk a little too fast, but definitely not enough for me to get so sick. I'm sure of that.

That's when I remember the whisper of suspicion from the night before.

Arabella.

Did she fucking *drug* me? Is she that bad?

There's a sound from the other room and I sit up fast in surprise, then regret it as pain shoots through my skull as if I were being hit by a hammer.

"Fuck," I say out loud.

I manage to creep out of bed, seeing that I somehow got into my big old Nike T-shirt that I've had since high school. I go over to the door and open it, hoping that it's not Arabella. I don't have energy for her. Who else could it be? Alistair, I assume. He's the only one I can imagine.

But it's neither of them.

"Cynthia?"

She jumps and then turns, almost dropping the ice tray in her hands.

"You're up," she says.

"You're here."

"You're welcome."

Another wave of pain passes through me. "Can you catch me up? I don't . . . I don't know what happened last night. I never get fucked up like that. I feel like maybe someone spiked my drink or something."

"Go sit down, I'll bring this stuff over to the living room. I don't know everything, but I think I figured some of it out. Here," she says, handing me a one-liter bottle of alkaline water.

I look at the clock on the wall. It's almost eleven. In theory, I'm supposed to be performing opening night in one day. And I have less than twenty-four hours to be at the theater for my last rehearsal and prepping for the night's performance.

Fuck. I thought one glass of champagne would be fine. I thought one shot would be okay. Sometimes it helps get me out of my head the weekend before a big performance. How had I been so stupid?

She comes over with a bowl of chicken soup and a small bowl of white rice.

"It's probably not what you'd normally eat before a show, but trust me, it'll save your life."

"It looks delicious, actually," I say, sitting on the ground to eat it from the coffee table. "But I'm confused, why are you doing this? Why are you helping me? I thought you hated me."

"I don't hate you. I hate Arabella."

"I thought—"

"Yeah, well." She sits down heavily in the armchair beside me. "We've been doing whatever we've been doing for like a year. She won't commit. I get it. It's fine. But sometimes it seems like she does things just to hurt me. She gets fixated. Like how she's fixated on you. Not in a romantic way, but just like . . . an obsessive way."

The first spoonful of soup seems to run through my body like magic. It courses through me, warm and reinvigorating.

"She set you up last night. She drugged you and she came home drunk, laughing about it. She was being such an asshole." She shakes her head. "She said she used your phone to text Alistair, saying you needed help. But pretending to be you. Then she called Clementine from her own phone and told her what was going on. Clementine booked it down here and discovered the whole thing. Including the apartment, which I guess she didn't know about?"

I nod. I'm starting to feel human again, but everything Cynthia's telling me is making me feel like retreating back to bed.

"I don't think she knew. No."

"I guess from that she figured out you two really were having an affair. Which . . . I don't know . . . were you?"

I look at her and I don't need to say anything for her to understand the confirmation.

"It's none of my business. No judgment," she says.

"I don't even know where my phone is," I say.

"Oh, I found it over here, one sec."

She gets up and then brings it back to me.

I open it and look through my texts with Alistair. Sure enough, last night, just before ten, there's a text I never sent.

Come to the flat. I need help.
Emergency

"I don't even know how she knew where the apartment was."

She exhales. "Yeah. That's how I found the apartment. Can I see your phone?"

I hand it to her and she sits down on the ground next to me, opening one of the apps that came with the phone. The Find My app, which is supposed to be used for finding lost devices and sharing locations with trusted people.

And yet, under the People tab, I can see that my location is shared with Arabella.

"What the fuck?"

"Yeah, she did the same thing to me when we first started hooking up. That's how I knew to look. That was back when she gave a shit about stalking me." She laughs gravely.

"This is insane. How long has she been—"

As I ask the question, I realize that there's a very good chance she was the one to send the paparazzi to the Seven the other night. That would make sense. But why? Why does she want me punished?

I remember now that, last night, I'd had a moment of confusion about how she knew where to take me when we got in the cab to go home.

"She's pretty nuclear when she wants to fuck someone up," Cynthia says.

"Why does she want me destroyed like this? If she wants me fired, why the hell did she ever even get me connected to the company? It was her help that got me in. I would have had no way in. She worked so hard to help me in the beginning."

"I don't know. I'm sorry. The only thing I know is that it probably has something to do with the fact that . . . fuck."

"What?"

"Last night, after she went to sleep, I went through her phone. Everything seemed off, and I'm not proud of it. I shouldn't have done it, except—I don't know, if I hadn't come over here . . ." She gives me a look and then says, "You were in pretty rough shape."

"Thank you for helping me."

"That's not why I'm saying it, I'm saying it because I kind of can't believe that she left you like that. I knew she was catty. I knew she was a bitch when she wanted to be. But you could have died. You were on your back in the bathroom—I mean, if you'd been sick again . . ."

The awful truth of what could have happened hangs between us.

"Thank you," I say again.

She waves away my gratitude, blushing a little. "Anyway, when I was going through her phone, I discovered that she's been cheating on me. Or I guess not cheating, since she wouldn't commit, but she's been having a full-on . . . I don't know, *thing* with—god, this is so weird—it seems like she was having an affair with Clementine."

This shocks me, somehow. After everything.

"Oh my god. That explains so much."

"Right?" she says, bitterly.

Yes. It does. I had thought, at some point, that maybe she had a thing going with Alistair. The way she acted was like a jealous lover. I knew she couldn't feel that strongly about me, and the fact that she seemed so weird when I got sponsored by the Cavendishes—it makes so much sense now.

I'm so disgusted with Alistair, I can hardly breathe. He left me there. They all left me there on the floor. Regardless of whether they thought it was my own fault or not, they knew I was sick.

My memories may be vague, but I remember that he said they needed to call 999, but when Clementine threatened to leave, he followed her. He'd rather walk out the door with his meal ticket than take care of me when I really needed him. Needed *anyone*.

"It seems like Clementine is going to, or is at least *saying* she's going to, leave Alistair. He's running around trying to make money and hide it all over the place and Clementine knows all about it. She just didn't know about you."

Shame swirls in my chest. I take another life-giving spoonful of the soup and then chug some water.

"So did Arabella drug me?"

She nods her head sadly. "I feel like she did. It seems like it was her whole plan. To frame you. To show Clementine the apartment and fuck you up so you looked like a mess. Get you fired."

"Yeah, I'm definitely fired."

"I'm sorry. I'm sorry for Arabella and what she did. She's like a one-woman Shakespearean play. I'm sorry you got swept up in it. I'm sorry I did, too, but at least she didn't come after me. She used to go through my phone and read everything and block people she thought were going to steal me away or who she just didn't like or whatever. She's vicious like that."

"Right." Then something occurs to me. I open my phone and go to Jordan's phone number.

He's blocked.

What the *fuck*?

"Oh my god, she blocked my ex-boyfriend. She blocked Jordan. She blocked my—oh my god."

My hands start to shake and my delicate-feeling heart starts to pound uncertainly as I realize that this means Jordan maybe *did* try to reach out to me. Maybe he *did* try to contact me. Maybe he called me when it was late and he was alone and missed me. Maybe *he* thinks I blocked *him*, or at least didn't answer.

Oh my god.

Somehow, this is actually a silver lining. Arabella is obviously a monster, but at least this means all is not, maybe, lost with Jordan.

I unblock him immediately and then open the text screen, wanting to send him something. But what?

I shut off the screen.

"But why would she block my ex-boyfriend? What does she care if Jordan can reach me?"

"My theory is she wanted you and Alistair to blow up so Clementine was forced to end things. The more public it is, the better."

"So she probably did send those paparazzi. God damn."

Cynthia nods slowly. "I'm sorry I was ever a dick. I should have seen it sooner with her. It's obviously over with her now. I'm not going back to that bullshit."

"Good for you." I finish the last of the soup. "Thank you for this. I feel almost totally normal again. And I owe you an apology. I'm really sorry I ever crossed a line into your and Arabella's relationship. That was not okay of me. I just never felt very clear on the rules."

"Ha. Neither was I. Anyway, I appreciate that, but we were never going to make it anyway." She pauses. "And you're welcome for the soup. Salt and protein, can't go wrong."

We smile at each other, and then I push myself up off the ground. "Okay, still a little shaky. What do you think I do? I haven't heard anything from anyone about the show tomorrow night."

She shrugs. "Just go in like everything's normal. They'll talk to you if they're going to talk to you."

"Yeah. Okay." Something occurs to me. "Was it you who sent me that text? A while ago. *Don't trust him?*"

She laughs. "Yeah. Sorry for the cryptic way of saying it. I just didn't want to get in the middle with Arabella and her vendetta."

"Right. But why shouldn't I trust him? It sounds like the whole thing was Arabella."

"I just thought he was a dick. But then, Arabella was talking shit about him all the time. I guess it got in there. Maybe he's not. I guess I knew something was off, just didn't know where."

CHAPTER THIRTY-FIVE

Walking into the theater Monday morning was as tense as trying to get out of a grocery store with a stolen watermelon hidden under a T-shirt. I felt like I was getting away with something, waiting to be caught. Waiting for someone to say, *What the fuck are you doing here?*

But no one said anything. And then no one else said anything. Just like the week before. And then the day kept moving forward and before I knew it, I was in hair and makeup. The poker face this company holds is unbelievable.

I'm grateful that Arabella isn't here so far. I wouldn't put it past her to show up, since she's made it her life's work to torture me.

We're about an hour from showtime when I decide to bite the bullet and send a text I've been meaning to send for a while now.

> Hey . . . long time no talk. Sorry about
> things at the gallery. I think we need to

talk. If you're willing to? I have a show tonight actually in an hour, but I'll be free around eleven? Any chance you'd meet me for a drink?

The idea of a drink still makes me feel a little woozy, but once I spend three hours under the stage lights, I know I'll be able to rally for a glass of something. If he's willing to meet me.

For the next forty-five minutes while I do my warm-up, I check my phone every five minutes—and that's me having self-control. He doesn't answer me, and a big part of me fears that he's just not going to. That him being blocked didn't matter, because he was never going to reach out anyway.

They've just announced the fifteen-minute warning until curtain up and my dresser has knocked on my door asking if I'm ready for costume.

I tell her I need a few more minutes, then I take a deep breath. I'm alone. When you dance a principal role as a soloist or corps member, you get moved to a principal dressing room for the show. I reach into my bag and pull out the photos I grabbed from my spot in the shared dressing room.

I smile at the one of Sylvie and me, then the one of Mimi and me.

Then I pull out Jordan's picture. The two of us kissing, full rom-com style.

And then I pull out the picture of my mom and me.

It's after my first show with NAB. She looks so proud. I'm smiling, but she is glowing. I look at it now and feel ashamed of my behavior. She was just doing the best she knew how. I grab a piece of tape and I put it up on the mirror. It's the only one I'm putting up tonight. This show is for her.

The show is a dream. It doesn't top the studio run-through on Saturday, but it's up there. I receive a standing ovation and numerous bouquets of flowers. When I bring the conductor on-stage for his bow, I finally have a chance to glance at all the flowers I'm holding. I can see on one tag a simple *For you—Jordan*.

I smile and take a few more bows and curtain calls before finally the audience have exhausted themselves. And the curtain closes for the night.

I feel exhilarated. My skin is damp with sweat, my muscles are on fire. I started the day at such a deficit, but somehow I managed to push through to where I am now.

My heart almost stops when I see Sarika and Charlie walking out from the wings. Fuck. Is it going to happen now? Is my reprieve over?

Sarika comes up to me and shakes her head, smiling, saying, "You were brilliant. Absolutely mesmerizing."

Charlie smiles, too. "Well done."

I laugh, relieved, and say, "Thank you so much. Thank you."

I wait for them to add that, of course, I am fired. But they say nothing.

A bit confused, I excuse myself and move past them, rushing to the dressing room. I wait impatiently as my dresser undresses me, then I reach into my bag and pull out my phone.

There's the text I was hoping for from Jordan as soon as I saw the flowers. I had checked after act one and act two and there wasn't anything. Fucking finally. I smile.

**You were amazing. Hope it's okay I got
a ticket at the last minute and was able**

to watch the show . . . I'll be in front of
the theater when you're through.

I start laughing as I read the text. He came. He fucking came. Tears start to come, and I wipe them away.

I hurry to get ready, cleaning off my makeup and throwing on a pair of jeans, a tank top, and a big, thick turtleneck sweater.

I put my hand on my excited heart and then run through the hallways. I avoid the backstage exit and take a shortcut to the front through the door to the lobby and see him.

I don't even think about it, I don't even hesitate before pushing open the doors and running up to him and just throwing my arms around him.

I know it's the wrong thing to do. I know he doesn't know everything that's been going on. But I can't help it.

Thank god, he doesn't shrug out of my embrace or pat me awkwardly. He hugs me back. A little stiffly at first, then I feel his body relax against mine.

I breathe him in, the scent of him, the warmth of him. I miss him so much. I can't believe how much I've missed him.

It's so clear to me in that moment that I have never, not for one second, stopped loving him.

Finally, we break away from each other.

"Do you know where you want to go?" he asks.

"Let's go to Bluebell."

Bluebell is a quaint little pub right around the corner from our—his—apartment.

We go outside, the balmy spring air damp against my cheeks, and we catch a passing cab.

We don't talk much on the way, just amicable silence and

observations about the things we pass. It's like we're saving the *real* talk for when we're sitting down, looking at each other. With a confidence-giving drink in front of us each.

The pub is busy and cozy, but we find a table near the fireplace in the back corner.

"I'll have a stout," he says, when the server comes over.

"Same," I say. As much as I love champagne, I kind of feel like I could go the rest of my life without expensive wine ever again after the last few months.

"So how have—" he begins, but I cut him off.

"This psycho ballerina Arabella blocked your phone number. Actually, you met her. That night after New Year's at the burlesque place. But the point is, she blocked you and I didn't know. Did you—have you tried to text me? Or call me? At all?"

He looks confused for a moment, and then nods slowly. "Ah."

"What?"

He pulls his phone out, pulls up our text screen, and puts it on the table in front of me.

Text after text after text after text.

The most recent ones say things like:

I get that you've probably blocked me, but I feel like if I keep texting, one day you'll answer.

Last month:

I hope you're doing okay. I know we're not talking, but I wish I could get ahold of you.

And back in January:

**Please come home. I love you. We'll get
through this.**

I look up at him. "You texted me."

He laughs. "Yeah, you could say that."

The server puts our beers down in front of us and we both
thank him.

"Cheers," says Jordan.

"Cheers."

We both sip, and then we start talking.

I tell him everything. What happened the night I left. Everything about my mom's estate. Mimi's bills. I even tell him how I
fell in with Alistair.

Laying it all out the way I do, like a story, it feels like it happened to someone else. Someone I have compassion for. Someone
who was really lost.

Someone who tried to blow up her life.

Alistair. He feels like a person from my life a million years ago.
I can't figure out why, at first, but the more I talk, the more clear
it becomes.

I just needed protection. Security. Safety.

That night at the Seven, he had said all the right words. He'd
said, *Maybe your problem isn't that you're going to turn into your
mom, maybe the problem is you can't accept peace when it's on offer.
Maybe your life is actually falling into place, not falling apart.*

Then he'd said I should let go. And then he'd said, *Maybe I'm
not going to betray you in the end. Maybe you're actually hanging
around with a good guy who's really just trying to look out for you.*

His words had had the ring of truth, but something had felt wrong. They'd felt almost right, but not quite.

Jordan was the good guy. Jordan was the one I didn't need to push away. He was the one trying to look out for me. That relationship, its peace, was something I couldn't accept. I was so used to turbulence that I couldn't let things be still.

My attraction to Alistair was real, but it was based in nothing but sex. I never thought about the future. I never fantasized about growing old together. You could argue that I didn't because it was just too early, but I thought about that the first *night* with Jordan. Not all of it, and not to a psycho amount, but I thought about it. The future was always a part of our present.

When I finish telling Jordan everything, all the way up to yesterday, he's silent for a long moment.

When he speaks, he's gentle.

"I love you, Jocelyn. I am so sorry I wasn't there for you. If I had known you wanted to hear from me, I would have done anything I could. But I didn't know where you were. I knew I couldn't show up at your job. When I saw you at the gallery that night, I could barely keep it together. I wanted to reach my arms out and just never let you go."

My heart feels carved out at his words. "I love you, I love you so fucking much, I'm so sorry I ever—"

"No, no apologies. It's okay. It's okay."

I start to cry and he pulls me in toward him, allowing me to hide my face in his chest.

"Shh, shh, shh, no worrying now. It's okay." He gives a soft chuckle. "I always thought we had such good communication, but we just keep ending up on different planets. First after Vienna, now this."

I laugh a little, too, pulling back and wiping the tears away. "I know. I'm so sorry."

He nods. "It's okay, Jo."

We both take a sip of our second round of beers and then he asks, "So what now?"

"Well, now I'm probably going to get fired. And then . . . I don't know. I really don't. I missed ballet. I was right to go back to ballet. But something about this just felt wrong the whole time."

"Maybe it's just not the right company for you," he says.

There's a simplicity in his words that almost shocks me. I hadn't really considered that this was an option.

"I . . . well, I don't know."

"You're a good dancer, Jocelyn. A great ballerina. You're not trying to prove yourself. The world knows you're a great dancer. You don't have to accept anything that doesn't feel right. Maybe in the beginning, but not anymore. You don't have to wait to be fired by this company. You just lost your mom, Jo. Whatever happened here, it happened, and it's okay."

"You think I should quit?"

"I didn't say that. I would never tell you what to do with your career. I'm just reminding you that you don't need to beg for anything. You don't need to fight for a place."

Now that he's saying it, I realize that I didn't feel completely relieved when I stepped offstage and saw Sarika and Charlie and they didn't fire me. I had dreaded getting fired before going on-stage, but after, it felt different. I had expected them to take me into the office and tell me I was through. And there was a part of me, I realize now, that had wanted that.

The idea of trudging through the next weeks, months, or even years in that environment made me feel completely miserable. Arabella and her harem of lovers eyeballing me. The Cavendishes and Mary Simon involved in my life. Even if I *didn't* get fired, I would just be given to some other donor, and as Arabella told me all those months ago, it's just different here. The donor-dancer relationship is different. It demands more. It demands something besides dance.

I think about a text I received from my old ballet mistress back in February. She told me to reach out if I ever needed anything.

Maybe I could do that. Maybe I could go back.

"Jordan," I say. "Do you want . . . to be my boyfriend again?" I ask.

I'm so nervous I feel like I might slip out of my seat and onto the ground, but I have to ask. "If you need more time, I get it, I just—"

But I stop speaking when he shakes his head.

"No? No? What do you mean, I'm sorry, Jordan, please . . ."

I feel suddenly desperate. Angry at Arabella for everything. Frustrated that I got so distracted by Alistair. Missing the warmth of the Waverly Inn and the chaos of Washington Square Park.

"I'll do you one better. Marry me, Jocelyn."

I miss a step as I try to replay his words, making sure I heard them correctly. "Did you—"

"Marry me. Let's not lose each other again. I love you."

I look at his beautiful face, his earnest eyes, and I want to kiss him. But first, I have to say, "Yes. Hell yes."

CHAPTER THIRTY-SIX

I wake up the next morning to the smell of coffee being made. I'm naked in Jordan's bed, warmed by the different layers of wool blankets we picked out together when deciding to make the bed of our dreams a priority when we first got the flat in London.

I smile as I lie there, feeling so soothed by the familiar setting. The wonky window that needs a book to prop it open to let in the breeze coming from what is, evidently, an unseasonably warm day outside. The twinkle lights on the bed frame. The glass on the bedside table that holds my water from last night.

I'm so happy to be back here.

I get out of bed, wrapping one of the blankets around my body as I go.

Sunshine pours through the open kitchen window and I see that he's made scrambled eggs.

I don't know why, but the scrambled eggs he makes are just the best.

"Still want to marry me?" he asks, with the easy smile of someone who knows the answer to his question.

"Uh-huh," I say. I drop the blanket and run over to him.

My life has had so much uncertainty. All of my life. It was always about preparing for what was to come. It was about withholding. It was about trying to earn the life I thought I deserved. I was lost, waiting, earning, proving, asking, begging.

Now there's a dense weight of assuredness that has settled into my bones, grounding me, reminding me that I am the one in control. Teaching me that I'm the one in control.

I find my phone and see that I have a message from Charlie.

Please come to my office after class for a meeting at noon.

"Well, there it is," I say, reading the text aloud to Jordan.

"How do you feel about it?"

I scan my heart for my truest feelings, and then say, "I feel excited. I needed to find ballet again, but I feel really sure that this isn't right."

He nods. "Okay."

I grit my teeth and gear up to acknowledge the elephant in the room. "You know . . . if I quit, then I'll have to move out of London."

He waves a hand. "I'm done with London."

"Are you sure?"

He nods. "Between Artie's article and that asshole's big purchase that night, I'm kind of . . . I don't know, I think I'm sort of rich now?"

I laugh. "I don't know about *rich*."

"No, I kind of am. That painting sale made everyone there start asking about prices. I sold my whole show."

I drop my fork. "Shut up. Are you serious?"

"Dead serious."

"That's . . . that must mean . . ."

"Yeah. Lots of fucking money. We can probably get a place with heating and air-conditioning. At the very least."

He takes a bite of his eggs and I stare at him. "That's insane."

"We can go anywhere. Let's just make sure you're happy this time. It's completely up to you. Paris, Madrid, Sydney, the moon, I don't care. As long as we go together."

I beam at him. It doesn't matter to me at all that he has money now. I'm happy that he's having success. I know that he's worked his ass off and he's been buffeted by the winds of his career for too long. We both were.

But now we both have control. I don't have to panic.

After eating, I kiss Jordan goodbye and take off for the long walk to the theater.

I think about my mom with every step. The heels of my shoes click against the pavement.

My mom was always so obsessed with status and wealth, always looking for a way to move up in the world. She was flawed, no doubt about it. She made so many mistakes along the way, chasing after the wrong men and getting caught up in her own desires, being distracted from any of her own potential and greatness by either assuming she needed the help of someone else or by putting all of her energy into me.

I feel a sense of acceptance, shrouded in sadness for my mom. I never got to be a peer to her. I never got to be a fellow, flawed woman beside her. I never got to give her compassion. I never got to ask her what she wanted. What *she* wanted. Not what she wanted for me. Not what she thought she couldn't have, but what she *wanted*.

I step into the theater and take a deep breath, the smell of old wood and dust filling my nostrils. It's a familiar scent, one that I've grown to know well over the last few months. I can hear the faint sound of music in the distance, the orchestra rehearsing for later tonight.

I make my way toward the offices, my heart pounding in my chest as I climb the stairs.

When I get to the office, I knock on the shut door, hesitating when I hear voices on the other side.

Inside, I find Arabella, Clementine, and Alistair with Charlie. What the fuck?

I was prepared to find Charlie, of course, and I feared that Clementine and Alistair might be here. But Arabella being here is just a bridge too far.

I remind myself that Jordan is waiting for me at home. That he has promised me ramen and cheap beer tonight. That we have started to plan our lives together again. That the world is our oyster.

"Please, come in," says Charlie.

I do, and I shut the door behind me.

Alistair won't meet my eyes. Clementine looks livid. Arabella looks overall tragic, but I can see the devilish look behind her eyes.

"I assume we're all here because I'm promoted," I say, not caring that my joke falls like an uncaught water balloon on the floor between us all.

"Jocelyn, there are some very serious allegations at play here. I'm sure you already know what they are."

I hang my head and prepare to take responsibility.

"Yes," agrees Alistair. "I think we need to talk about your completely inappropriate behavior."

I look at him and then feel my mouth open in shock. He still won't meet my eyes. I see that he has a hand on Clementine's leg. This absolute *wimp*.

Oh my god, *really*? He's going to pin this whole thing on me?

"You have allegations, Mr. Cavendish?" I ask, my tone bitter and full of rage.

He shifts uncomfortably, and then says, "I have felt very uncomfortable at times around you, Ms. Banks, and—"

But that's when I realize . . . I have a few allegations of my own.

"You know what, Charlie? You're completely correct, there are some very serious allegations that need to be made. Firstly, Arabella. I would like to acknowledge that it's with her help that I arrived here and secured a donor."

After briefly tensing up, she visibly relaxes and says, "You're welcome."

"Yeah, thanks for that. But on the other hand, Arabella has also assaulted me. She bit my ear so hard that I still have a scar, in fact. I can show you if you want. It's also on the cameras, since it was on company property. On Saturday night, she also drugged me. I was incredibly sick. Of course, I still managed to perform last night."

The room has turned tight and strained. This isn't what anyone expected.

"Jocelyn, this—" begins Charlie.

"One moment, Charlie. I know that you want to accuse me of an inappropriate relationship with my donor. And you're not wrong. I have had relations with Mr. Cavendish. If you want to examine the intricacies of that relationship, then we can have a very long, complex conversation. We can do it publicly, if you like, and allow everyone in the city to weigh in on whether they think I am the one to blame. And we can even pit it against the other inappropriate relationships between the donors and dancers at this company. I know of at least one other highly questionable relationship in the company, and if it would be helpful to let *everyone* know about that, then I am more than happy to share."

I don't blink. I don't look at Arabella or the Cavendishes, even though all eyes are on me.

"I don't think that will be . . . I don't think that will be necessary," says Clementine. She clears her throat. "After all, my husband has a history of trying to buy whatever pretty little thing he wants. Paintings. Women. I'm sure a public display would only make things harder on us all."

"Especially the company," I say, with a tone of immense agreement.

She nods, looking a little panicked.

"Mrs. Cavendish, I thought—" starts Charlie.

"I'll make it easy for you," I say. "I'm going to resign from the company. I haven't found it to be a healthy environment. And if you prefer, then I won't tell anyone about my experience at this company. I can keep everything to myself. If we all agree that's best."

Everyone in the room knows what I'm saying. I'm saying that we all better keep our mouths shut or I'll go nuclear. Maybe I did learn something from Arabella and her wicked ways.

She looks furious. Like a bomb about to explode. And then she does.

"You cannot be serious," she says loudly. "Clementine, do something!"

Clementine gives her a look that means *Shut the fuck up, now.*

Arabella laughs angrily. "Clementine, after all this? You're going to let it get swept under the rug?"

"Swept," says Clementine.

I stifle a laugh.

Arabella shakes her head, looking furious that her plan to take me down and force Clementine to go public hasn't worked. I don't know if Cynthia was right about all her conjectures, but it's really feeling like she nailed it.

"I'm going to go now," I say. "Oh, and Mr. Cavendish, did you want Jordan to send you the painting you purchased under my name? Or did you want to continue to use it as a tax write-off? I wasn't sure if you actually wanted it or just wanted the money, or . . . what do you think?"

He seethes at me, and then says, "You can keep it."

"Great."

I shut the door behind me and then run down the stairs feeling liberated. Free. Untethered.

I burst out onto the street, into one of the first sunny days London has seen in months and months. I pull out my phone. At first unsure of what to say. But I decide to keep it simple. We'll have loads of time to catch up in the future.

When I type them, the words feel right, even though I'm not quite sure yet what they mean or what they will mean to me. I just know that they're true.

Sylvie, I'm coming home xx

ACKNOWLEDGMENTS

I would like to acknowledge all the extraordinary artists I worked with during my time as a ballerina. Your stories and craft inspire me to bring ballet to a wider audience. Thank you to my friends, family, and fellow dancers for your incredible support.

Paige, Annelise, and Cindy—I couldn't have done this without you!

THE
UNRAVELING

MELANIE HAMRICK

READERS GUIDE

QUESTIONS FOR DISCUSSION

1. Jocelyn struggles with expressing and accepting her emotions, even though she is self-aware of how her denial and weaponizing of emotions negatively impacts her life and relationships. Why do you think that is?

2. Jocelyn feels like she must play the lead in *Manon* because she sees many parallels to her own life. When was a time that life imitated art for you?

3. Jocelyn's flashbacks reveal the dynamics between three generations of women in her family: grandmother, mother, daughter. How do these relationships shape Jocelyn as an adult?

4. As a part of pursuing Jocelyn's career as a ballerina, Jocelyn's mother begins to control her daughter's diet. How does this impact Jocelyn's relationship with her mother? How do you think young girls' role models shape their dreams, aspirations, and attitudes toward how they see themselves?

5. Jocelyn has two primary love interests: Jordan Morales and Alistair Cavendish. Why do you think she was drawn to each of

them? What do you think the differences in her relationships with these two men say about Jocelyn throughout the story?

6. What do you think of the stark contrast between Jocelyn's childhood in Louisiana and her penthouse life funded by Alistair?

7. What do you make of the donor culture in the ballet world as Jocelyn experiences it?

8. Arabella has many complex roles in Jocelyn's life: savior, friend, lover, rival, enemy, threat. What do you think of her character?

9. Art is an essential part of life for Jocelyn as a dancer and for Jordan as a painter. What art form resonates the most with you, and how do you think art enhances life?

10. The feeling of home is important to Jocelyn—she finds home in her grandmother, in ballet, in Jordan. What does it mean to feel at home? Where is home for you?

Photo by Andres De Lara

Melanie Hamrick is an author, ballerina, producer, choreographer, and mother. Born and raised in Virginia, Melanie began dancing at a young age. Her career as a ballerina spanned over sixteen years with American Ballet Theatre. While traveling the world for work and with her family, Melanie has always carried novels and notebooks with her. Her passion for reading and dance inspired her to begin writing. Her first novel, *First Position*, was published in 2023. She continues to be inspired with ballet, which is also the subject of her second novel, *The Unraveling*.